THE
LESS DEAD

Also by Denise Mina

Garnethill

Exile

Resolution

Sanctum

The Field of Blood

The Dead Hour

The Last Breath

Still Midnight

The End of the Wasp Season

Gods and Beasts

The Red Road

Blood Salt Water

The Long Drop

Conviction

THE
LESS DEAD

DENISE MINA

Harvill *Secker*

LONDON

3 5 7 9 10 8 6 4

Harvill Secker, an imprint of Vintage,
20 Vauxhall Bridge Road,
London SW1V 2SA

Harvill Secker is part of the Penguin Random House group
of companies whose addresses can be found at
global.penguinrandomhouse.com

Penguin
Random House
UK

First published by Harvill Secker in 2020

A CIP catalogue record for this book is available from
the British Library

penguin.co.uk/vintage

ISBN 9781787301726 (hardback)
ISBN 9781787301733 (trade paperback)

Typeset in 13/19 pt Bembo
by Integra Software Services Pvt. Ltd, Pondicherry

Printed and bound in Great Britain by Clays Ltd, Elcograf S.p.A.

Penguin Random House is committed to a sustainable future for
our business, our readers and our planet. This book is made from
Forest Stewardship Council® certified paper.

For DM, KM, LM, MR, JG, TW, ML, EC
and all who loved and cared for them

HOPE DIES SLOWLY BUT it does die. Even though it's obvious that Margo Dunlop has been stood up she can't seem to make herself leave. She's a doctor and well knows how stubborn and pernicious hope can be. Without confirmation, in the absence of direct contradiction, hope will linger long beyond the point of being useful. The speed of death is often determined by the degree of initial investment.

She has been waiting for an hour and forty minutes, alone in this odd-shaped room, listening for the lift and staring at the back of the door, willing it to open and change her life. She has come to meet her birth family for the first time. Not her birth mother though, it turns out that Susan died a long time ago. How wasn't specified in the contact letters but Margo very much needs to know. She's a doctor. She's pregnant and afraid of her own genetic legacy. She has suspicions.

She's too invested. She shouldn't have come here. She should have been more careful.

The birth family are very late. Deep down Margo knows that they're probably not coming now but she's trying not to get angry. She's still clinging to an outside possibility that they have a good reason for being late – a train crash or a stopped watch, as if that still happens. If they turn up late and blameless she doesn't want the meeting to turn into a fight about punctuality. There are questions she needs answered.

She's waiting in a room at the top of an old office block in the heart of Glasgow, just off George Square. It's hot and smells weird, as if something is rotting deep in the fabric of the building. The adoption charity have tried to make the room homely but the furnishings are cheap and somehow ominous, like a police reconstruction of a family sitting room where something dreadful happened. There's a sagging sofa with a low back, a coffee table with a box of tissues on it and a dining-room chair. An Ikea bookcase holds torn children's books and a sticky game of Hungry Hungry Hippos with no balls. She's been here long enough to look.

The shape of the room bothers her too. It's square with a low ceiling of glass squares, all painted opaque with white emulsion. She thinks the inside of the building has been gutted and modernised and this must have been the top of a grand old staircase, that what she's sitting under is the old skylight. Thinking about it makes her feel the void beneath her and her shin bones tingle, like a memory of falling.

Margo found the contact letters from Nikki hidden deep in a drawer in her mum's bedside table. The first was dated several years back, the latest just a few months ago. They were addressed to Margo, care of Janette and asked Margo to please write back? Nikki said she was desperate to see her because she really needs Margo's help with something.

Janette was dying and rarely conscious when Margo found the bundle of letters. She has tried to understand why Janette didn't pass them on. Nikki did sound mad, all that stuff about

'Glasgow's Jack the Ripper' hunting her for thirty years, but Margo is less interested in the substance of her delusions than the tone. Margo's not entirely sure of her own mental health. She wants to know if Nikki was schizotypal, if there is a genetic likelihood of her getting it. But Nikki's not coming.

Margo looks at the back of the little door to the room and imagines what she would look like to a stranger walking in. She's tall and the ceiling is low, her hands are on her knees, feet are flat on the floor. She'd look intimidating and monumental, like a statue of Queen Victoria discovered in a crate. She attempts a welcoming smile but tension instantly warps it into a growl.

But no one's coming anyway. She drops the scary smile and lets her face idle in neutral. No one. She picks up her coat from the settee and sits it on her knee, a first move towards putting it on.

Now she'll never know what happened to Susan or if she gets her height from her, if she's mixed race. Her hair says yes but her skin tone says no. She won't get to ask anything. No one is coming.

So bloody rude. Selfish. What kind of people agree to a meeting this emotionally charged, pick the place and the time, and then don't turn up? She checks the time on her phone; it's an hour and fifty minutes now. She's on an indignant roll but gets distracted by an unanswered text from an hour ago.

Her best friend Lilah asked:

How about now, lambchop, anything yet?

Margo still hasn't replied. She kept hoping to have a better answer.

A very careful knock is followed by the little door being opened. It's Tracey, the counsellor who gave Margo a long talk about limiting her expectations on the way in. Margo dislikes Tracey for reasons that she can't quite fathom.

Maybe it's the tense situation. Maybe it's Tracey's belligerent walk. She sways her shoulders and enters the room belly first as if she's pregnant and wants to talk about it, or is fat and doesn't. She has thick glasses that distort her big green eyes and wears a dress with a low neckline displaying four inches of cleavage. A gold chain with a green pendant surfs her record-breakingly long boobs, bobbing around, going under sometimes only to be unthinkingly fished out by Tracey's chubby forefinger.

'Hello again,' she whispers as she comes in, head tilted sympathetically, lips pressed tight in a very sad sorry as she sits on the sofa and clasps her hands together. She's going to tell Margo to give up and get out. She'll dress it up but that's what she'll mean.

Tracey doesn't get to speak before Margo blurts that she'll just wait for another half-hour, if that's OK?

'Well, see now,' drawls Tracey in a breathy Northern Irish accent that sounds like a melancholy old song, 'the problem with that is we're supposed to actually shut the office in a wee ten minutes. I sort of just wanted to have a wee chat with you before that happened so that you don't leave feeling that you might have liked to have talked to someone? Would you maybe like a wee chat about it? About your feelings?'

Every sentence ends in a tonal upswing, every statement is littered with infuriating conditionals – maybes and mini-misations and perhaps. But Margo is a doctor and has been on the receiving end of enough impotent rage from patients to know that Tracey isn't to blame for how she feels.

'I'll just wait on for the last ten minutes, if you don't mind.' Margo says it softly, overcompensating for her white-hot fury. 'At least then I'll know for sure that Nikki didn't come. It's just ten minutes. I may as well.'

'Aye, yeah, may as well, grand, grand. May as well.' Tracey pats her own knee while looking at Margo's. 'You don't owe them anything, you know? You've given them a good long time to get here. You've done what you can. You don't have to wait.'

Margo doesn't know why Tracey is using the plural. Is she being formal? Or does Tracey know something Margo doesn't? Is Nikki trans, or has Margo just been stood up by several people? Is that better or worse?

'Well, I'll wait for the ten minutes.'

'Sure.'

'If that's all right.'

Tracey nods and smiles vaguely. She air-rescues the green stone from the ravine of her cleavage but doesn't move to leave. She's trying to be kind, waiting with her and giving Margo space to talk about her feelings if she wants to. Margo doesn't trust her.

What Margo does say is that it's very quiet in the office, is it always like this? Tracey tells her that, to be honest about it, they don't really do reconciliation mediation very much any more. They used to but people tend to trace their birth families on Facebook. She wouldn't recommend that. That can go very, very wrong. Being stood up isn't the worst, believe-you-her. You've no idea. Honestly.

Margo was still clinging to the faintest possibility of car crashes or excitement-induced heart attacks but Tracey knows no one is coming. She works here, she's seen it all before. Margo is suddenly so angry that she feels sick and Tracey sees that. She reaches over and squeezes Margo's hand pityingly, which makes it worse.

Margo puts her own hand over Tracey's and squeezes back, maybe a little too hard, and begins to rage-cry. Lilah calls this the ugliest cry of all.

Tracey says kind things: listen-you-to-her-now, you're all right, you're all right, now. It could be worse.

Margo yodels: 'What could possibly be worse than this?'

Tracey talks softly: this is not the worst I've seen, not by a long way. It can go *very* wrong, especially if there isn't a mediator. The state of some of them! Wouldn't you look in the mirror and wash your hair? They've had some right arseholes in here. Tracey's being a lot more frank than she was on the way in. It can be dreadful and she should know because she's been through this herself, oh yeah, and that is why she works here, as a volunteer, because of her own terrible, terrible experience.

She looks at Margo, waiting for a prompt but Margo doesn't care what happened to Tracey. This is happening to her right now and she's overwhelmed.

It takes a moment for Tracey to realise that she isn't going to ask about it. She blinks, shuts that box of horrors and moves on, talking in abstracts: when people meet on the Internet, well, a lot of people are far too young. Don't all teenagers resent their parents? Tracey knows she did. That's part of growing up, isn't it? It's tempting to look for a different family to connect with. There's often an initial delight because, you know, they've kind of solved a mystery, haven't they? Everyone is focused on what they have in common and they ignore the differences, points of conflict, all the while being that wee bit too open with each other. And the birth families, huh! Well, that's a whole other barrel of fish. Most families have stuff going on, don't get her wrong, but sometimes they're just dealing with bad people who want money, for example. There have been situations ... stalking, police involvement ...

Tracey's eyes well up. This is her story. Margo didn't ask when prompted but Tracey has managed to share it anyway. She's making this about her. Her chin twitches, she's about to cry and that's it for Margo. She holds up both hands.

'Tracey, no, look, I'm really sorry – this is all too much for me already. My adoptive mum died recently, I've split up with my partner ...' She stops short of blurting that she's pregnant. 'Can you leave me alone?'

Tracey takes it well. She says of course, no problem at all, take your time, and she gets up and goes out, shutting the door behind her carefully as if she's trying not to wake a sleeping baby.

Margo covers her face and sobs. She's been fantasising about this moment since she was tiny. She'd rather that it went horribly wrong than that no one turned up. She wants to know what Susan died of, do they have genetic mental health issues, she needs to know for her own sake, for the baby's sake. Are they prone to postnatal depression? But she also wants to know more mundane things: did Susan want to keep her? Did she try to get her back? Are her birth family rich or poor, Catholic or Jewish, Irish or Romany? Are they musical? Athletic? Margo has always felt diluted by possibilities. Splintered. She imagined all of these alternative selves existed in parallel worlds and these other lives have meant so much to her. They fostered possibilities and comforted her when things were miserable at home.

But she'll never get to ask. Nikki isn't coming.

The hope she harboured is finally gone and she realises that she shouldn't have come here looking for answers to all of that. She shouldn't have come here at all. It's too much for her right now.

It's over. Fuck it and fuck them. Fuck death and her ex-partner Joe and the smell in here and Tracey's mad intonation. Fuck everything. From now on it's just Margo and the Peanut in her uterus.

Tonight she's going to cheer herself up, go to the movies alone and see something with explosions in it, she's going to drink a bucket of fizzy sugar and eat a family bag of chocolate raisins. She stands up, pulling her hairpins out and scratching at her scalp, shaking her hair loose, letting it stand up and stick out and do what it wants. She rubs her hot eyes, smearing mascara down one side of her face.

This is what she looks like when there is a change in the energy outside the door. She feels it before she hears it: the muffled shriek of a lift arriving.

2

A SUDDEN COMMOTION OUTSIDE, a shrill voice saying indistinct words and Tracey calling a nervous 'hello?' from her office as the new voice cuts high and turns towards the door.

The door is hurriedly opened before Tracey can gallop over from her desk and a very small woman steps into the room and presents herself.

'Oh my God!' shrieks Nikki. 'I can't believe what you're wearing, Patsy!'

There's a lot going on at one time: *Patsy* is the name on Margo's birth certificate, the name given to her before she was handed over at two days old. Margo isn't wearing anything extraordinary, just a cotton shirt and black jeans, so that's odd. She's also distracted by Nikki's voice which is not loud or angry, just a very particular nervous timbre, pitched to be heard over blaring televisions and people screaming at each other. It's a voice she hears patients use in the surgery, the voice of very anxious people and mothers who can't control their kids.

'Hello?' says Margo. 'Are you Nikki?'

'Is that you?' says Nikki.

They examine each other with the bold regard of small children meeting for the first time.

They look nothing alike. Nikki is small and blonde and underweight. Margo is tall with thick black hair, deep-set brown eyes and pearlescent skin.

Nikki's clothes are strange, she looks as if she is wearing a costume. Everything she has on is brand new and slightly too big for her: an immaculate grey trackie top straight from the packet, cuffs rolled up, matching lumpy trackie trousers. Over the pristine grey she wears a beige overcoat with a dangling cloth belt that has never been tied. She looks as if she's had an accident and been given someone else's clothes to wear home. Such plain clothes don't really fit on a woman like Nikki because she's strikingly good-looking. She has good bones, she's graceful and moves with the consciousness of her core that dancers sometimes have: Margo is struck by the slow ease of her long neck, her spine snakes as she slides into the room, her hand movements are eloquent. None of it seems affected either but unconscious and natural.

Her blonde hair is pulled back tight to the nape of her neck. She wears no jewellery and her face is heavily powdered, like the first frame in a YouTube make-up tutorial. Margo thinks it was because she was coming to meet her. It wasn't. She'll soon find out that Nikki has been in court all day and her dull, asexual appearance is a pointed message to old acquaintances and adversaries that her life is very different now, that she is very different now.

She's trembling with nerves but glides across the room, places her arms around Margo's upper arms and gives her an awkward, obligation-hug. Margo is suddenly afraid that Nikki might cry. She sees a lot of emotional displays in the surgery and knows that expressions of emotion and depth of feeling are not the same thing, that sometimes they're opposites. She's suspicious of big dramas and, if she's being honest, finds them a bit vulgar.

Not knowing what else to do, she reciprocates the hug, keeping ahold of Nikki for slightly too long. Reticent, they both bend away from the embrace, keeping their faces clear and throwing themselves off balance so they have to sway from foot to foot like crabs having a fight.

Finally they let go and look again. Margo suddenly sees her own face.

She sees deep-set brown eyes and a pointed chin. She sees good skin under all that powder and stray eyelashes in the inner corner of eyes that mirror her own. She sees things she has never noticed about herself before: eyebrows that threaten to arc into a Ming the Merciless point in the middle, an uneven lip fold.

Margo looks at these echoes of her own face and feels herself change. All the splinter-Margos come together and form a whole, taking up more space in the room. She is a balloon being blown up for the first time, a line drawing becoming three-dimensional.

Nikki sees the likeness too. For a still moment there is nothing in the room but two sets of the same eyes, drinking each other in.

They sit down with their knees touching, Nikki on the sofa, Margo on the office chair. Tracey takes a seat further along the sofa and sits back, a referee giving the fighters room to hurt each other, smiling and tipping her head in a way that feels phoney. Margo senses that she isn't quite wishing them well and tries to bring Tracey into the conversation.

'Weren't you about to shut?'

'Totally happy to wait on.' Tracey gives a slow blink, showing she is being patient but says to Nikki, 'You are nearly two hours late.'

'Got caught up.'

Margo asks, 'In what?'

'Stuff. I's waiting for a thing to start,' says Nikki, 'but they've never called it and they've never said they weren't going to call it until like ten minutes ago. I couldn't know.' She shakes her head as if she can't be bothered talking about that and looks at Margo's hair. 'Our Susan had mad big hair like that. Thick black hair. That's how she got her nickname. "Hairy" they called her.'

Margo grimaces. Hairy is old-lady derogatory Glaswegian slang for a rough, low-class girl. It's a hangover from Edwardian times when low-born girls didn't wear hats. Nikki can see that Margo doesn't like it.

'No, I know,' she says, yanking her coat shut defensively. 'I know calling her Hairy isn't very nice but we all had daft names back then, it was how it was. They used to call me "Goofy". My teeth used to stick right out.' She salutes from her top lip, showing Margo what they used to be like. Margo only now notices that she has false teeth. 'Yeah. Got smashed out by a boyfriend.' Nikki flinches, knowing she's getting everything wrong. 'I mean, thanks actually, because he's done us a favour in a way.' She looks at Margo imploringly.

'What was Susan like?'

'Wee. Smart as a whip. Funny …' She smiles at the memory of her young sister but her expression collapses, suddenly desolate, and her eyes well up. She whispers, 'She was awful bad with the drugs. Heroin. She was small. She never had a chance,' and blushes, blinking back tears as her eyes dart back and forth to Margo, taking her in by bits: hair, clothes, posture, handbag.

This isn't going very well. The class divide between them is glaring and it shames Nikki. It's a source of intense discomfort to Margo too, because she doesn't like to think about class or how privileged she is. She just thinks she's normal.

There are scars between the knuckles on the back of Nikki's hands, emphatic white against the pale pink skin, healed track marks: white station stops on a map of her circulatory system. She has been injecting but stopped a long time ago. She doesn't have the sleepiness of a methadone user or the drowsy disgust of someone on Valium. She doesn't seem to be on anything else.

'I was so sorry to hear that she had died.'

Nikki drops her hands and nods and says, 'Awful sad.'

Margo suspects a heroin overdose. Glasgow suffered an epidemic of overdoses in the years around her birth and now she's seen Nikki's hands it seems even more likely. She hopes it is that and not suicide or anything to do with catastrophically poor genetic mental health.

'You didn't say how she died in your letters.'

Nikki either cringes or winks. Margo hopes it's a cringe. 'I didn't think it would be right …'

'Can I ask you something quite frank?'

Nikki nods that it would be OK.

'Did you have a heroin addiction too?'

Nikki glances at Tracey and suppresses a smirk. It wriggles around behind her lips but her eyes are steely. 'Why ye asking me that?'

'Your hands. I know you've been using intravenous drugs, I can see that you're not on anything now.'

Nikki tugs her coat sleeves down and over her hands and tips her chin defiantly. 'Clean and sober four years.' Her eyes are angry that Margo asked, more so because it was in front of Tracey.

'Four years? That's amazing,' says Margo. 'Hard work.'

'Using is harder work. If you could harness the work ethic of addicts Glasgow would be a paradise.' Tickled by her own wit Nikki smiles, defensive walls down for a moment.

'I've seen a lot of addicts in the surgery,' says Margo. 'I have got some small idea of how momentous what you've done is.'

'You're a doctor. You're amazing.'

Margo isn't really amazing. She's not coping very well. She had a bit of a breakdown after Janette died and has been avoiding work ever since, afraid to admit to having fragile mental health in case she never gets to work again. So she bats the compliment back, 'No, Nikki, *you're* amazing. Four years is amazing. Thanks so much for coming. And for writing.'

'But I've been writing to you for years and you didn't reply.'

Margo doesn't want to blame Janette for hiding the letters but can't think what else to say. She shrugs. 'My mum – my *other* mum. She didn't pass the letters on. I don't really know why. She died quite recently and that's when I found them.'

She expects Nikki to ask about Janette, who was she, did she do a good job bringing Margo up, what was her childhood like, but Nikki doesn't. Her eyes dart quickly to the side, flicking the unwelcome topic off a mental dishcloth.

'I was thinking you didn't want anything to do with me,' sighs Nikki. 'But the timing of this couldn't be better. See how you're a doctor? The case right now … you can help.'

Nikki waits for Margo to ask about this *case right now* that is clearly so important to her. She watches Margo's mouth, slowly nodding. But Nikki didn't ask about Janette and that's important to Margo. She's been waiting for two hours. She doesn't know why she has to be the compliant one all the time.

'Anyway, Nikki, I've got so much I want to ask. When did Susan die?'

'What?'

'How long after I was born?'

'Not long.' Nikki is not pleased about the change of subject. Her eyes harden.

'And she gave me up two days after I was born?'

'No, she gave you up right away.' She can see that goes down badly. 'Look, Susan wanted to keep you, but the way things were … she'd a whole lot of problems, drugs. *Bad*. So … there it is.'

'I'm sorry. I phrased that badly. I'm not reproaching anyone.'

Nikki nods and blinks and looks at Margo's shirt then half smiles and changes the subject, 'OK, look, I need to ask: are you psychic?'

'Am I what?'

'Psychic. There's a lot of that in our family. Seeing the future, stuff like that?'

'No, I'm not, I'm afraid.'

'Oh.' Nikki is disappointed. 'Shame, because the sight does run through us, very strong. I wondered if that's how you became a doctor.'

'No, I'm, um ...'

'I mean, I'm asking because – see that? What you're wearing?' She points at her red shirt and black jeans. 'That's a bit psychic. Look –' She reaches into her shoulder bag and takes out an old yellowed photograph. 'I brought this to give you. This is Susan.'

She hands her the small picture.

A long time ago Susan Brodie stands in a living room, in front of a sideboard and a painting of an Alpine scene, and grins into a camera. She has a more symmetrical nose than Margo and a twisted right front tooth but she has Margo's bushy black hair, her eyes, her skin, her face. She wears a silky red shirt with a big collar and a black pencil skirt, like a waitress in a steakhouse. It's basically what Margo is wearing now. Margo is entranced by the picture.

'Wow.'

'I know. See the clothes, see what I mean?'

'Yeah.'

Nikki giggles, delighted. '*That's your mum.*'

'That's my mum,' echoes Margo.

They sit with that for a while.

'That's for you. You keep that,' whispers Nikki.

'Thank you.'

Margo puts it away in an inner pocket in her handbag and sees Nikki's eyes following it. Giving up the picture is a loss. People didn't used to take a lot of photos. She thanks Nikki but it doesn't feel like enough.

'I'm sorry if I sound dismissive, Nikki, it's just that I'm a scientist and I don't really believe in that stuff.' Her scepticism is not well received. She tries to soften it. 'Do you think you are psychic?' She's wondering if she hears voices.

'Oh, no,' Nikki says, serious, 'I don't have the gift. It's just – we really need a doctor and then you are one. I thought you'd known, sort of psychically …'

That statement doesn't seem to go anywhere.

'I see,' says Margo, 'sorry, it's just, as I say, I'm a scientist.'

'Oh, you know everything then.'

They stare at each other unkindly and Margo breaks first. 'Did Susan know who my dad was?'

Hesitation. 'Yes.' Slow blink.

It feels as if Nikki is about to fabricate a lie. There is no father's name on Margo's birth certificate.

'I mean it's OK if she didn't –'

'Barney Keith.'

The name sounds fictional. 'Right? But she didn't put that name on my birth certificate.'

'You wouldn't want his name.' Nikki can't look at her. 'She's done you a favour there. He's probably dead now anyway.'

A coldness settles between them. Margo doesn't know what she's done wrong. She wants to know if Susan died of something hereditary but she doesn't know how to ask now.

'Poor Susan …'

'Aye.'

'I'm so sorry.'

'Oh aye, yeah. She was *it* for me. She was my wee sister. She was the world to me and I was it for her. Know what I mean?'

'How did she die … ?'

'Got murdered.' She says it carelessly, as if they're talking about a lost scarf.

'*Murdered*?'

'Yeah. There was a lot of that back then.'

'Oh? Back – when is this we're talking about?'

'Aye … late eighties, early nineties. Lot of it.'

'I'm so sorry, I didn't know. Who murdered her?'

'A stranger off the street.'

'Oh God, how awful, I'm so sorry.'

'I know who it was, I know where he lives, I know what he did, I just can't get him.'

'Oh!' This is what she was hinting about in her letters, this is the Jack the Ripper stuff. Margo wants to steer her away from it. 'Well! What else can you tell me about Susan herself? Was Susan tall?'

'No. 'Bout five foot three.'

'Did she do well at school?'

'No.'

'Did she like to read?'

'No.'

This isn't going well. Margo thinks Nikki might like to talk about herself. 'Do you have children of your own, Nikki?'

'Ah no, sadly.'

'Did you want children?'

'Of course I did. I'm normal.'

Quite an odd reason to have children but Margo has patients who've had kids for less cogent reasons.

'When did Susan –'

'Look, this is a whole lot of questions,' says Nikki, blinking nervously. 'I thought we were just going to meet each other.'

'Sorry.'

''S OK but – it's a lot. Today has been – a lot.'

'Fair enough. Thank you so much, again, for the photograph. It means a lot to me.'

'You're welcome. Can't believe your hair is her hair.'

'I've never seen anyone else with my hair before.'

'I know, me neither, it's unique! That's what she used to say. Unique!'

Confident that the meeting is going smoothly, Tracey stands up and says that the office is about to shut but maybe they'd like to stay on for a wee fifteen minutes or so and have a cup of tea? It's very kind of her. She's already staying late, past the end of her shift, hoping that the meeting can be salvaged. Mindful of this, Margo says no thanks but Nikki says oh, aye, please, she's dead thirsty. Tracey goes off to get it, leaving the door ajar.

Nikki watches her leave, keeping her eyes on the corridor as she whispers urgently to Margo:

'She was murdered by Martin McPhail. They never got enough on him, but you and me, you being a doctor, we can catch the fucker.'

Margo blinks. In the distance she can hear a kettle boiling.

3

'You're a doctor, right?'

'Yes.'

'Patient records are all on computer now, yeah?'

'Yes.'

'OK. They interviewed him about Susan's murder but say he was in hospital at the time. You're a doctor, you can see his medical records, you can tell us for sure he wasn't in hospital and we can prove it was him.'

'Sorry – why don't you tell the police about this, if you're so sure?'

'The cops know. The cops covered it up. A conspiracy.'

Margo feels herself withdrawing. The police don't do that, have no reason to do that. From her experience of working in the large organisation of the NHS, there isn't time to elaborately cover things up or conspire because so much time is spent infighting, and she's fairly sure the police are the same.

'They lied about his alibi but you can prove he wasn't in hospital that night. I've got all the other evidence we need. *I've got it.*' Nikki stares at Margo, mouth agape.

'I can't do that.'

'But it's all on computers. You can go into his records –'

'Not unless he's my patient, I can't. That's illegal.'

Nikki tuts dismissively.

'No,' says Margo, 'you don't understand: I could have my licence to practise medicine revoked if I access the records of someone who isn't a patient. We're not allowed to just go in and have a rummage around. It's not like a dating app, you can't just check out the records of your family and friends. People have lost their jobs for doing things like that.'

'Well, I mean, I won't tell on you.'

'If the records were released they'd go into the system to see who accessed them. It would bring them straight back to me.'

'But we'll leak it. They won't know it was you. We'll leak it.'

'You're not hearing me: I have to sign in, there are security checks on the way *into* patients' records. They can trace the individual users who access any record.'

'You could if you wanted to.'

'That's right. I don't want to and I'm not going to.' She doesn't want to be rude but she does want to be very clear.

'You're just going to let him go?' Nikki looks disgusted. 'He murdered your mother and you're just walking away?'

'Well, what's interesting about what you're saying, what's occurring to me as I listen to you now ...' Margo has techniques. Most doctors don't have terribly good social skills but she does. She can shape and direct a conversation from annoyance at a neighbour to the giant, ever-changing mole on a patient's neck. She hears a surprising number of conspiracy theories in the surgery and listens carefully. Sometimes it's an indicator of an underlying mental illness. Sometimes it just means they spend too much time reading rubbish online and have to get out more. '... is why would the police give an alibi to Susan's murderer? What interest do they have in doing that?'

'McPhail was a cop at the time.'

Margo blinks.

'They'll never go after him. They'd be liable for a big payout if he was found guilty. He's untouchable. He knows that.'

'Oh.'

'Aye, I know. There was nine lassies killed in Glasgow back then, they got two convictions of other people, they were fit-ups. Smoke and mirrors. Cover their backs. I know there's other families feel the same way I do, but they're not being hunted the way I am. I can't just do nothing. It's getting worse. He's still writing to me.'

'Writing to you?'

'Threatening me. He's letting me know he knows where I live, he says he's going to kill me.'

Margo says it reflexively: 'You should go to the police ... oh.'

'See what I mean?'

'Oh.' She tries to think of something positive to say but, really, she just wants to get away from here now. 'Does this McPhail man sign the letters?'

'As good as. He sends me bits of the clothes Susan was wearing when he killed her, describing her, things about her, stuff only he could know.'

'Has this just started?'

'He's been doing it for thirty years. Since she died, he's been doing it. Years in between the letters but he always knows where I live. When I move he writes to me.'

'Still, if you've been getting them for thirty years and nothing has happened? That's quite a long time to threaten someone for, isn't it? Probably means he won't actually do anything?'

'Until he does. I know he's enjoying upsetting me.' Nikki gives a bitter smile. 'I know that's why he does it. But know that film? The one about the cop? With her in it?' She clicks her fingers, trying to remember. 'You know the one: he's a psychiatrist in the FBI and she's a cop? If they don't catch him in time he'll kill again?'

'Isn't that all of them?'

'But in that one he doesn't care about killing them, he wants to scare them. He does kill them at the end but what he enjoys is their fear, he's getting off on it, like –' She mimes masturbating a man slightly too vividly. She all but spits on her hand.

The conversation has taken quite a bizarre turn. Margo's already allowing for the fact that long-term drug misuse would leave Nikki disinhibited, with strange patterns of speech and odd coping strategies, possible memory gaps, but eloquently miming a handjob is quite hardcore especially when it's done in the first five minutes of a family reunion by a woman in her mid-fifties. Nikki knows she's done something wrong but rattles on anyway. 'If you won't look up his record, you could get someone else to do it, couldn't you?'

Margo shakes her head. 'I'm not doing that.'

'OK.' Nikki huffs in exasperation. 'Well, here's another thing you can do: I've got samples of his DNA. I can prove that he killed Susan but the cops won't even test it.'

'Where are the samples from?'

'On the letters.'

'Well, if that pans out what you've got there is proof that he wrote the letters, not that he did the murder.'

'But only the murderer could write the letters because he sends me things she had with her that night, the night he killed her. I've got the proof. What I need is a doctor to test it.'

'You don't need a doctor, you need a DNA lab.'

But Nikki isn't listening. 'See today? I was at that High Court, some poor guy with a Russian name, Moorov, he's up for one of those old murders. DNA. He wasn't even in the frame back then, they thought it was her boyfriend.'

'You were there?'

'I was waiting for the case to come up but they didn't call it. We were all waiting for hours. I had to be there, for Susan. This is what I'm saying about being psychic, the timing and everything.'

Margo concedes. 'Well, that *is* quite weird.'

And Nikki warms to her. 'Isn't it? Isn't it, though?'

'Yeah.'

'But I mean, what does it mean? Meeting you on the same day that that comes up: nothing. It means nothing. But it is weird.'

'It is quite weird.'

They have reached a consensus: *this is quite weird*. And somehow it bridges the gap between them because the will to connect is there. But Margo sees Nikki suddenly wonder how she can use her to get what she wants.

'I thought McPhail might be there today.'

'Why?'

'He did this one as well. He'd be there enjoying it. Watching all of us. They're saying they've found this Russian's DNA on the lassie. Does that mean he's killed her? I don't know. Could have been McPhail again. The girl was working the streets, for fucksake, she'd have been teeming with DNA. But see –' she leans in to Margo – 'the DNA on those letters – *that's definitely just him.*'

'So ... sorry, what actually happened to Susan?'

Nikki takes a breath and slows herself down. 'She was abducted in a van. She was murdered. Her body was dumped at a bus stop in Easterhouse and found the next morning.'

'Gosh, and this was ... ?'

'October 12th 1989. The anniversary is just by. I light a candle ... No one else really remembers but back then it was like Jack the Ripper times. Girls were dropping like flies out there and no one remembers. Cops didn't bother their arses, no one cares, but you could help me if you wanted. You could look at his record. You could test his DNA.'

'I see.' Margo has partially shut down. She's a public servant herself and knows that police officers don't do things like that. People don't get murdered and no one cares. She has information to harvest and then she wants to go. 'How old was Susan when she had me?'

Nikki shrugs. 'Nineteen?'

'Oh, not quite as young as I thought ...' She had supposed Susan was a mid-teen, perhaps too young to look after a baby. Nineteen seems quite grown up.

'So, the cops refused to admit McPhail could have done it. Still refuse. But he was corrupt. He was giving out baggies for blow jobs, was rough, was taking girls in his car, two, three at a time, he had a thing about pissing. I mean we all knew him, me, Susan, all the lassies out there, working on the street for our drug money, oh aye, we *all* knew.'

Did Nikki just tell Margo that her birth mother was a drug-addicted street prostitute? Margo looks up and sees that she did. Nikki watches it land. Margo doesn't think she meant to be mean when she told her though. It just seemed to come out.

'Right?' says Margo. 'Susan? She was ...' Descriptors fail her. '*Out there?*'

'She didn't want to be. No one does. She was doing it because she was desperate with the drugs, our Susan. Just, incredible, the worst I've ever seen. Never seen anyone as bad with it. She was spending three hundred quid a day.' Nikki flattens her hand to her chest. 'Me? At my worst two hundred, and I was bad.'

'And this addiction led Susan into ... sex work?'

'Oh yeah. Worked the Drag down Anderson way and men was down there, preying on us like Jack the Ripper. Just like him, just as vicious. Some people think it was one guy, some folk think it was all McPhail –'

'Nikki ... this is too much.'

'Yeah, I know, so – not the records but will you help me with the DNA?'

'No, I mean this whole thing, it's too much. I'm just here to find out where I came from, this isn't for me.'

'But she's your *mum*.'

'Not for me.'

Margo clears her throat. She's afraid to look up and meet Nikki's eye.

Out in the office they can hear Tracey fixing the tea, opening the fridge door to get the milk – pphhut – closing it – poup – laying a tray. Margo is planning how to get away from Nikki. When they get down to the street she'll run or jump a cab, because fuck this.

'You're like everyone else,' whispers Nikki. 'You don't care.'

'I do, Nikki, but I'm not here to get involved in something … it's a lot to take in.'

'You could help if you wanted to.' Nikki narrows her eyes. 'You're clever. A clever lassie.'

Nikki doesn't know if Margo is clever; what she means is Margo is middle class and people will listen to her, that she has access to resources and medical files and DNA labs and Nikki doesn't. Margo does have access to those things and she retains access because she plays by the rules, understands the limitations, knows when to shut up and knows not to accuse the police of conspiracy.

'I think Tracey wants to shut the office.'

'You don't care.'

'I really think you should give the letters to the police.'

'I did. They said they meant nothing.'

'Well, if the police say that –'

'You could do the DNA on them.'

'Look: DNA tests are only confirmatory and they cost money and would be completely pointless in this instance because I don't have access to a database to compare a sample to.'

'Can't you get access to one?'

Nikki's upset but there's so much to explain that Margo doesn't know where to start. She just wants to get up and leave, but just at that moment, Nikki wipes her nose with her hand. She wipes left to right and left again, using her index finger, curling her hand on the recoil. It's a very specific gesture executed in a very specific way. She has a mild crease on her left nostril showing where she has been repeating that exact movement for years. Margo did that. She used to always do that until Janette berated her to stop – use a handkerchief, for goodness' sake, that's revolting. She still has to remind herself not to. She has never, ever seen anyone else do it.

'Because you're a *doctor*. I mean, if you can't do it, who will?'

'Nikki,' Margo says carefully, 'please listen to me: I'm not getting involved in that. It's not that I won't help you, it's that I can't help you. I'm trying to be very clear. You've misunderstood the procedure involved in getting access to medical records and what is achieved by sampling DNA.'

'Oh. OK.' Nikki crosses her legs away. 'OK, well, fine. What do you want to talk about then, if you don't want to talk about Susan?'

Me, thinks Margo. I want to talk about me. 'I do want to talk about Susan –'

'It was hard for an addict to go through with a full pregnancy, you know, it was hard for all of us.'

That's the end of it for Margo. 'Look, I know Susan was clean when she had me.'

Nikki looks guilty. 'No, she wasn't. She was a heroin user, she was caning it up to the last minute before you were born –'

'No, she wasn't. I know that's not true.'

She can see Nikki trying to work out how she knows that. 'No, but –'

'Because I was handed over to Janette at two days. If Susan was using when she gave birth to me I would have been kept in for longer. Any baby born to an active drug user would be kept in intensive care, they'd be monitored and bloods would be taken, they wouldn't be released for weeks. My birth weight was over nine pounds. Susan must have been clean. If there was any suggestion that she was using they would have kept me in for observation.'

Nikki blinks hard. She half shakes her head and whispers, 'Yeah, well, the gear was a lot weaker then.'

But Susan was clean. Margo has thought hard about that over the years. It matters to her because she has worried about damage that might have been done to her *in utero*, missing neurological paths and attachment issues. She has obsessed about genetics, most adoptees do, and as a medical student her interest took on an extra dimension.

Nikki is lying but patients lie to doctors all the time, as if the counter-evidence isn't carved into their lungs and ventricles and livers. Sometimes it's not because they're ashamed or malicious. Sometimes it's a coded way to impart important information: I am in pain, I'm depressed, my drinking is compulsive.

Margo suddenly thinks that maybe Nikki isn't lying about Susan because she's vindictive and manipulative. Maybe she's just nuts and people can't always help that. Is Nikki really saying: I cared for you before you were born so be nice to me? Maybe Susan is alive. Maybe Nikki *is* Susan. Maybe she couldn't face Margo as herself, but why would she choose that story? She could have said Susan died arranging flowers or saving a dog from a river or something because this corrupt cop murder story isn't making Margo interested. It's making her want to run away.

'Here we are!' Tracey comes back in with a breezy smile and a tray with a mug, a selection of sugar sachets standing upright in a glass, a carton of milk and a plate of biscuits. 'Tea!'

There's a lot of messing around with the tea, does Nikki want milk, sugar or sweetener? Biscuit? Have you tried these ones? Nikki answers politely, fluent in the universal coded language of biscuits: these are lovely, I've had them before, have you tried the Lidl version? They're great. These have nicer chocolate though.

Margo nods and shakes her head and wonders about Nikki having the presence of mind to wait until Tracey was out of the room before saying all that mad stuff.

'Where was Susan living when she had me?'

'Wi' Barney Keith.'

'Can you tell me more about her? Anything?'

'Looked like you. Same hair.'

She's already said that.

'Did she like music? Did she keep well? Did she have asthma or eczema?'

'Oh, now *you* want *me* to help you?' Nikki eats her biscuit angrily and looks at Tracey. Then she downs her tea in a oner and is on her feet, indicating that Margo should get up.

'OK. Come on then. We'll go to a pub and I'll answer your questions and we can talk about the DNA thing.' She says to Tracey, 'Thanks for your help. We're offski.'

Tracey isn't sure about them leaving together so soon after meeting and she asks to talk to Margo alone. They put Nikki out in the corridor and shut the door and Tracey asks if Margo is happy to leave with her aunt. Margo isn't but she just wants to get out now so she says it's fine. Thank you for your patience. Tracey'll phone Margo tomorrow and check everything is OK.

Nikki is invited back in and sees that she has won without being told. They gather their things, sign some papers and Nikki apologises to Tracey for being 'that wee bit late' as they pull on their jackets and scarves.

They leave the office and walk downstairs together, their steps slowing as they move from oppressive warmth to the cold. The strangeness of the situation dawns on both of them: they look alike but they're not alike. They're family but they're not family.

As they pass the glass door into a dark office suite Margo catches their reflection. She looks like a stodgy social worker, escorting a difficult client to an appointment she simply must attend. They don't fit together at all.

Margo has not had a cloistered life. She worked in Accident and Emergency for two years and has dealt with people from all over the city, set bones, extracted knives from legs and glass from faces, but this is too much for her. It's mad and sad and makes no narrative sense. Nikki doesn't care how she feels about this.

They pass through the foyer and step out into the cold street.

It's dark. The temperature has plummeted. A crisp frost is forming on the pavement and the bonnets of parked cars. It was sunny and bright when Margo went in. She feels as if Nikki has stolen the day from her.

'Mon, well,' Nikki pulls her by the elbow to George Square.

Shoulder to shoulder with her confabulating aunt, she walks towards the corner. There's a pub across the street – that's where Nikki is taking her. It has steep stairs up to the entrance. Margo has been in George Square hundreds of times, for concerts and demos and Hogmanay parties, cutting across it to Queen Street Station. She'd swear on her life that she has never, ever seen that pub before. Red blinds are pulled low in all the windows. She feels as if she'll never get out if she goes in.

The traffic favours them and they cross straight over, dazzled by the headlights of waiting cars, stark against the dark. Nikki is walking so fluidly that she seems to be falling forwards in a dance, leading with her chin, hardly breaking step as they reach the kerb and she skips up the steps to the pub door. Margo knows that whatever is said in there will just involve her saying more noes to Nikki, no to losing her licence to challenge a conspiracy that doesn't exist, no to trying to save a mother who has already died.

'Nikki.' Margo stops at the bottom of the steps and looks up at her.

Nikki turns back, smiling, her face a question.

'I'm sorry, this isn't ... I just don't know how ...' Margo backs away, turns to the road. She waves a panicky arm and a passing taxi draws into the kerb. She's opening the door and scrambling in before the driver even gets the handbrake on.

The taxi pulls away and she keeps her eyes front, sees Nikki's silhouette from the corner of her eye as it slides past the window. The taxi turns a corner and she sits back, taking deep calming breaths.

She did the right thing. She did what she could. She doesn't owe Nikki anything. She did the right thing. She's allowed to leave. She can choose.

The taxi rumbles down through the town and she takes her phone out and googles 'Susan Brodie', 'Glasgow' and 'murder'.

And this is how she finds out that Nikki was telling the truth.

Mostly.

4

WATCHING THE TWO OF them coming out of the door, walking down the street like a pair of bitches with somewhere to go. Two of them. Nikki and a woman who is Susan Brodie's double. But older than Susan. Susan if she'd got older.

It's exciting, watching the traces of the long-dead girl in a new face, shuffling along behind Nikki, along the pavement to the lights, over the road, going straight for a pub.

Nikki's doing her usual: looking for something to take the edge off.

Nikki Brodie looks a million years old now. Skinny, nothing to her, face like a bag of balls, teeth all different. The new teeth change the shape of her face completely. She's dressed up all clean and normal like she's going to a probation hearing. No pelmet skirts or bra tops, none of the shit she used to wear. She looks boring and respectable. Ridiculous for someone like that, who's done the things she's done, things she's done with that dry old body.

How many did she take on? How many alleys and billboards did she go behind, demean herself, dirty herself, rolling in the filth there and smiling when the money was put in her hands? Yet there she is, walking along a road like a clean, normal person, pushing the button at the lights. Anyone could touch that button after her. A clean, decent person could touch it, a child could press it and get the traces of Nikki Brodie on their hand. She dirties everything she touches.

Something happens on the pub stairs, can't see what, can't hear, but then the Susan-looking one is backing away, she seems scared. Maybe she has seen the filthiness of Nikki Brodie, the squalor of her, and got disgusted and needed to run.

Maybe other people can see it too, that Nikki Brodie is nothing but a stain.

5

IT'S DARK INSIDE THE taxi cab but Margo is staring into the bright face of her phone. She's mesmerised by only the second photograph she has ever seen of her birth mother. Susan looks even more like her in this one than the one Nikki gave her because she's not smiling.

Susan is sitting against a blank white background. She looks unsure, her expression wary, as she watches someone to the left of the frame. Someone behind the camera seems to be directing her. She's wearing a coat with a furry collar and is catastrophically thin. Her cheeks are hollow, she has a cluster of cold sores on one side of her mouth but has lip-pencilled over them. She looks very young, still very much like Margo but a splinter Margo, one who lost a bet with life. It's a strange photograph for a newspaper article to use of a victim.

The legend underneath reads: *Susan Brodie: Vice Girl's Body Found*.

Margo pinches in so that the photo fills the screen. She's avoiding the text of the article because the contrast between the story and the algorithmic setting is too much. The story is a retrospective of a dark episode in Glasgow, a time when nine young women were murdered less than a mile from

George Square, when drug deaths hit an all-time high, when her mother was stolen and killed. This is intercut with animated offers of free online bingo games and an advert for package holidays: a woman in a red swimming costume singing show tunes about being happy on a beach.

She's focused on Susan. Stray, fractured words from the article hit her eye: '-ecially brutal', 'several murde-', 'McPhail', 'plague'. She doesn't want to read much more about that, her mood is so low already.

The photograph holds her there. Susan. Other Margo. She's looking off to the side and Margo dips her head as if, through time and the magic of a Google search, she could catch her dead mother's eye and smile and reassure her because Susan looks poor and lost. She looks drug-addled. She looks like a casualty. Maybe she was using when Margo was born. Janette could have lied about the timing – she had books about attachment in the house and must have worried.

To make herself leave the screen, Margo takes a screenshot and saves it. Then she phones her brother in Saudi.

Thomas picks up. 'What?'

'Where are you?' she says, because that is what she always says when Thomas picks up.

He's in some bloke's apartment, watching rugby. She can hear from the background burble that there are lots of people there. He says they're all drinking beer and eating curry. What's she phoning for?

'I went to meet my mum ...'

He's distracted by the match and says he forgot she was going to the adoption agency today. 'How'd it go?'

'I met an aunt. I saw a photo of Susan and she's got crazy hair, like mine. Same eyebrows as well.'

'Wow.' She's not sure if he's commenting on the rugby or her news about the hair.

Riyadh is only three hours ahead but she and Thomas always seem to be in different moments: she's having a busy morning and he's full of lunch. He's falling asleep and she's just got in from work. Their moods never match.

He's a year older than her. They were kind to each other growing up but he's a hard man to stay close to. They're very different. Margo works for and loves the NHS. Thomas hates rainy Glasgow and lives in Saudi for the tax breaks. All their friends visit him for free holidays but Margo only went once and had to come home early. She said she couldn't cope with the heat but, really, she hated the compound lifestyle and told Joe, her ex, that Thomas was living like a factory animal. Now she worries that he'll tell Thomas she said that. She knows they're still in touch.

He asks if her mum was fourteen when she had her.

'No, she was nineteen,' says Margo.

'She wasn't forced to give you up, then? A nun didn't rip you from her arms?'

'No.'

'She just gave you away.'

Thomas is bitter about being adopted and always has been. He has no interest in tracing his own birth family. Margo has always been more sanguine. Thomas was an unhappy child and thinks it's because he was adopted into a family that fell apart. When he speculates about his birth mother he says she was probably a fourteen-year-old slut who left him in a McDonald's. He never speculates about his birth father. He doesn't think that's relevant, says it could be anyone, that his imaginary teen mother probably serviced all comers and got paid in packets of crisps.

Margo snickered when he said those things because she was young and he was her big brother. She laughed with Thomas about his slut mother, about promiscuous girls, at jokes about the local bike. She laughed along and absorbed the implied set of rules about the dangers of enjoying her own body, about keeping it controlled, appropriate, thin, young and white. They sneered together because they'd been rejected and it felt empowering to reject back. But now she sits in the taxi, looking out of the window at the acres of overgrown waste ground in the Gorbals and imagines a pregnant fourteen-year-old Susan eating crisps, not knowing who the father of her child is because she could have been impregnated by so many men. It's horrific. She'd take Susan straight to social services and call the police, get them to find the men who did that to a fourteen-year-old and get them off the streets. She can feel the hairs on her neck stand up when she imagines that. Excitement. The thrill of righteous anger.

'So, is your aunt as rough as buggery?' says Thomas.

Margo can't bear to lose a fight to Thomas. 'No, Nikki's very nice. She's a nice lady.'

'Yeah? What does she do for a living?' He's shooting questions as if he's making conversation at a company drinks party.

'Works in a cake shop.'

It's the only non-professional middle-class job she can think of. She's trying to sell Nikki to Thomas but, really, Thomas doesn't care about that. It's Margo who would like Nikki more if she worked in a cake shop. If Nikki bred labradoodles or had a rose garden or lived in the country Margo might read Nikki's crassness as her being straightforward, her lateness and no-nonsense manner as eccentricity. Now she just thinks Nikki's a scary ned. She can never let Thomas meet Nikki because, if he does, Margo will be the only thing worse than a snob: she'll be an exposed snob.

'You going to see her again?' asks Thomas.

'Nah, think we'll just leave it there.'

He likes that. His voice is lighter when he says, 'Will Janette's be cleared for the estate agent next week?'

'Getting there.'

'Is it going OK?'

'Oh yeah.' It's going incredibly badly. She's mostly crying in different rooms but doesn't want to tell him that. She said she'd do it and she hasn't.

'Hey, well, I'm sorry it's all down to you, Margie, but thanks for taking it on.'

'No worries,' she says, though she is nothing but a big bag of worries.

She's scared that Thomas will float away from her when it's all sold and settled. Until now they've been held close by the crippling cost of Janette's care and she's terrified she'll lose him. She's worried she did the wrong thing, walking out on Joe, and she hasn't told anyone she's pregnant yet. She was hoping Nikki would be warm and motherly, maybe present her with a warm extended family and invite her in, that it would be straightforward.

'Anyway!' she says. 'Anyway, clearing out is keeping me busy. Nikki gave me a photo of my mum and she looks exactly like me.'

Thomas tells her to send him the picture and she has to hang up to do it. She doesn't want him to see the newspaper one. She takes a picture of the photo Nikki gave her and sends it. Thomas texts back in seconds.

Don't be a bloody dork. He sounds like all those ex-pat arse-holes out there.

She doesn't know what he means. She texts back, *?*

Not of you. Send pic OF HER.

She takes a deep breath. She isn't imagining it, he can see the crushing likeness between them too. She texts back telling him to look carefully at the teeth. A moment later Thomas replies with a surprised emoji.

She sits in the dark taxi staring at the photo of Susan on her phone, willing Thomas to call or text again, but he does neither.

Susan looks so much like Margo it's frightening. Same face and hair and long neck, same stubby fingers, same eyes. She wants to phone Joe and talk to him about it but that's not fair. It's not fair to call him for emotional support. She left him after all.

The image dims and dies, leaving her alone with her thoughts and a rising sense of panic.

Margo stabs in her security code and buries her face in her phone, skimming the article about long-ago dead women and far-future holidays. She backtracks and opens another one about the case today. It was brought against a man called Moorov from Blantyre. Police took a DNA swab from him when the garage he worked in was robbed and got a hit for the thirty-year-old murder. He was not interviewed at the time and had never been a suspect. He was expected to plead guilty.

An inset paragraph gives a recap of all the murders and Susan Brodie is fourth on the list. She was nineteen when she was killed, her body was dumped in Easterhouse. No one was ever charged with her murder but Martin McPhail, a police officer who left the force shortly afterwards, was named as her killer in a book about the killings. He is currently suing the author.

Margo looks out at the dark wasteland and then glances up to the rear view mirror. She sees the taxi driver's eyes slide towards her. Suddenly self-conscious, she arranges her face for viewing and looks back out of the window.

They stop at the Eglinton lights, where a train line to London cuts beneath the road and the M74 to Carlisle fly-over passes above.

With every passing moment she feels more adrift and alone.

6

THE CAB PULLS UP in Holly Road and Margo pays, gets out and lets the taxi draw away behind her. Unaware that she is being watched, she stands on the pavement and looks up at her flat. She is still paying rent on the flat she shared with Joe and this is all she can afford. She can't face living all alone in Janette's house but she hates it here.

It's a new building, positioned in a vacant space between nice tenements, facing pretty old town houses across a narrow street. The neighbours hate the people who live here because it is ugly, the work was contentious, the sound insulation is awful and they're all short-term tenants in an area of proud homeowners.

She thumbs the code into the keypad on the door and pushes it open, tramping up to her sterile rented flat in this sterile rented building.

The building isn't good quality. There's a parsimonious-ness to everything: the rooms are too small, doors are hollow, sinks and baths are shallow. Nothing is scuffed or broken but it's just a matter of time. She moved in two months ago when she left Joe because it was available, cheap and close to Janette's house. Now she feels shaped by the meanness of it. A single vase makes a room feel cluttered. The heat rising from the flats downstairs makes it too warm. She's always got a headache because she grinds her teeth when she's here.

She opens her front door, drops her coat and bag in the tiny hall, goes into the bathroom and starts running a bath. She wants to wash the night off herself.

The man downstairs is playing a computer game. He plays it at night and the soundtrack is thunder or explosions or something but, heard through the floor, it sounds as if he's moving furniture all night for hours. She can feel it in her bones as she texts a prompt to Lilah:

Aunt turned up. Hello and goodbye. Bit mad. How was baby shower?

She gets nothing back. Lilah turns her phone on and off like a pensioner conserving the battery because she can't always be bothered talking.

In the living room Margo opens her laptop and turns it on. She looks at the screen for a moment and then she does exactly what Tracey warned her not to do: she looks up Barney Keith.

Facebook has only one Barney Keith living in Glasgow but he doesn't look anything like her. He has fishy lips and yellow skin and small eyes and he's ancient. He lives over in Nitshill, on the far southern outskirts of Glasgow, and isn't a big Facebook slave. His posts are intermittent. He can't spell very well and uses a lot of text speak, numbers for words and emojis for emotions. He expresses his identity through strings of emoji flags. She works out his address from his posts complaining about the bin men. On Google Street View she can see a grey pebble-dash terraced council house and a front garden littered with a washing machine, skip bags of rubble and dog shit. Her heart sinks until she realises that this can't possibly be her father, he's twenty or thirty years older than Susan would be now if she had lived. She's surprised, she'd have thought it was an unusual name but there must be another one and he's not on Facebook. She's quite proud of that in a way. Maybe he's got a life going on, doesn't feel the need to advertise. Maybe this Barney is some sort of relation to him.

The pitch of the running water changes and she gets up and goes into the bathroom, leaning over to turn the tap off. She stands up and catches sight of herself in the mirror. It's Susan Brodie, back from the dead, standing in Margo's horrible flat, caught unaware.

Back in the living room she looks up old newspaper articles about Susan Brodie. There aren't many. Mostly Susan is in a sidebar, a bit of backstory to a series of murders a long time ago. A disgraced ex-police officer, Martin McPhail, was interviewed about her murder but no charges were ever brought. Over the course of a decade nine different women were killed in the same small area of Glasgow, all sex workers. Police struggled to get information from the public or make arrests until Tanya Williams.

Unlike Susan's photo, Tanya's picture is of a smiling blonde, very thin and young. She looks sweet and giggly with big eyes and backcombed crazy hair. Her grey-haired mother is pictured too, holding a family photo of Tanya riding a horse. Tanya wanted to travel and hoped to study nursing one day. Her grandmother had died and Tanya turned to drugs to cope with her grief. They had been very close.

The other women are represented quite differently, in what seem to be arrest photographs. Their murders are listed chronologically. It gives each woman's name, her age, whether or not she had children and the method of her death: strangled, stabbed, beaten with a brick. Susan Brodie is listed as: age nineteen, no children, abducted, body dumped in Easterhouse. Margo was four months old when Susan died. She would have been cosily tucked up at Paul and Janette's, long before their marriage went sour.

That's all the papers say about the other murdered women. It's a cold, factual list that could be about someone stealing park benches: an old one was taken from here, a green one from there, are these bench thefts connected? What are the police doing to stop the bench thieves?

In all of them Susan is just a detail. Margo wonders if Nikki made up the killer-cop story as a counter to Susan's roaring insignificance. But the articles mention him too.

Some of the tabloids even have a photo of McPhail. He's fat and square and red-faced, looks as if he has high blood pressure but he's smoking in the street, looking to the side as if he has spotted someone he knows. Next to him is a picture of a very good-looking man. He's blond, tanned and lean, wears a cotton shirt and has a big, handsome face. It's the author Martin McPhail is suing for defamation, Jack Robertson.

Robertson left journalism in 2003 and wrote a book about the case of the Glasgow murders, *Terror on the Streets*. A search of his name shows Robertson at a variety of book signings, wearing various noisy shirts, giving talks to adoring crowds of, mostly, women. Robertson's book theorises that a serial killer committed 'most, if not all' of the murders. There's a profile interview where he poses in a dank alleyway at night, looking worried. His book was a bestseller and he's reported as having sold the film rights for a six-figure sum. Margo isn't sure that's true. It's on Wikipedia and could have been written by Robertson.

Lilah finally texts back:

CARNAGE. Massive fight.

Margo replies:

OMG?

Can't talk. Still here with police.

You OK?

No one hurt but very annoying. Broken window.

Margo half laughs to herself. It was supposed to be a bunch of women in their thirties drinking wine and cooing over baby clothes, not a drunken brawl, but she stops suddenly as she realises that it's bound to be something to do with that wanker Richard. She knows it is because of the minimising tone of *'very annoying'*. Lilah makes everything else more dramatic and downplays every outrage by her mental ex-boyfriend.

M and P tomorrow am?

Margo replies:

Deffo. 10am?

After a pause Lilah texts back:

Unable to locate thumbs up or whichever emoji is taken to indicate the affirmative. In summation: yes.

Margo smiles at that, even though she knows Lilah is being playful because she doesn't want Margo to ask for details. Margo doesn't want to be quizzed too closely either so they're quits.

She goes back to her laptop. There must be more about Susan than an odd paragraph here and there. When patient files are lost at work Margo always tries a variant spelling, so she tries a search for 'Suzanne', 'Brodie' and 'Glasgow' and this brings up a different set of hits, mostly for a radio presenter, but on the second page, right at the bottom, is a heading: REALCRIMESCENE.com. She opens it to a page with blood splattered across it and a series of numerical links, one of which has 'SB' next to it. She clicks on the listing.

A photograph of a cold blue morning. A bus stop in a grey place: a kerb, a pavement and a naked body lying on trampled mud. The crime picture is wide, taking in the overall scene. Gathered in the gutter are soggy cigarette ends, dropped by people getting on buses. The cob-orange filters have unravelled in the rain and lie around like little square sweetie wrappers. The bus stop is just a pole with a timetable attached, tagged and unreadable.

Beyond that is Susan. She's lying on her back on a red and yellow tartan rug. It's a lap rug, too small to protect her from the cold ground. Her skin is pearlescent, radiant white because it's so bloodless. Susan has been stabbed through the heart, in the upper left thoracic quadrant, six or seven times. The blood has been washed from her body, the skin has contracted around the wounds and they gape, a cluster of tiny mouths screaming in chorus. Her arms are limp, one thrown out to one side, the other draped across her chest. She looks as if she's been thrown out of a van. She has the waxy pallor and sunken sockets of a day dead. Her breasts rest on the side of her ribcage. She isn't underweight. Most addicts are. Both upper arms are bruised where she has been restrained but there are no track marks, none on her legs or feet either. Susan wasn't using when she died.

Margo has dissected corpses. She has removed and weighed livers and lungs. She isn't shocked by the sight of death or injury but she isn't ready for Susan's vulnerability and how young she is. She's small for nineteen, childlike, and dead and dumped, naked on frozen mud.

It doesn't feel as if she's looking at someone else at all but a younger self, a splinter Margo. No one was punished for this. They did this to a young woman and they're still out there, walking around, eating biscuits, drinking tea, having Christmases. She feels the injustice of it deep in her gut, the way Nikki must have for decades, a cross between fear and nausea. It's wrong.

That picture should not be in the public domain. How did a police photograph come to be on the web? What purpose does it serve? At medical school students were tutored over the course of a full term in how to approach a cadaver with respect, but Susan's body is just an object, up on a web page for people to use. What are they using it for? A cheap, horrified thrill? Are men masturbating to this picture? Susan's just a kid. They wouldn't have posted it if she had a family who were able to stand up for her.

A flash of silver skin catches Margo's eye on Susan's lower abdomen. It's a stretch mark, the trace of a full-term pregnancy. It starts just above her pubis and branches out, growing and widening over her stomach like the ghost of a silver birch.

Margo touches the screen, feels the warmth as if it's from skin, from her mum, as if she has wished her alive again. Foolish. Magical thinking. Silly.

She drops her hand, and sees it then. A yellow puddle.

Footprints in the mud by her head, two of them with clear treads, big, about a size ten or eleven, and deep, as if someone has been standing there for a while looking down at her. It's urine. Someone peed on her.

She slaps her laptop shut. No.

She goes and climbs into the barely warm, shallow bath, hugging her knees. No. When she gets out she's careful to keep her eyes down to avoid the mirror.

She crawls off to bed, sad and sorry she ever went to meet Nikki, and listens to a podcast about the myths surrounding the Ark of the Covenant to stop herself thinking as she falls asleep. She can't think about that. She doesn't want to know about that. She wakes in the middle of the night, the phone still burbling about a completely different topic now – she's been listening for hours. She slaps it to turn it off and rolls away, settling into a warm, delicious foetal position. Then she realises that she really, really needs to go to the toilet.

Drowsy, she staggers a little as she lumbers from the bed to the corridor, steadies herself on the wall as she crosses the hall. It's six thirty and she leaves the lights off, trying not to wake up too much so that she can get quickly back to sleep, and sits on the loo. A vague, nagging awareness makes her glance back out to the hall.

There, lying on the floor, is a letter.

The envelope is blue, small, from an old-fashioned letter-writing set. It has been dropped in through the letter box and slalomed halfway across the hall. Puzzled, she goes out and looks at it. The envelope is lying face up and the writing is unfamiliar. There's no stamp on it. It has been hand-delivered. She snaps the hall light on and reads the address.

BITCH PATSY BRODIE
TOP RIGHT FLAT
3 HOLLY ROAD

Nikki Brodie must have done this. She's the only living person who knows Margo's birth name and she's trying to scare Margo. She's trying to rope her in.

7

MARGO PICKS UP THE letter carefully, holding it out in front of her like a dead mouse as she carries it into the kitchen, puts the lights on and drops it on the table.

She looks at the address again. Is Nikki angry? Is she dangerous? Calling her 'BITCH' does sound angry. How did she get into this building? How did she even find out where Margo lived? Because all their correspondence has gone through the adoption agency and they sent her letters to Janette's house, not to here.

Margo makes a big mug of tea and thinks through the mechanics of what happened last night.

She was in the street with Nikki, then she was in a taxi, came straight here. She was looking at her phone most of the time, a bright screen in a dark cab. She wouldn't have noticed another taxi following them. There were lots of cabs around George Square at that time of night, Nikki could easily have followed her.

Then she'd have to get through the keypad security entrance downstairs. She imagines herself arriving, seen from behind, getting out of the cab and standing on the pavement, looking at the building, hating it.

Approaching the door, keying in the security code. In the early-morning kitchen Margo lifts her hand and mimes thumbing the code in, she is muscle-memory remembering how she moves when she does that. Her arm reaches out quite far, there's more than a foot and a half between hand and shoulder. She does tend to stand quite far back when she keys it in, anyone watching carefully enough could see the numbers she was punching in – 2 7 3 9. The numbers are widely spaced – they could probably see that from across the street. Nikki could easily have seen that.

Watching from the street then to see which lights go on after Margo goes in. 'Top Right Flat' sounds like a description from the street. Her actual postal address is 3/3.

Nikki's a nut job. Maybe she killed Susan.

She rips the envelope open and takes out a single sheet, flattens it on the table and reads.

The letter says she looks like the fucking whore, Susan, like the whore Patsy too, though Margo doesn't understand that reference. It threatens to batter her, rape her, to stab her fucking tits until her whore blood pours out and then piss on her. It seems to have been written in a rage but still sounds stilted, staged, like a disguised voice. The grammar is woeful, the spelling not much better. It's signed 'the Ram'. There's even a PS, added on in a different pen at the end: 'I can smell youre cunt through this door. I will bleach you clean.'

More swearing, she thinks to herself, and hears Janette's voice in her head: neither shocking nor clever. You'll have to try harder than that. Swear words are for people with a limited vocabulary. Margo doesn't really believe these things, she likes a good swear, but she's invoking her mum because she's a bit frightened by the raw venom in the letter. She's frightened that Nikki found her here.

She should call the police but it'll take them hours to get here and it's not that serious. It's a rude letter, people hear worse online all day and nothing has actually happened, but she gets up and starts pacing the kitchen for reasons she can't quite fathom. She gets out one of the letters Nikki wrote to the adoption agency and puts it on the table.

Nikki's handwriting is big and uneven, joined-up, and tumbles gracefully across the page. The threatening letter handwriting is small and square, individual letters stand apart from their neighbours and the full stops are punched almost through the page. This handwriting looks different but how can she really tell?

Would it be an escalation to call the police? She knows Nikki will be at the High Court later today, she could just go and see her there. Be straightforward, just address the thing head-on. It's not a bad idea. The court is a public place, it's safe and she could tell her that she'll call the police if it happens again. That'll let Nikki know that she's not scared of her, not scared one bit.

She goes back to bed and tries to sleep but can't. She tries the podcast trick again but it doesn't work this time. Finally, she just gives in and gets up and makes herself some porridge. It's a quarter to nine.

The letter is still sitting on the table as she turns the radio on for the morning news. More bad stuff. She sits down, keeping a wary eye on the letter. But she's not scared, she's not even going to move it. It doesn't bother her – Nikki'll have to do better than that. She got a creepy letter. It's not that big a deal.

Her mobile rings loud and she fumbles and jumps and throws the bowl of porridge at it, spraying milky lumps across the table. God, she's wired, but it's only Tracey at the adoption agency, calling to see how she is after her wee meeting yesterday. Did it go all right in the end there?

Managing to sound calm, Margo gives her a brief outline of all the mad things Nikki told her about Susan's murder by a serial killer policeman.

Oh, says Tracey, that's a new one. Well, poor you, that's not very nice, is it?

Margo says, well, it gets worse: this morning she got an abusive letter and she's sure it's from Nikki and it was hand-delivered.

Oh dear, that's worrying.

Well, no, she explains, it's not worrying at all, actually, because she knows where Nikki will be this afternoon: she's going to watch a murder trial at the High Court and Margo is going to go and see her and give her the letter back and tell her to stop it.

That's a really bad idea, says Tracey, please don't do that. Stay away from Nikki because, to be honest, you don't really know anything about this woman and you have no idea where that might lead. Margo should call the police and they can go and find Nikki and warn her to stop.

Margo says she has considered that but, on balance, being completely straightforward seems the better way to go. If she gets the police to confront Nikki that would make Margo look intimidated, which is exactly what she thinks Nikki wanted. Better to go and say, in front of everyone, look: fuck off, take this letter and don't do it again or I will involve the authorities.

No, says Tracey, don't. Just, please, don't. Do not do that. You don't know her.

She says it so adamantly and solemnly that Margo wonders if Tracey knows something about Nikki that she doesn't. Margo hums and says she's sure it will be fine. It's a public place and is probably full of police officers.

Sounding panicky, Tracey tries another tactic: perhaps Margo would like to come in and talk about it first? Bring that wee letter in and they can look at it together? Or Tracey could come to Margo's house this morning if she'd prefer? Where is this she is now, Marywood Square? Tracey only lives round the corner, it'd be no trouble at all.

Janette's house is in Marywood Square. Tracey thinks Margo is there and she doesn't want to correct her.

No thank you, says Margo, but she'll call back if she needs to talk. Thanks for the offer, it's not necessary, seems over and above. A very kind offer though.

Look: to be clear, says Tracey, I really think you should stay away from Nikki. Going to the High Court, that's what she wants. She wants a reaction and more contact and that's what you're giving her. Please call the police?

Margo says she'll think about it but she won't. She's not going to do that.

Tracey says, anyway, all that stuff about murder must have been frightening? Not really what you came here for, is it?

No, says Margo, not really. She thought Nikki was making it all up until she checked the Internet and found the articles and a crime-scene photo of Susan's dead body. That part makes her cry because Susan's so young and vulnerable in the picture. She can't bring herself to mention the cluster of gaping wounds on Susan's chest so she says it was the piss that really upset her. That someone would do that. It's so denigrating, so dismissive, and she looked so young.

Tracey is kind and says nice things, she's sorry, it'll-be-OK, and waits for her to calm down.

Why is that photo even up there? asks Margo. Why is it in the public domain? What purpose does it serve and who's looking at it?

I don't think it should be there, says Tracey. But there might be something I can do. Would it be all right for her to contact the website on Margo's behalf and ask them to take the image down? Worth a try anyway?

This is actually really helpful. Margo says thank you, she'd appreciate that.

She gives Tracey the domain name and the misspelling of Susan's name. As she's spelling it out she gets weepy again. They didn't even spell her name properly.

'OK, well now, I'll call you right back about that as soon as I hear anything, let you know how I get on. OK now?' says Tracey. 'Don't go to the court. Call the police.' And she hangs up.

Margo dries her face and admits that this is upsetting, it's an upsetting situation and she's not in a good place anyway. She shouldn't go to court or try to see Nikki. She should go and see Lilah and the dogs and then just go straight to Janette's and start the clearing out.

She scrapes up the porridge and folds the letter away, puts it in the envelope and puts it in her handbag, more to hide it than because she wants to take it anywhere. She gets dressed and puts on make-up, looking in the bathroom mirror, insisting to herself that this is her face, only hers, and the un-likely spotting of Susan Brodie last night was just because she was surprised and blindsided by Nikki, by the articles, by the mad story. It's a cruel story to tell a stranger. Asking for things. Demanding things. It's not her problem, all these long-ago things. She's got enough going on.

She's thinking all these sensible thoughts when her phone rings in the kitchen and she goes to answer it, expecting it to be Tracey again.

It's not. It's Joe.

Margo's thrilled to hear his voice but tries to sound offhand. 'Oh, yeah, all right?'

'Yeah,' he says. 'How'd it go yesterday? OK?'

'Odd. Very odd.'

'Good odd or bad odd?'

'Dunno. Interesting. Bit mad.'

Margo thinks she's bad to Joe. Joe thinks she's bad to Joe. Margo has all the money and all the power and she doesn't know how to stop being so controlling. He's a lovely man, he deserves her respect, but he terrifies her. Joe doesn't know she's pregnant. When she tells him he'll be delighted. He'll accept her behaviour, disregard the meanness, tolerate it for the sake of the baby. Now every word from her mouth has the world-changing phrase *I am pregnant* behind it so she sounds stilted all the time.

'Are you OK though?'

She sighs. 'Well, yeah, I'm OK. I'm tired. Didn't sleep much.'

'Was the prick downstairs calling forth mighty thunder all night?'

The hum of Joe's voice tickles her ear. She slowly bends her head to her shoulder, trying to trap it, shuts her eyes and conjures his bare back in bed. He's asleep on his side, facing away from her, she's close and his shoulders rise like a wall. It's early in the morning and she watches each breath spread the ribs and bring them together. His skin is a galaxy of freckles.

'How was the baby shower?'

'I didn't go. Lilah texted me and said that the police were called.'

'Did you hear about Richard? He turned up and smashed a window.'

'Shit!'

'Yeah, he was trying to get in, to get to Lilah.'

Richard is Joe's half-brother. He was a wealthy antiques dealer in London but is currently Lilah's full-time ex and stalker. Joe has tried to intervene but is mostly paralysed with shame and worry about him and what he'll do next.

'Joe, how did Richard find her?'

'She must be telling him, he finds her all the time.'

Richard's stalking was not spontaneous. He and Lilah lived together for four years until she left him and ran away back to Glasgow. He claims she stole from him and he just wants the money, which is almost certainly partly true, Lilah does steal things, but it's not just about that. He was threatening suicide for the first couple of weeks. Joe said he was holding himself hostage to get her back. It's messy and they've all been sucked into the collapsing star of Richard and Lilah's relationship, but they can't just opt out because it's so tangled. Richard is Joe's brother, Richard and Lilah introduced Joe and Margo, Thomas and Joe are best friends. It used to be cosy but is suddenly suffocating, like a wet duvet over the face.

'How's the clear-out at Janette's going?'

'Really well. I'm getting it done. I have to go, anyway, I'm dog walking with Lilah.'

They listen to each other breathing for a moment. The tension builds in her and she tries not to scream that she's pregnant.

'Get off the fucking phone, you weirdo wanker,' she says and flinches at the edge in her own voice.

Joe laughs, because what else can he do, but when he speaks his voice sounds tired and miserable.

'OK, Margie. Talk later.'

And he hangs up.

8

'IT's ONLY FIFTY FUCKING quid,' says Lilah.

'I'm not going to Iceland tonight, no.'

They're walking up to the first floor of a close with an oak balustrade and exquisite wall tiles in watery green and yellow. Lilah gets out a set of keys with a balding rabbit-foot key chain, makes a disapproving face about it to Margo and does a squeaky voice, 'Thanks for the leg, Mr Bunny!'

'Whose flat is this?'

'Some old bloke, I think.' She opens the wooden storm doors. 'Judging from the coats in the hall cupboard. Got a pair of gorgeous corgis though.' She slips the key in the inner glass door and swings it open to a musty-smelling hall with a threadbare antique rug on the floor and dark wood dressers with so much unopened correspondence piled on top that the horn-handled letter openers and stained glass lamps have been shoved over to one side.

Margo hasn't been to this flat with Lilah yet. It's one of those Victorian West End flats that seem to go on forever: a huge hallway with lots of doors into large, bright rooms and a low corridor at the end. She has been in flats like this before and knows that it will lead to a more modest set of rooms for the servants.

Two old black-and-white corgis mosey out of a front room to greet them. One of the dogs attempts a jump onto Lilah's thigh but he doesn't make it, lands heavily on his front paws and seems to instantly regret trying.

'Oh, Mr Muttley!' Lilah crouches down to him and cups his damp jaw. 'Poor old dear, did you do a big jump and hurt yourself?'

They lead the dogs down the dark servants' corridor to a bright kitchen with a big black range. Lilah pours dried food pellets in their bowls and replaces the water.

Muttley and Pitstop are her current foster-dogs but she still misses her original foster charge. Huntly, thin as a string and almost blue in colour, was an Italian greyhound who hated walks, food, noise and people. Margo thinks Lilah loved him so much just because he looked like her. Pitstop and Muttley's owner is in hospital, no one ever said what the old man had or if he'll be coming back, but Lilah has volunteered to look after them. She wants a dog of her own but she's not ready for the commitment.

Lilah has just moved home after ten years in London. She has left yet another disastrous relationship, one in an on-going series, and Margo is struggling not to blame her for being victimised, while working out the pattern: are the men giving off potential stalker signs or is she doing something to them? What the hell keeps happening with these awful men she's going out with? This is the third time it's happened and Lilah is so deep into it she doesn't seem to know that it's not normal for couples to spy on each other.

They put coats on the two dogs, attach their leads and carry them down the stairs to the street. Margo takes Pitstop, a wiry bitch with a warm, bald belly freckled with enormous nipples. The old dog pants happily, watching where they're going and Margo finds herself unthinkingly kissing the dog's soft ears.

Outside, they put the dogs down and walk straight to a cafe in Kelvingrove Park. Lilah says it's OK, the dogs can't be arsed walking about in the cold any more than they can.

They sit outside for the dogs' sake and order hot chocolate. The dogs lie down at their feet and Muttley instantly falls asleep.

'It's only two hours away,' Lilah says.

'Are you aware that the world is on fire? We shouldn't be flying around all the time.'

'The flight is going whether we're on it or not. In many ways it's worse if it goes and we're not on it, Margo, that's actually really wasteful.'

Margo smiles despite herself.

'I know it's wrong but it was a last-minute deal. Fifty quid each and I could do with getting out of here.'

'What about Muttley and Pitstop?'

'I can get someone to cover for me.'

'You're not supposed to do that, Lilah. What if the house gets robbed or something? What about the dogs?'

She considers this. 'We could leave out loads of grub and let them piss and shit in the house and clean it up when we get back?'

'How is this a "we" thing?'

The cafe is next to a swing park, deserted during school hours. Lilah seems to know all the dog owners in the park already. A broad, bearded man proudly walking two small French bulldogs with muzzles and harnesses waves to her from the side gate. An old lady dressed in a fur coat trills Morning! to her as she walks along with a rough collie on the path by the cafe. A professional dog walker with five random dogs calls to her in a crackled voice and asks after Muttley and Pitstop's owner.

'Still no word, Shirley,' Lilah calls back.

'You're like the mayor of the dog owners,' says Margo.

'Because I'm fostering. They like me because they're thinking about what would happen to their own poor dogs if they got ill,' says Lilah.

She's an unlikely hero. Lilah's tall and skinny and looks like an art deco ornament. She wears charcoal eyeliner on her big blue eyes, and a Louise Brooks bob so dark that it sheens blue. As with all great natural beauties, she simultaneously doesn't feel attractive and frets about losing her looks. She once flew to London and spent two hundred and fifty quid having her hair dyed the same colour as it was when she left. Recently, at a Botox party, the man got drunk and injected her too much. Lilah says her forehead now looks like a really good skin graft after a really bad fire.

'The Blue Lagoon is fabulous.' Lilah catches the waitress's eye and waves her empty cup to ask for another hot chocolate. 'It's a geo-spa and the hot springs are outside, you're surrounded by snow, they have mineral exfoliating treatments, your skin feels amazing.'

'A rough flannel in the bath at home does the same thing.'

'Don't you ever want to just fucking run away?'

'Right now, very much. I got an abusive letter from that auntie I met last night. Said she's going to stab my tits.'

She shows her the letter and Lilah reads it.

'Well, she's quite the crazy bitch!' she declares.

'Major,' agrees Margo. 'It was hand-delivered in the middle of the night and I can't work out how she got into my building or how she knew where I lived. That's what really bothered me, not the threats or whatever, just: how did she get in?'

Lilah gives her the letter back. 'Quite shit threats as well.'

But she doesn't know about the scene-of-crime photograph.

'Yeah.' Margo looks at the letter again. 'Threats have really come on in leaps and bounds over the last decade or so. Reading this is like a twelve-year-old telling you you're smelly.' She fits it back in the envelope. 'Think she's trying to suck me into her crazy world view. She thinks a killer is on the loose.'

'Well, that does sound fun.'

'Yeah, I've got windmills of my own to tilt at just now. Are you going to tell me what happened with Richard last night?'

'I will, I will, I will, darling ...' Lilah's accent has changed since they left school but so has Margo's. They never talk about it openly but Thomas, drunk, once said that Margo's accent had gravitated down, Lilah's had gone up and if you split the difference you'd get somewhere near the truth.

When they were younger Margo loved Lilah so completely that she half hoped she would end up with Thomas. She imagined them all forming a family unit together, Christmas dinners at home and Margo fussing over their many, many children. She found ways to engineer nights when they were all together, trips to the movies and nights in student unions, but Thomas never made a move. She couldn't understand it. Lilah was adorable, everybody agreed. She never understood until Thomas told her: Lilah is a pain in the arse, he said. No one needs to be that charming. She'll end up in prison. She's feckless and goading and she'd steal the eyes out of your head.

Margo and Lilah's friendship is intense, they see themselves in each other, which can be good and bad. Lilah lost weight in fifth year, really a lot of weight, going from a plump girl to underweight in just a few months. Margo hadn't cared about her weight before, never really thought about it, but then she lost weight too. Slimness was suddenly a currency between them. They got thin at each other. Whenever Margo went to bed hungry or found clothes were too big for her or bought a size XS in a sale, it was Lilah she thought of, and it wasn't kindly. She loved Lilah and Lilah loved her but the competitive undercurrent was occasionally tinged with malice.

Lilah almost never forgave Margo for getting into medicine because she wasn't academic. She couldn't sit for hours the way Margo did, copying out textbooks or underlining passages and reading them three times. Lilah was good at everything else but Margo could do this. Lilah might be what got Margo into medical school. When their class gathered in the school hall to get their final exam results it was Lilah that Margo was scanning the crowd for. She was the person Margo wanted to crow at. She loved being kind about Lilah's failure.

Margo sometimes wondered if they actually hated each other, if they were secretly attracted to each other or thought they were each other. There was always something of the other-self in her feelings for Lilah. But Margo didn't have that relationship with other female friends and Lilah always seemed to. Whatever it was and wherever it came from, Margo didn't feel right when she didn't see her regularly. Maybe it was love. Maybe it was sisterhood. Maybe it was competitiveness. It was no accident that they ended up going out with brothers.

She was down visiting Lilah for New Year and Richard invited his brother over. Margo was half expecting more of the same when in walked a hippy in ill-fitting cycling tights and a hi-vis jacket. Joe cut across Richard's braying monologues and made them all get food-van dinners and walk along the South Bank. He was like the anti-Richard. They'd been together for two years and she often wonders why she isn't with him now.

Lilah is telling her the story of last night, trying to make light of it but it's an uphill struggle.

The baby shower was going well, they were all tipsy, apart from Emma, obviously, because she's eight months pregnant. They were in the kitchen and Deborah (they both hate Deborah) was in the middle of a brilliant drunk confession about Paul (this is delicious because they both hate Paul even more than they hate Deborah. He's a humourless know-all who stands too close when he talks to you and is always doling out advice about things he knows nothing about). Anyway, Paul hasn't touched Deborah for ten months, she thought he was having an affair but it turns out that he watches porn all the time and is functionally impotent. They're going to couples counselling and Deborah is livid that Paul has to do a sex-fast for two months and that'll be a year since she's had sex. She was sobbing into her Chardonnay because she's so 'lonely'.

Lilah and Margo laugh unkindly but Margo feels bad and tuts and says, 'Oh, poor Deborah!' and then they laugh even more because it's such a half-arsed attempt at disguising schadenfreude. Lilah says they were all being kind and trying to listen without laughing when they heard someone kicking the front door. It was Richard and he was screaming for Lilah.

They piled into the front room to see what was going on and Richard saw Lilah in there, lost it and smashed a big window, all the glass fell into the living room, and then he just stood outside, in a state of utter broiling annoyance, didn't even try to come in, he just stood outside shouting in at her about his money.

Well, Lilah shouts back to Richard, this isn't exactly restoring my faith in your mental health, is it? Following me around and smashing bloody windows. This isn't even my house, Richard. You're smashing windows on other people's houses. Do you see how mental that is?

Anyway, one of the girls got freaked out and called the police, so annoying, and when they came Richard said it was just an accident, that he turned round too quickly, his bag banged on the glass and it was really heavy because it had his laptop in it and that was what smashed the glass. It would have been fine, they'd have let him go of course, but because Joe had reported him to the police that other time, well, they looked it up and things got serious from there. They took him in and held him for hours and he's fucking furious now. She flashes Margo a reproachful look, as if she's responsible for Joe calling the police. They were in a restaurant and Richard threw wine over Lilah. No one was even looking at Joe, they were caught up in the fight at the table. Margo moved out shortly afterwards during an argument. Nothing has been the same since.

'I'm sorry,' says Margo.

'Oh, no,' says Lilah, reaching across the table and squeezing her forearm, 'I didn't mean that.'

They look each other in the eye and smile because she did mean that, she meant exactly that, and they know each other too well to lie.

Margo shouldn't have told Joe all the things Lilah told her about Richard, the passport confiscation, the punching her ribs when no one was looking and taking her keys so she couldn't leave the house. Lilah told her those things in confidence, she loves a secret. Now Margo is shamed for letting Lilah down and she's furious with Joe for telling. She's a bad friend. Joe says Lilah's secrets are bullshit, that she uses them to control her friends. Now he won't even talk about it because he says that's what he thinks and what's the point?

'How does Richard know where Emma lives? I thought she'd just moved. Did he follow you there?'

'No, he got there two hours into the evening. Someone must have phoned him.'

'Give the money back for Godsake, Lilah!'

'I didn't take it.' But Margo can tell she did from the way she dips her chin to let her hair fall over her face and changes the subject. 'You in touch with Joe again?'

'No!' But Margo is lying too. She's lying to Lilah, trying to set an example because she's afraid that if Lilah knows she's seeing Joe sometimes then Lilah will immediately get back with Richard. Joe is problematic but Richard is dangerous.

Lilah shakes her head sadly. 'You're taking Richard's side on the money issue?'

'It's not about sides any more. Give him his stuff back and sue him for back wages. If Joe's right –'

'*If?*'

'Well, he says when you leave an abusive relationship, that's the dangerous time. You might need to do more than pretend it isn't happening. Maybe you need to go to the police about him and get a restraining order.'

Lilah is quiet for a moment. Margo thinks she's still a bit in love with Richard. He was very glamorous when they first met. He flew all over the Middle East on buying trips, drove a big car, had a house in Mayfair.

'Come away with me, Margo. I want to get out of here.'

'No. You always want to get out of here.' She sighs and stirs the chocolate up from the bottom of her drink. 'This woman, the auntie, she was a drug user and she said Susan was using heroin when she had me. She wasn't though. Why would she lie about that?'

'Is she slagging her? Did she hate her?'

'Don't think so.'

'Maybe she didn't remember? If she was off her face a lot of the time she might just not know.'

'She doesn't seem uncertain. She thinks she knows who killed her.'

'Maybe she killed her.'

'I wondered.'

'Well, this is too sad for me. I just want to go away some-where lovely.' Lilah sucks her cheeks in. She looks amazing when she does that, she knows she does. 'I mean, Margo, as you know, I sweat justice but I'm also a fan of deep-tissue massages, so ...' She pretends to weigh up the two options and makes Margo laugh.

Lilah says that, before Richard had his little drama, the girls were asking why Margo wasn't there and Lilah told them she was at the adoption agency meeting her birth family. They were all very sympathetic.

Margo doesn't want to be pitied. As Lilah talks on about Richard, about how having a restraining order will just wind him up and Joe should fuck off and mind his business, she composes a heavily edited paragraph about Nikki that makes it sound good: we did meet and it was lovely. She's a lovely lady. Overcome so much. Tried so hard to find me. She works in a cake shop. She tries it out on Lilah and it works.

So Margo tells the rest of the depressing story in a funny way, tells her about Nikki's conviction that she was in *Silence of the Lambs*. '*He still writes to me* ...' She does it in a witchy voice. She mimics Tracey's odd walk. They laugh about that for quite a long time.

Then she tells her about the photograph of the crime scene. She can't make that bit funny. When she thinks about it, it makes her feel cold and sad and afraid. Lilah says ooo, yeuw, the letter writer mentioned that, didn't they? Maybe they saw it on the Internet too? She should get that picture taken down. Margo tells her Tracey is trying to do that for her but she's a bit odd, Tracey. Margo's not sure about her at all.

'Come away with me?' whines Lilah, clawing at the table.

'No.'

'I'll pay for you if the fifty quid is an issue?'

Margo drops her spoon and looks at Lilah. 'You know I hate spas. I hate that bit where a teenager in a lab coat explains that rubbing jam on your shins will reverse your kidney function. Can't listen to that crap.'

They've had this conversation before.

'The great thing here,' says Lilah, 'is there's a language barrier, that's what's so great about this one, and swimming ...' She knows Margo likes swimming. 'I thought it would be nice for us to spend a bit of time together because, you know, of all the stuff going on.'

Is Lilah finally admitting that she's in an abusive relationship? Margo looks at her and sees that she isn't. The stuff Lilah's talking about is Margo's stuff. Janette's death and the split from Joe. She feels bad every time she does this but she tries again.

'You've got a bit of "stuff" going on too, Lilah.'

Lilah shifts uncomfortably in her chair. 'Who hasn't got stuff? Dead people and dogs.'

Margo realises that neither of the dogs has moved for ten minutes. 'I'm scared to look down.'

Lilah does, kicks Muttley gently in the side and asks him if he's dead. Both dogs stir and then fall back to sleep.

'Not dead,' she says and smiles. 'See? Another great day for Lilah.'

9

GLASGOW'S HIGH COURT IS shoved over to the edge of the river, facing away from the city like a naughty child sent to a corner to have a think about its behaviour. The building is low, blackened and neoclassical with three sets of grand double doors facing the street, flanked by six massive columns. Litter and leaves tumble about lazily on the stairs behind railings that are shut and chained. The real entrance is a modern extension tucked round the corner in the shadow of a disused railway high line. Margo has seen it often on the nightly news but has never been there.

It's a cold, blustery morning as she walks from her car, passing an artisan bakery, a designer wool shop and a dingy porno outlet with windows pasted with offers of trade-in deals on XXX DVDs. The Saltmarket is a mixed area, up and coming but still with pockets of rough-as-fuck.

She turns the corner to the entrance and finds the door ringed with giant concrete balls, defensive measures against car bombs and ram-raiders. Uniformed police officers gather in clusters, smoking near groups of lawyers in long black gowns. They linger near the door but the public smoke their cigarettes further away, aware that this is someone else's turf.

She passes through revolving doors into a high-ceilinged lobby with a balcony running around three sides. There is a metal detector and airport-style security run by a uniformed guard who takes her handbag and shakes his head kindly when she asks him if he needs to check her shoes. He asks her to open the bag and prods the contents with a stick, nudging used tissues and receipts out of the way to check for guns or knives. He nods her through the metal detector and gives her back the handbag on the other side.

The lobby is busy. Rows of seats are bolted to the floor under a big window, half full of people watching the comings and goings or staring up at TV screens that hang from the ceiling like information boards in an airport. Nikki isn't there. Margo has no idea what to do now. She's facing a reception desk of fine blond sandstone and a white-shirted usher waves her over but she doesn't really know what to ask him.

'I'm looking for a murder case,' she says. 'Um … a man … very old case, happened in the early nineties? The man has a Russian name? Something-ov? I'm looking for someone who has come to watch the case?'

The usher's eyebrows rise as his lids lower slowly. 'I need a name.'

'Nikki Brodie?'

'We have no case with that name.'

'No, she's come to watch it. She'll be in the public gallery.'

'Will she?'

Margo's suddenly aware of having no idea what she's doing. 'Sorry, I don't know how it works, she said she'd be here.'

'I see,' he says. 'Well, we don't keep a register. I have no idea who's in where.'

'Oh.'

'We have one case being heard against a man with a Russian name. North Court.' He shows her the listing on the overhead screens and looks up to the top of a staircase snaking up to the balcony. 'That case is winding up now. The public will be coming this way. You can wait over there and they'll come past you.'

'I'm not here for the case, I'm not terribly interested in that sort of thing,' she says, trying to impress a disapproving stranger she didn't know existed until two minutes ago.

It doesn't work.

'Aren't you?' He thought she was stupid a minute ago and now he thinks she's an idiot. 'Well, you can wait over there.' Wryly adding, 'With all the other people who aren't terribly interested.'

He points to the front row of chairs and a couple of baffled-looking pensioners in matching purple cagoules, one of whom is asleep. Margo doesn't think the usher's being rude, he's just entertaining himself.

She backs away, feeling foolish and a bit giggly. She sits where he pointed but finds herself facing the usher from twenty feet away. It's quite awkward so she turns and stares up to the balcony, anticipating Nikki's arrival.

She's nervous to be here, she knows it's not the best idea, but the alternative is going to Janette's and failing to clear the house. She's not sure what she should say to Nikki if she does find her. Should she threaten her with the police? She can't quite remember why she was so certain the threatening letter was from Nikki now.

Lawyers in suits and gowns sweep along the balcony walkway, going through doors, followed by clerks with trolleys of files and boxes. Behind them, a man comes out of a door wiping his hands dry on his trousers. It seems to be a toilet but it's too high up to see the signage. A door tucked deep into the high corner opens and a woman with a distinctive walk emerges onto the balcony. She's swaying from the shoulders, wearing a dark overcoat and thick glasses that distort her eyes. Margo stands up. Is that Tracey? But the figure disappears into the toilets. That looked a lot like Tracey.

Her eyes are still on the balcony when the door the Tracey-type came out of bangs loudly against the wall. The sound clatters around the foyer, drawing the attention of all the people waiting.

A trio of weeping women stand still, aware that they have done something wrong. They see all eyes are on them and freeze for a moment before linking arms defensively and helping each other along to the stairs.

They're all dressed a bit like Nikki was yesterday. Her clothes suddenly make sense to Margo. These women are poor and they've dressed up and come here for a bad day. They don't belong here, aren't comfortable, but they've dressed the way they imagine people who do belong might: tidy clothes that don't fit or flatter them, boring clothes in tidy, boring colours. Their hair is pulled back tight to be neat and out of the way. They very much want to get out of here.

'Wait!' A well-dressed woman hurries to get from the door to catch them at the top of the stairs. This woman does belong here. She wears a black skirt and top under a leather biker's jacket. She's tall and handsome and has thick white hair that suits her well. Margo can hear fragments of conversation.

'DCI … ?' she says.

'Course we remember you,' says one of the women, her voice breathy and grateful.

'Very pleased …' says the woman. 'Very brave … be proud.' Her voice is formal and crisp.

The white-haired woman is a police officer. Probably retired. Possibly the investigating officer on the original case. They all shake hands at the top of the stairs but one of the women is crying so hard her companions make their excuses and help her down the steps. She can't stop crying but is trying hard, convulsing her face and chin as her eyes drip and burn.

Margo looks up and sees the policewoman looking straight at her, head tipped, lips parted, looking at her and wondering.

Nikki suddenly appears behind the woman, scuttling along the walkway with her head down. The cop startles, reaches out and touches her sleeve to get her attention.

For a fleeting moment Margo thinks Nikki's being arrested. She drops her bag to the floor, ready to run to Nikki's defence, but that's not what's going on at all. Nikki turns to the tall woman and falls face-first into her chest. The policewoman hugs her, rocking slightly, cupping the back of Nikki's head, sobs racking her body like a cat bringing up a hairball.

This is what Margo should have done for Nikki last night. This is what she didn't do. It must have been a hard, hard day for her yesterday. Guilt and empathy trump her scepticism, wiping it out completely. Nikki had been waiting all day yesterday for a proxy win in a cold, unfriendly court and then came two hours late to meet cold, unfriendly Margo. Small wonder she was fraught. Small wonder she seemed strange.

The guilt Margo feels about her aunt is so much more comfortable than hostility that she welcomes it and drops her defences entirely. Bad Margo. Poor Nikki.

The three weeping women pass in front of Margo, blocking her view until she looks back up to see Nikki wiping her face on her sleeve and the policewoman pointing at Margo and asking a question.

Nikki slumps when she sees her. She cringes and shuts her eyes, scratching her scalp hard with both hands, covering her face. She drops her hands and gives Margo a tired, reluctant wave. She doesn't want to see her.

The policewoman links arms with Nikki, guiding her down the stairs to meet Margo.

'Hi,' says the woman.

'Hello,' says Margo, addressing Nikki.

Nikki nods but can't look at her. She rubs her nose, finger to tip, covering her tiny face with her hand as she swipes up.

'I'm Diane Gallagher.' The woman holds her hand out to shake Margo's.

'Margo Dunlop. I'm – Nikki's niece, I think?'

Nikki nods and rubs her forehead with her palm. She doesn't want to be here. 'Upsetting,' she says, pointing back to the stairs. 'Awful –' Her face crumples and she covers it with her hands to hide her upset.

Margo finds Diane Gallagher frowning at her, nodding her a prompt to comfort Nikki. She's so authoritative that Margo obeys instantly, wrapping her arms around her and rocking her gently the way she saw Gallagher doing it on the balcony. She hugs her until Nikki catches her breath.

Finally Nikki steps back, drying her face with a shredded bit of ruined tissue from her pocket.

'I have to go.' She looks shyly at Margo. 'Why're you here?'

'Looking for you. About last night.'

Nikki nods. She thinks Margo is here to apologise and a half-smile flits across her face. It's suddenly very obvious that Nikki doesn't know anything about the threatening letter.

'Maybe we could try again?' says Margo. 'Maybe meet for a drink?'

'Oh no, not today, I'm not fit today.' Nikki scratches her head again.

'How about tomorrow? In the pub we nearly went to?'

'OK.' She nearly smiles. 'At six?'

'I'll be there. I'm sorry for –' She gestures upstairs, to whatever happened.

Nikki nods and hurries away, pressing the scrap of tissue to her eyes. Margo and Gallagher watch her leave through the doors, the wind blowing her overcoat into wide wings as she makes her way down the street.

'Brave woman,' says Gallagher.

'Nikki?'

'Yeah. He pled guilty but they had to go into details about what he did to her. It was harrowing.'

'Nikki says it might have been someone called Martin McPhail.'

Gallagher rolls her eyes. 'I don't know if you know how much Nikki's been through. She said Susan was your mum?'

'Birth mother. Nikki and I just met last night.'

'Well, those girls, Nikki and Susan, all those girls, they went through hell and that was a reminder. They're all traumatised and certain people have, I don't know, *exploited* that. Sold them a story. But the man's DNA was on her, he pled guilty, so ...' She's smiling at Margo, looking hard at her face. 'I had pictures of all the women above my desk for six years, you know.' Her eyes roam to Margo's hair, to the shape of her eyes, to her neck and Margo knows that she's seeing her mother.

'Did you know Susan?'

'Yes.'

'Did you know her well?'

'No. I only met her when she was pregnant with you.'

'Ah, well, that was brief.'

'I respected her though,' says Gallagher. 'Do you know what she did for you? She gave up heroin for the duration of her pregnancy. She did that for you. I can count on the fingers of one hand the number of girls who got clean. Quite a lot tried, believe me, but if you ever doubted that Susan cared –'

Margo thinks she's reflexively coughing, that a speck of dust is lodged in her throat but she's shocked to find tears leaking from her eyes. 'Oh.'

'Yeah,' says Gallagher, 'she was quite something. No one could believe it. They didn't think it was possible, a lot of them. She was something of a touchstone.'

Margo swallows the emotion immediately. 'Nikki seemed to think Susan wasn't clean when she had me.'

'Oh, but she was. Everyone knew she was.' She looks away, hiding some private thought.

'I wonder, would there be any chance I could meet you for a cup of tea at some point? I'd very much like to ask you about her, even if you didn't know her very well at all, there's so little …'

Gallagher gives her a business card. 'Contact me and we'll make an arrangement. What's your name?'

'Dr Margo Dunlop.' She watches her write it down in a small address book.

'A doctor?'

'Yes, a GP.'

Gallagher is very pleased about that. 'Well, just shows you. Contact me and we'll make a time.'

'That's tremendously kind of you.' Margo's trying to sound posh and unthreatening but she looks up and sees that Gallagher doesn't care about that at all. She's not even looking at her any more.

'Jason!' Gallagher is talking over her shoulder, calling to a man a bit younger than Margo who is walking across the lobby alone, hands deep in his pockets.

Jason turns back and she tells him who she is and why she's here.

She wows at him, look at you, she says, so tall! (He's not very tall.) So grown up! (He has the old-man skin of a kid who grew up hard.) This must have been very difficult for you, hearing the details about what happened to your mum and seeing him there? Jason nods at the floor, grinding his jaw as Gallagher says nice things: she would be so proud, son, she was a brave and determined young woman, just as the judge said, and nothing can take that away, not the manner of her passing, not anything.

These are pleasantries, it's obvious Gallagher is just trying to be kind, but Jason seems like a man who doesn't hear many pleasantries and they matter to him very much. He nods his way through them, smiling at the ground, never meeting Gallagher's eye. Only when she finishes does he look up and smile and then he is suddenly very young.

'Your mother was dealt a hard hand and played it with great dignity. You should be very proud.'

Margo thinks she's really talking about Jason. He mumbles a thank you and walks taller as he heads towards the door.

'I'm sorry for your loss,' Margo says quietly as he passes, regal in his grief.

'Disaster,' says Gallagher, when he's gone. 'That girl's death was a disaster for her family. You were adopted?'

'Yes.'

'How was that for you? Were they nice people?'

Margo's gripes about her childhood seem frivolous now. She's about to answer and say it was nice but Gallagher stiffens and mutters *shit*.

A tall, slim man with thick grey hair takes the last step down to the foyer. He and Gallagher lock eyes. Margo instantly recognises Jack Robertson. He is stately and wears steel-grey leather trousers and a grey sweater under a faded black denim jacket. He sashays over to them.

'Diane? Hello.'

'Jack,' says Gallagher. 'Didn't see you there.'

'I saw you. I was at the back. What do you make of all that?'

'I've got to go.' Gallagher turns to leave.

'It's ridiculous,' Robertson says to the back of her head, 'isn't it?'

Gallagher makes for the exit and Robertson follows her. She manages to shrug him off at the metal detector and Robertson stands and watches her through the window.

'Excuse me?' Margo touches his elbow. 'Are you Jack Robertson?'

'Yeah?'

'Hi, I'm Margo Dunlop.'

They shake hands and he looks her over. 'You were talking to Diane Gallagher just now?'

'Yeah, you wrote the book –'

'Yeah, yeah. Who are you? You a cop?'

Margo feels a bit insulted – her clothes aren't that dowdy, although they are quite dowdy. 'No, I know the families. Can I ask you if you heard anything about nasty letters being sent to relatives of the murdered women?'

Robertson snorts. 'What – recently?'

'Recently and historically. Specifically related to the Susan Brodie murder. Letters from someone calling themselves "the Ram"?'

Robertson looks away and purses his lips, looks back, appraises Margo. 'The Ram? What do you know about that?'

'Some of the family have been receiving correspondence. I wondered if you –'

He steps a fraction closer to her. 'You read my book?' He sounds a bit accusing.

'I meant to. I was going to buy it today actually.'

'Well, you can't buy it in the shops just now.'

'Is it out of print?'

'No, it's more complicated … Are you a lawyer?'

'No, I know Susan Brodie's family and they're still getting abusive letters. I thought you might know something about the Ram.'

'*Still?*'

'Yes.'

'From "the Ram"?'

Margo nods, 'That's what they said. Got one this morning.'

Robertson takes that in, snorts to himself and nods at the stairs. He looks Margo over. 'Can you get hold of that letter? Is that possible?'

Margo shrugs.

He nods at her. 'What are you doing tonight?'

Sitting in a flat I hate, wishing everything in my life was different, thinks Margo.

'Dinner,' he says, 'eight o'clock in Andolfo's on Bath Street. I'll bring you a copy of my book *as a gift*.'

'Thank you so much.'

'Don't thank me, you're buying,' says Robertson and he swaggers away.

Margo watches him waving at the security staff. She picks up her handbag from the floor and makes her way towards the door.

'Goodbye.'

It's the usher standing behind the reception desk. His face is soft and he nods respectfully. He saw her with the women, all the women, and he wants to be kind.

'Thank you,' says Margo. 'Thank you very much.'

IO

IT WAS WAITING THERE at the end. Susan. Sitting in the lobby. Alone. Waiting. Then talking to Gallagher, listening for the juicy details. She knows Gallagher and Robertson and Nikki and all of them. Has she been around for ages? Hanging around, picking up titbits, tricks, meeting the rest of them, from back then?

Watching them all. Were her lips wet? She was looking around, watching, seeing them crying. She was into it.

She was sitting on the edge of the seat as if she was about to bolt. A runner, like Susan, leave you on your uppers.

Who'd want to be there? It's a choice. She's making a choice to be in it. You'd have to be vermin to take an interest in that, to sit there with your whore mouth hanging open, listening to that.

Susan did. She chose that for herself. Having the baby was too long off her back, gave her time to think.

This new Susan, this new one, she's got pregnant tits. Can tell. Swole, like Susan was then, same way.

Add a five-quid baggie and she'd spread them for anyone, take it from anyone that paid for it. Just holes.

The smell of her had soaked into the chair. She smelled of sweet puss, like meat turning bad.

Odds are that she's going down to the Drag right now. Might as well just follow and have a see.

11

MARGO CAN'T FACE GOING back to Holly Road. She feels even less comfortable there now, so she goes to squander a couple of hours in the Mitchell Library. It's near Andolfo's and one of Margo's favourite places on earth. She'd happily be locked in for a month.

The Mitchell is a huge, rambling reference library in the centre of Glasgow. Built over the course of almost a century, it incorporated other buildings and extensions so that the interior swings wildly through time frames. Brushed-steel lifts arrive in tiled Victorian corridors, Edwardian wood-panelled rooms lead into stairwells with smoked-glass bannisters. Margo squandered her teenage years here along with other swotty kids. Medicine tends to attract kids with control issues, kids who can ignore distractions or hormones or the need for sleep in order to study hard. Margo spent days here, weathering the storm of adolescence by ignoring it. She knows the warmest corners and hiding places, which toilets are always clean, what the cafe sells and what it used to sell.

Night is falling as she pulls into Granville Street and spots a handy parking space.

She notices lights in her rear-view mirror; a car close behind hers is hesitating, apparently unsure whether she is stopping in the middle of the street or waiting to reverse-park. She waits for them to draw back but they don't.

She can't get in if they don't move. She flicks on her indicator, asking them to pull back, but they stay still. She puts the car in gear so the reverse lights will show but the car behind her pulls towards her slightly, nudging forward, coming too close. Margo reverses an inch. The car closes the gap. There are plenty of spaces, she doesn't think they'd secretly bagsied that one, but they won't budge.

She raises her hands so they can see her exasperation.

They nudge forward again. She can't reverse at all now.

Muttering curses, she changes gear and pulls slowly forward, driving straight into a space nose-on to the library building, watching the car behind in her mirror.

It does nothing. The engine is still running but the car hasn't moved.

She pulls on her handbrake and gets out, standing on the pavement to look, thinking maybe the driver has been taken ill or they are on the phone. The car is a big old boxy Honda, green-coloured, about thirty years old and quite dirty. The sun visor is down, though evening has fallen and it is getting dark. The engine revs.

Suddenly the car shoots along the road to the junction. Her eyes are on the driver's window and she sees an upraised palm facing her as if they're waving.

She doesn't recognise the car, even though it's quite distinctive, but the driving style is attention-grabbingly erratic. Is the driver ill? Are they going to crash? At the last minute it takes a fast, neat turn into a side street, heading away from her, and, as it turns, the slim hand drops from the window. It turns again and is gone. She thinks that the hand was not a wave after all but the driver hiding their face from her. Odd. A little bit threatening.

Still puzzling over it, she goes into the library. She wants to check something out before she goes to Andolfo's. She's pushing the doors open before she even thinks about the threatening letter to her house. And the ones sent to Nikki. It makes her shiver, the notion of that dark malevolence lurking everywhere, but the incident in the street was unconnected, she's sure. She's looking for patterns in pebbles on the beach. She's being paranoid.

Inside the doors, the building opens out into a big bright courtyard with a shop and a cafe and a bank of computers. The cafe is shut but something is on in the theatre next to it and people are gathering at the tables, waiting to go in. She walks over to the lifts and takes one up to level 5: the newspaper archive.

The lift doors open to a swirly 1970s red carpet and smoked-glass bannisters. The reading room is quiet. It has magazine racks filled with obscure titles, football history, types of trains. A few readers, mostly men of retirement age, sit scattered at tables, poring over old newspapers and maps, reading quarterlies and staring into space. White filing cabinets form a wall down the centre of the room.

A librarian standing behind a low desk beckons Margo over. Margo asks how she would get to see newspaper coverage of an old murder trial in Glasgow in the early 1990s.

Possibly a tabloid would be best?

Yeah, says Margo, that's a good bet.

At the filing cabinets the woman explains the chronology, which drawer has which paper, and opens one to show her rows of white boxes, dated. They find the relevant dates for four months after Margo's birthday and take them over to a screening machine perched on a table for one at the side of the room.

The machine consists of a screen at the back of an upright three-sided box with protruding wings at the side to shield the viewer's face and a spooling mechanism at the front. The librarian takes one of the rolls of microfilm, threads it through the glass clamp and onto the receiving spool. She turns a switch at the side and a light shines up, projecting the image through the glass onto the roof of the box where it's mirror-reversed and reflected onto the screen at the back.

This is the button for scrolling forward. This is for re-winding when you've finished each spool. Please return them as you found them and be sure to put them back in the right filing cabinet. She leaves Margo to it.

Margo isn't sure how to operate the machine. She was trying to pay attention but got distracted by thoughts about the driver of the Honda. Were they ill? Rude? Mad? Maybe it just didn't mean anything.

She sits down at the basic machine and sees handmade signs stuck all over it: '*PLEASE* rewind', 'DO NOT REMOVE', 'Push *gently* to rotate image'. Margo already feels as if she's done something wrong and she hasn't even touched it yet.

She scrolls through to a date four months after her birthday and starts to read.

The paper is tabloid and unfamiliar. It's more than thirty years old and the values are quite shocking. She skims stories about a by-election in Govan and sex and football. A lot of the paper is about sex. Teen sex, kiddie sex, teacher sex. Are Women Finished By Forty? The women pictured in it are all in luridly sexualised poses, legs apart, blouses undone, looking over their shoulder. Margo sees a TV presenter, now considered grandmotherly and dowdy, but back then she's biting her own shirt collar and smouldering out at the audience through lowered eyes. By contrast, all the men in the paper are solemn meaty lumps who have done things or had things happen to them. They gaze out, unperturbed by being observed, certain of the audience's empathy.

Margo feels as if she's reading in a language she doesn't understand, as if she's eavesdropping on aggressively hetero-sexual Victorians.

Two weeks in, she finds a three-inch column on page 7: DEAD VICE GIRL'S FEAR OF STALKER.

Here is a photo of Susan that she hasn't seen. She is out of focus, as if she moved just at the moment the picture was taken. It's tightly cropped on her face and she is laughing, her eyes are crinkled shut. Her wild hair is wet, as if she has just come in from heavy rain, and it glitters with sparks of light, as if all the wild kinks are filled with pearls. She smiles wide and her twisted tooth is bare and sweet, there's no shame here, she doesn't know anyone is looking at her. She's young and her cheeks are pink and wet.

Margo cranes into the box, towards the screen, trying to fill her eyes with the image. She feels a yearning for her mother roll up from her stomach in great, warm waves, the desire for connection shoving her into the image. She mouths her mum's name.

It feels cruel to pair that picture with the story. Sad to have to read those words. She forces herself.

Tiny vice girl Susan Brodie was murdered plying her trade in fear of a crazed stalker. Susan, 19, was found dumped on the busy Edinburgh Road in Easterhouse on Saturday morning. Devastated sister, Nikki Brodie, made an emotional appeal last night: 'Somebody must have seen something. Lassies are dropping like flies out here.' Susan had been living with boyfriend Barney Keith, 38, since she was 15.

Margo sits still. There's a picture of him. The legend underneath reads: *Devastated: Barney Keith.*

Barney has grey teeth, sunken cheeks and Margo's round brown eyes. She blinks. That's her dad. His girlfriend was a fifteen-year-old sex worker. Mr Nitshill Complaints-to-the-council is her dad. She's glad he's devastated. She hates him. She hopes his entire life was shit.

Mothers are different. Susan carried and formed her, cupped her stomach when Margo was inside. Janette raised her, fed her, saw her through fevers and taught her how to make a bed. Barney is just a sperm donor, really, a genetic reference point. He's not who she is. He's just a ball sack with a backstory.

A little shocked at her venomous thoughts, Margo sits back to take a deep breath and meets the eye of a man across the room. His eyebrows tent suddenly as if he can hear what she has been thinking. Embarrassed, Margo slides back into the screening box.

The article quotes Barney. He says Susan had been raped quite recently by a client who was known to the police. She had seen him hanging around again in his van and was afraid. The last time Barney saw her was the night she went missing, as she was getting into a taxi for the city centre. He is devastated.

She scrolls on, putting Barney's devastation in the past with the press of a button. She stops at a photograph of DI Gallagher looking almost exactly the same as she does now but with brown hair and tighter skin. She still has the same patrician bearing, the same hard stare, and is quoted saying that Jack Robertson's claims last week that a serial killer is on the loose are irresponsible, not true and causing mayhem. What the police need are witnesses, not theories. 'We know it is easier not to get involved,' says Diane in the past. 'We know who was in the area at the time. If we don't hear from them soon we will have no option but to visit these men in their homes and places of work.'

Margo likes the veiled threat of that, of cops turning up at a man's door to ask his wife if they can have a word about a sex worker's murder. She spools on and finds nothing more. No more comments, no arrests, no more appeals for information.

The story seems to die as Susan died: dumped at the side of a road in the dark.

12

THE FOOD AT ANDOLFO'S is startlingly bad. Margo's linguine tastes of nothing but calories and water. The chef has tried to dress the plates with fresh parsley but it's still basic super-market pasta with one-note tomato sauce. She didn't know people went to restaurants this bad any more. Even the decor is awful: the tables are grey marble, too cold to rest a hand on, and the bare stone walls are varnished with wet-look gloss. It looks like a Bond villain's cave. The place is busy and bustling though. Everyone else seems to be enjoying the tasteless food except her.

She begins to doubt herself because Jack Robertson is so enthusiastic. He smiles and nods and hums at his plate, sends his compliments to the chef.

'Isn't this delicious?' he says, ripping off a portion from the garlic bread they're sharing.

It tastes of oily tinfoil. Margo wonders if pregnancy has changed the enzymes in her saliva, or the consensus in the room is an elaborate practical joke, but it isn't. Either this level of bland is the perfect level of bland for the clientele or no one here has ever been to another restaurant.

She tries to think of something to say that isn't about the food. 'I've never actually been here before.'

Jack smiles and nods. 'I hear that all the time! This place is one of those well-kept Glasgow secrets.'

Jack is very likeable. He has the unshakeable self-confidence of a man in his mid-fifties who has neither lost his hair nor gotten fat. His skin is sun-kissed, as if he's just back from having an adventure somewhere exotic, and his hair is a loose, silver mane framing his brown face. He's still wearing his grey leather trousers but has changed into a yellow and black Versace shirt. He wears an antique Rolex and a chunky gold chain around his neck that rests on stray grey chest hairs. This feels like a date or, more specifically, as if Robertson is on a date and Margo is here for an interview. Sartorial flair is eyed with suspicion in the medical profession. She's wearing clothes that mark her out as a sensible person who will do her job, turn up on time and not steal meds.

'Why has your book been withdrawn from sale?'

'Legal reasons.' He puts his beer down. 'Martin McPhail is suing me for naming him.'

'As responsible for the murders?'

'Yes.'

'Including the one that was tried today, where another man pled guilty?'

He shakes his head, reaches down to his large leather messenger bag on the floor and pulls out a brick of a paperback. As if to emphasise the weight of his work he drops the book and makes the table shudder. 'My opus. This is where I make the case against McPhail. You can have that. It's a gift.'

'Thank you,' says Margo. 'I should give you some money for it –'

'No, no,' he puts his hand on the book, still convinced that this might be some form of legal entrapment. 'You pay for dinner and we'll call it quits.'

The meal is going to cost quite a lot more than she would have spent on the book but Jack smiles and waves a hand as if she should let the enormous favour he's doing her pass. 'I've got boxes of them at home. Can't sell them while this case is hanging over me so the garage is full. Self-published. Didn't want to go with a commercial publisher because we knew it would be big. It was.' His eyebrows bob.

'You made a lot of money?'

'Well, define "a lot of money". I made a good chunk of change. Put it this way: McPhail thinks he'll get a decent pay-out just for threatening me. I'm worth suing.' He looks terrified and proud at the same time. It's a salty mix. 'Benefit of not going with a publisher. Get a bigger share of the profit.'

Margo hesitates, unsure of how well it will go down but then just says it. 'But a bigger share of the liability. I suppose a publisher would have been more circumspect about what you said.'

'Yeah. *Yeah.*' He looks at Margo with a respect she didn't know was missing until it arrived. He points at his book with his fork. 'Have a look.'

Margo gladly abandons her soggy linguine to flip through the book.

It looks serious and scholarly and dense. There's an index and pages of photographs in the middle but the cover is lurid. It's red and black like a tabloid front page. In the foreground are a woman's legs in fishnet stockings. In the distance, a faceless man in silhouette crouches, holding a knife, ready to pounce at her. Along the bottom are individual photos of all of the women who were killed, their eyes redacted.

'That cover is an embarrassment,' frowns Jack. 'We changed designer four times over a year and a half.' He stabs at the fish-netted legs with his fork, leaving four tiny teeth marks on the woman's calf. 'Gaudy. The PR people were trading bitch-slaps the whole time.' His grin falters. 'Sorry. Is "bitch-slap" OK to say now … ? Everything changes so quickly I don't know what's all right any more …'

Margo doesn't know either but she's only half listening. Mostly she's looking at the photo of Susan.

There's a black bar across Susan's eyes but it's still definitely her. Her squint tooth is visible between her open lips. It's a head and shoulders shot. She's wearing a yellow vest top, red lipstick and a toothed hairband that flattens her hair away from her face and lets it puff out at the back. Margo wore that style to a school disco when she was thirteen.

'Did you have to use mugshots?'

'They're the only pictures we could find …'

Margo knows they weren't. The papers had better pictures of Susan than this one. This makes the victims look like crim-inals. This makes them seedy and problematic.

'Susan Brodie,' she says. 'What a life she had …'

'Oh, not just her. They all had hard lives. You heard them talking through that girl's last night in court today?'

'No, I just came at the end.'

'Well, it was a fairly typical night down on the Drag: she was at the needle exchange, popped into the Jesus bus for a cup of tea at two a.m., two thirty she went out on the streets again, picked up a punter. Next thing she was found dead in Wellington Lane. Strangled. Naked. Teeth marks punctured the skin on her shoulder. Pretty sad.'

'And you thought Martin McPhail was responsible for that?'

'I did. I *do*.'

'But they found someone else guilty today.'

'Yeah, well, they didn't prove his guilt, he pled guilty. There could be *a lot* of reasons for that, I suppose … Doesn't definitely mean he did it …'

But they both know that it probably does. Robertson can't meet her eye.

'Who the hell knows what was going on today? His lawyer said the case was defensible but his client *wanted* to plead guilty, said in court that he was "reluctantly following instruction". Was he convinced to plead guilty by the powers that be?'

'Maybe he just did it.'

'No. I can see why you might think that. His DNA was all over the poor girl but that doesn't mean anything. Vicious, what he did that night, McPhail …'

He looks at Margo, as if he's trying to get her to agree that it was McPhail. Margo nods and this pleases him.

'*Injustice*. See, this is what happens when policing fails,' he says and stabs the tabletop with his forefinger, 'fools like me, nuts like me, we can't stand it. We can't just throw our hands up and accept that and walk away. We *can't*. This is how society breaks down, how feuds start, you know? You hit my brother, no one is there to intervene so I seek justice by hitting you back and on it goes ... It's a *failure of policing*.'

He's suddenly so adamant and off topic that Margo thinks he has said terrible, irresponsible things in his mad book. She can hardly wait to read it.

A sudden burst of high-pitched laughter draws their attention. Four middle-aged women at a nearby table laugh loudly. Behind them, at another table, a man knocks a beer bottle over and it clatters to the stone floor. The women all cheer and start talking to the man and his friend. Margo realises that the draw of the restaurant isn't the food, it's that they serve wine in enormous glasses. Everyone is here to get pissed in a civilized setting.

'See,' says Jack, 'you had to be there to understand: back in the mid to late 1980s, when heroin came to Glasgow, it changed everything. A whole generation was wiped out, parts of the city became chaotic.'

The tipsy women are inviting the beer spilling men to join them at their table.

'The Drag used to be down by the river but the docks closed and it moved uphill. Used to be older women. They knew how to take care of themselves. They met in the Waterloo pub at nine every night before they started, for a drink and so they'd know who was out each night, who to look out for. They knew what they were doing. One Christmas they even had a secret santa. If a woman looked too young they'd call the police. But that wasn't just out of the goodness of their hearts, younger women would take all the trade, but it meant it was less wild on the Drag.'

The two men are joining the women, dragging metal chairs around the stone floor and talking loudly.

'There were rules. Not to romanticise the past, I'm sure it was just as shitty but it was *safer*. Then heroin arrived and addicts flocked down there desperate for money. Girls from ordinary backgrounds, girls you wouldn't expect. Young kids, middle-class kids. Kelvingrove Park was where the guys went to prostitute themselves, all young, lots of them were straight out of childrens' homes.'

Robertson clears his throat and takes a drink of beer. He's sad, affected by the memories of that time and his voice is lower.

'Let me tell you,' he says, 'those heroin addicts were not sympathetic. They were scrappy and dirty. Blood everywhere, needles lying around. They'd spit at you to give you hep C or HIV. The numbers down there quadrupled over night. Girls were turning up in their school uniforms, nodding out in the street, fighting over pitches. Then violent sex offenders from all over the country started travelling up to Glasgow. Once the cops stopped a van of three men on the M74 out-side Lockerbie. Three rapists who'd been in Belmarsh Prison together, coming up to Glasgow "for a weekend".'

'Where were the police?'

He sighs heavily. 'Well. The police ...' He looks as if he doesn't know what to say and then catches the waiter's eye, signalling for another beer. The women and the new men friends are pairing off. Bizarrely, one of the couples are tonguing each other like horny teenagers. Jack doesn't seem to have noticed.

'Initially, the police didn't give a shit. There were too many of them to arrest. Women would be battered and left on the street and stepped over by uniformed cops, members of the public were no better. It wasn't until Diane Gallagher came in that anything happened.'

His beer arrives and Jack tries to smile a thank you at the waiter but his eyes are sad and tired. He waits until the waiter is gone before he continues.

Jack says Gallagher would never accept that McPhail was responsible for the murders. It was a blind spot. She was determined to believe that all the murders were by different men, intimate partners or drug dealers. She may not be his favourite person but she was a hell of a police officer. Pragmatic. Respectful. Gallagher moved the boundaries of the Drag from six blocks to four so that they could monitor who was there. They were taking down licence-plate numbers and descriptions of violent punters. She listened to the women. He says Diane was well aware of the problem and what she did was radical.

'Attacks were happening every night, it was horrific. At the height of it they hired a conference room in the Central Hotel and invited all the street sex workers to come to it. The room was full of women, some of them were falling off chairs, but they were all really angry. There must have been two hundred there. They were furious and wanted to know what the cops were going to do. Really bolshie. The police and the city council made a joint announcement: all of their funding would go into a single project – to supporting women leaving the life. They'd pay for rehab, give them new houses, move them, retrain them. An exit strategy from prostitution.'

'Wow!'

'Yeah, I know. Radical. Holistic. Thinking outside the box, all the buzz words. Problem is applying that. Messy people and messy lives. The people they were trying to help were a bit more complicated than anyone thought really. Getting off drugs isn't just about help being available, is it? This was during the recession so what are they retraining them for? There weren't any jobs.'

'It was a mistake?'

'Well, was it? Someone had to do something.'

'You know, in medicine we take the Hypocratic Oath and it says "First do no harm".'

'Sometimes it's just an excuse to do nothing, though, isn't it? At least they did something.'

'They must have had some successes?'

'Well, the numbers of service users aren't made public, so who knows, but the scheme hasn't been replicated anywhere else. Not even Edinburgh. That's very telling.'

'It didn't work, then?'

'You're not allowed to say that.' He frowns, mock-angry. 'Glasgow Social Work Newspeak. They just keep pouring money into it. Questioning it is one of the great unsayables of Glasgow public life.'

'What was it that made you suspect McPhail?'

'He worked CID down at the Drag. Seemed fairly straight for most of his eight years but something happened, don't know if it was a bang on the head or drugs, I don't know, but he went wild over a two-year period. He started using the drugs himself, they didn't test cops for drugs then, the closest they came was smelling their breath at the start of a shift. He was giving the girls drugs that he confiscated, bribing them to have sex with him, letting them stay in his flat, misfiling charges. His colleagues made complaints about his erratic behaviour and he got a brief suspension and it was then that things got really dark. The girls were so vulnerable. He was a really nasty man. He knew them all down there and they knew him. Girls started going missing or turning up dead. Some from ODs, some from violent attacks. But McPhail was always there, always nearby. I was expecting a backlash from other cops when I named him in my book but no one had a good word to say about him.'

'That doesn't mean he was guilty of a series of murders. It means he was unpopular.'

'True. McPhail was on suspension for some procedural offence, they already knew he was a liability, but he was still down the Drag every night. I saw him, I was a reporter at the time. Lots of people saw him. He was paying girls for sex with drugs he'd confiscated, paying them to let him piss on them. Then he started to get violent.'

'What happened to Susan Brodie?'

'That the one you're interested in?'

'Yeah.'

'Well, the poor thing was just nineteen. She'd been out working the streets for years. Went missing from her usual pitch in Wellington Lane about midnight on a Thursday night. Someone saw a white van and assumed she'd gone off in it with a punter but when she didn't make it back they told her sister she was missing. Her sister was out there as well.'

'Nikki Brodie. She was at court today.'

'Oh? I didn't see her.'

'She probably looks different. She's been clean for four years.'

'That's unusual. Anyway, Susan was missing for a day and a half and the sister kept trying to report her missing. Police wouldn't listen. Then she was found on the Saturday morning, at a bus stop, naked, dead. She'd been stabbed ten times or something like that, body had been washed clean.'

'Washed?'

'Suggests access to a bath, to a house or something, doesn't it? Also they found undigested toast in her stomach. They thought she'd been held in a domestic setting rather than as a hostage in the van. McPhail, supposedly, was in Hairmyres Hospital at the time, being treated for a collapsed lung. His wife was on holiday so he had the house to himself.'

'But you don't think he *was* in hospital?'

'No one remembered him being there. None of the staff or patients.'

'How long after did you ask?'

'About six months, a year.'

It's quite a big margin of error:'About a year later then?'

'Hmmm.'

'Was Susan a drug addict too?'

'Actually, I believe she was clean at the time of her death. Cops lied about that to the public but I thought they were doing the right thing there, really.'

'Why?'

Jack sighs over Margo's shoulder and bites his bottom lip as if he's trying not to say something. He takes another deep breath before he speaks. 'It was hard to make the public care. They hated those women and she was choosing to be out there. The police didn't want her to seem less sympathetic. If people knew she was out there by choice they'd have given McPhail a tickertape parade down Buchanan Street.'

'She wasn't a sympathetic victim?'

'No. She wasn't passive. She was stabbed with a knife she always carried. They didn't tell anyone that either. It was a little combat knife that fitted between her fingers. Tiny little blade.' He holds up a fist. 'McPhail knew she had that. All the street people did. He'd have asked to see it and then used it on her. He was a nasty man, you know? I was scared of him and I was a big beefy bloke.' A shadow of fear crosses Robertson's face and she thinks about him thirty years ago, how young he must have been. 'We all knew it was him but we couldn't say. Then he got done for an unrelated rape ten years later and I was made redundant from the *Scotsman*. I had all the materials so I sat down and wrote it in two months.' He shrugs and looks a little smug. 'When the book came out and named him other rape victims came forward. He got convicted of one of those as well.'

'But not the murders?'

'No. They never tried him for those.'

'Still think he did them all?'

'I must decline to answer that question for financial reasons,' he says and they both laugh. 'I don't know but he *did* kill Susan Brodie, the one you're interested in. Basically, the cops realised it was him, knew how bad that would look and they gave him an alibi.'

'Were they angry when your book came out?'

'Probably,' says Jack. 'I was pretty nervous when it came out but I heard nothing.' He gets his phone out and swipes through some photographs.

It's an ID photo of Martin McPhail. His lips are collapsed into his gums – he doesn't have his teeth in. He has shaved badly too, patchy tufts of grey beard over a grey prison pallor, silver-skinned and still bright ginger hair. Distinctive.

'This is McPhail now. A release photo. Pals on the force texted me it as an FYI.' An address is attached to the photo: 10a Nairn Drive, High Blantyre. Robertson puts his phone away. 'Thought I'd see him at court today, looking for me, crowing about the guilty plea. I know the lawyer who's representing him. I could lose my house, my car, everything.'

'I wouldn't have thought he could get that much. His reputation can't be worth much.'

'Not damages, it's the costs. I'd have to pay his lawyers if I lose …' He looks into the middle distance and pales when he thinks about it. 'I mean, he won't win. I can prove what I say in the book, he wasn't in Hairmyres, his lung hadn't collapsed, he had an empty house to take Susan to, he had access to a van and so on, but I still have to pay my costs. And obviously I've had to stop selling the book or giving talks.'

Margo thinks he's going to lose the case and suspects that he thinks so too. She's sorry for him.

They order coffee, macchiato for Robertson and a decaf Americano for Margo. Again, Margo pretends it's the best coffee she's ever had because she likes Jack now and doesn't want to be mean about his favourite restaurant.

'Delicious,' she says to be nice. 'There's a photo of Susan Brodie's dead body on the Internet. I came across it by accident. Pretty disturbing.'

'No,' Jack gasps, 'that should *not* be there.'

'I'm trying to get it taken down.'

He's looking at her hair. 'What's your connection to that family?'

'Susan Brodie was my birth mother.'

Jack is shocked. 'Oh God, I am so sorry.' He reaches across the table and crushes her hand. 'You're her family? So when you were saying about getting letters from the Ram, that was you? Have you got them?'

'Who was "the Ram" supposed to be?'

'I thought it was McPhail's nickname.'

It doesn't sound like a nickname to Margo. It sounds like something a man would call himself. 'Did you ever get threatening letters at that time?'

'Not me. The paper got quite a lot of nasty letters. It's not uncommon. People do that sort of thing ... people are very odd.'

'People? What sort of people?'

'Really, really normal-looking people. You know, after school shootings in the States they advise parents of kids who've been killed not to open their mail for a while because they get such vicious letters from random strangers.'

'About gun control or something?'

'No. Just mean letters. Defies belief, doesn't it? It's not new either. Newspapers got hundreds of Jack the Ripper letters while that was going on. Hundreds. Different people writing *as* Jack the Ripper. In his voice.'

'Prototype fanfic?'

He smiles. 'I suppose. Honestly, the public are a very strange lot.'

'They might have meant well, they might be trying to draw the police's attention to leads they think they've overlooked.'

'Yeah.' He's not convinced. 'Well, I'm not aware of letters specifically from someone called "the Ram" but it was a name that was associated with McPhail.' He smirks. '*Definitely* remember that.'

This is a lie. Robertson's making this up to support his case and he's doing it very badly. It's insulting how poorly he's lying.

'So,' he says, 'you were telling me about these threatening letters from McPhail ...'

Margo shrugs. '*If* he's the murderer.'

'Did you bring them?'

'Mostly they went to Susan's sister.'

'Can you put me in touch with her? I'd like to meet her.'

It seems quite shabby that he hasn't interviewed Nikki already, but she shows him her own letter. His face is suddenly very taut, as if he's excited and bad at hiding it.

'Gosh. Just this morning? D'you have CCTV on your house?'

'No, there's no CCTV.'

'You *must* phone the police.'

'I feel a bit silly, it's just a letter. Nikki's been getting them for years and she told the police but nothing came of it.'

'This could be good for me, you know? For my case.'

Jack asks if he can borrow Margo's letter, to copy it. He says he'll post it straight back to her. Might be really helpful.

Margo suggests taking a photo on his phone but he says he'd like to 'get it copied properly' and looks shifty. She thinks he wants a high-res scanned copy in case he writes a follow-up book. They swap contact details and he puts the letter in his bag. She's glad to get it off her hands.

'You should tell the police though, tell them that you think it's McPhail.'

'But I don't know if I do think that yet.'

'Trust me,' says Jack. 'It was him. You're just his type.'

She looks at the picture of Susan, aware of the likeness between them, feeling slightly sick. Robertson didn't need to phrase it like that. She's being threatened, it's not a Tinder date. She signals to the waiter for the bill.

The restaurant is in full drunken roar now. Tables of pink-cheeked women are talking too loudly, interrupting each other, everything is exaggerated. The atmosphere is febrile.

'Gets a bit wild in here sometimes,' he mutters as they get their coats and scarves on.

'Nice place,' says Margo, thinking that Robertson is one of those people who is attracted to chaos and maybe doesn't even know it himself.

Outside they find the street and the road filled with people leaving the King's Theatre across the road. The crowd are jolly and loud, dressed for the frosty weather, milling around at the lights and spilling into the road. The press of the crowd pushes Margo and Jack into the railings as they say their goodbyes. They don't know whether to shake hands or hug but settle on a handshake. Margo turns to leave.

'I'm so sorry about Susan ...'

'Fine.' Margo pats his hand away. 'It's fine.'

'I'm taking a cab. Can I drop you somewhere?'

'Thanks but my car is just round the corner.' She's glad because she suddenly realises that she doesn't trust him at all.

Jack steps back. A cheerful man slides between them, making his way to greet a friend ('Georgie!!') and Margo takes it as a chance to get away.

'Thank you for taking the time,' she calls back.

'Thanks for dinner,' says Jack and turns away. 'I'll post this letter back. Please get your aunt to phone me. Could be a great help.'

'OK, bye.' But Margo doesn't know if she'll even mention him to Nikki. She watches him weave his way through the crowd, tall, distinguished, handsome and feels somehow as if she's just been a bit part in a cheap true crime TV biopic:

Jack Robertson, Lady Saver.

13

JOE OPENS THE DOOR to her but keeps an arm out, barring Margo's way. She's suddenly terrified that he has another woman in there with him, someone nice and soft, who can see what a good guy he is, how funny and droll he is, who appreciates him and his cooking and his many, many opinions about everything. A woman who'll usurp her.

'I'm still paying rent here,' she says, sounding like a bitch.

Joe sucks his teeth and looks over the top of her head. 'It's ten thirty. I have to get up for work in the morning.'

Margo chews a nail and checks herself. 'Can I come in?'

Joe sighs. He looks really sad. 'What for?'

Margo wants to be with him. That's really all she's here for. Just to be with him for this one moment, to see his face and be near the certainty of him, the smell of him, the sweetness of him.

'Can I talk to you?'

He doesn't want to let her in but he does.

She follows him through to the living room. It's a nice flat in a bad area. The rooms are big and they've furnished it with second-hand finds and cheap Ikea essentials. Joe has no money and didn't want expensive stuff, which was just as well because Margo spent most of her income on Janette's care.

They did splash out on two things though, two things they really loved: a huge television and the sofa. She watches as Joe sits down slowly on it.

It's a big grey velvet sofa, bought less than a year ago. They got it on tick, are paying it up over a year. She remembers when they bought it. Ex-display in the New Year sales. Janette was quite ill but still aware, still happy in herself, tottering around the lower floors of her enormous house, waiting for Kiki to bring her dinner in. Joe had just taken over the bike shop a few months before and was working longer hours than Margo. He was tired all the time and they had fights, play fights, nothing serious, about him nodding off at night and drooling onto the precious velvet. A nice time. Before Lilah and Richard arrived back from London and everything got messy.

She sits down on a chair across from him, no longer welcome on the big spongy sofa, no longer part of that.

He looks up at her expectantly but says nothing. He needs a shave and a shower, she can smell his smell. He's just in from work and looks tired.

They don't usually talk when Margo appears at his door late in the evening. They usually start kissing and go to bed and hope that everything will be better when they wake up. They've talked out their relationship, talked as far as talking can go. Joe isn't sorry for reporting Richard. Margo can't forgive him for breaking Lilah's confidence. Lilah and Richard won't call a ceasefire so Margo and Joe can't stop fighting either.

'Did Lilah tell you Richard broke Emma's window?'

'Not really. You know how she is.'

'She told you in silly voices so she doesn't have to take it seriously?'

She thinks about the rabbit's foot on the key chain. 'Sort of. They kept him in for ages because of your complaint, you know. You shouldn't have interfered.'

'Margo, you think being cautious means you're not doing anything but that's bullshit. He could really hurt Lilah and it's a flashpoint – when someone leaves a relationship that controlling, this is when something serious could happen. I'm protecting him as much as her. But let's not pretend you're not doing anything. You're standing there, letting it happen right in front of you and not stepping in. That is doing something. It's just not taking responsibility.'

'She doesn't want you to protect her.'

'I don't care what either of them want. I did it because someone needed to do something.' Joe shuts his eyes and holds up a hand. 'Can we, just for one night, not talk about them?'

Margo doesn't know if they can. 'We should have stayed out of it until we knew what was going on.'

'Margie, we knew perfectly well. You did what you always do and did nothing, to be careful. You need to be reckless sometimes. At the moment you're just drawing back from the world inch by inch and blaming everyone else –'

'She's my best friend.'

'*He's my brother.* And OK: I don't like Lilah, I think she's a pain in the arse, but the irony is that I'm the only one who's concerned enough about her safety to do anything.'

'She's not in danger. You've no idea how many scrapes Lilah has gotten out of.'

'We're avoiding talking about us by focusing on them again.'

He's right. They are.

He holds up one adorable finger. 'I'm saying one thing and then we're not talking about it, even hinting at it, for the rest of this conversation: Richard has a history of violence with his ex-wife. He broke her arm. She said it was an accident but I know it wasn't, I saw the bruises on her jaw. That's all I'm saying.'

But they've made eye contact now, properly, and the tone has changed. Voices have dropped, eyes are hooded, they're craning towards one another and straining with the effort of not touching.

'Am I allowed one thing as well then?'

'Just one,' he says, leaning forward and touching her hand to distract her.

'If the H-bomb was dropped on Glasgow tonight I'd go and stand next to Lilah. She's indestructible.'

Their fingers intertwine.

'Finished?' he whispers.

'Yeah.'

'Can we talk about you now? About the adoption lady? By the way, I know yesterday was Janette's six-month anniversary. I didn't want to text you …'

Margo had forgotten. Joe remembered though. He's reminding her that she's this far away from her mum dying, that he's thinking about how she feels, that he's making allowances for her because he knows it isn't an easy time.

She almost tells him she's pregnant.

The world-shattering news rattles around her head like a stick being dropped down a well. Saying it will change the direction of everything forever, she knows it will, but she still doesn't know which direction she wants to steer in. When she looks at Joe, at his wide shoulders and his broad jaw, at the brown freckles in his green eyes, she knows she wants to keep on looking at him for the rest of her life. It's when they're not together that she doubts herself. She's bullying to him because she's afraid of the pull he has over her, frightened of his high-handedness, worried that he seems to be deciding who she can and can't be friends with. She saw fleeting glimpses of it before Lilah came home, his reluctance to socialise, how he didn't like a lot of her friends and accused her of being dishonest about her motives for a lot of things. She's not sure of him, she's defensive, and she's terrified of being trapped.

'Well,' she says, 'I met my aunt and you will not believe the half of it.'

Joe smiles. 'Is it a big, long story?'

'Yes.'

'Are there lots of side stories and irrelevant characters?'

'Buckets. Do you know how much you can charge for watery linguine?'

'I don't.' He draws her to him. 'Would you care to join me here on this hire-purchase velvet life raft and bore the shit out of me with every single detail?'

So she does.

At five in the morning she wakes, queasy and startled, and slips out of bed, leaving Joe to sleep. She makes a cup of ginger tea in her favourite mug, a pint-sized one with a photo of a grubby street pigeon on it. She settles down in the velvet sofa and opens Robertson's *Terror on the Streets*.

The style is tabloid and mildly hysterical. Sentences never seem to want to end. He gives a rundown of the first murder, which policemen were in charge of the investigation, who the important crime reporters were at that time, who the editors of the newspapers were and what they were known for. There are a lot of men's names and descriptions of them that mark none of them apart. It's all very chummy and, to an outsider, really quite boring.

He talks about all of the women who died violently on the Drag, starting with a woman found in a car park. He gets to the second death and then the third and then the fourth: Susan Brodie. It tells her nothing new in a lot of words.

Robertson gets to the night she went missing and sets the scene. Three 'prostitutes' had been murdered within five years. The atmosphere was tense on the Drag, everyone was afraid of the next murder.

He goes on: it was a cold Thursday night, Susan was feeling tired and depressed, craving drugs, missing her baby, when a white van pulled up and someone motioned to her to get in. Susan was unsure but desperate. Susan moved towards the van to see inside. Whatever she saw reassured her because she got in.

Margo sits back. Robertson can't possibly know these things, he's describing someone else's life in a subjective narrative. Margo doesn't know if it's all right to do that. It feels wrong and unkind and presumptuous.

Susan got into the van and was never seen alive again. She died as 'a bitter sun rose over Glasgow's mean and dirty streets'. He mentions that toast was found in her stomach at the post-mortem, that there must have been a toaster wherever she was, and finishes the chapter on that observation, as if the presence of a toaster has narrowed her whereabouts down conclusively.

The next chapter is about McPhail.

Martin McPhail always wanted to be a police officer. His brother went into the force before him, and was promoted up through the ranks very quickly. It's almost word for word what he told her in the restaurant. She's a little bit annoyed about that, but he makes a point of saying that in every one of the murders 'urine samples' were found at the scene. That's a bit thin – and, Margo notices, very carefully worded – given that most of the women were found in alleys in the city centre. In every single murder, McPhail, or someone fitting his description, was seen in the vicinity at the time. McPhail could not account for his whereabouts at the time of any of them except for the fourth one – the Susan Brodie murder – and that alibi was confirmed by only one source, Strathclyde Police. Later, when he was arrested for rape, he confessed to a cellmate, giving details of the murders that police confirmed could be known *only* to the killer.

Margo tuts. They weren't known *only* to the killer. They were known to the police as well and McPhail was in the police. It's a frustrating read. He's making logic leaps and assumptions, propelling himself through nonsense arguments with indignation.

She flips to the photographs in the middle. An image of the High Court, pictures of women in silhouette, gathered on street corners. Mugshots of some of the women. She gets to the middle image. It's Susan's crime-scene photo. Susan, naked on the rug, cigarette ends in the gutter. This picture is higher resolution than the one on the Internet. This is where they scanned it from.

Jack Robertson knew where the picture came from. He must have known but he lied about it to her in the full knowledge that she'd find out when she opened the book. He didn't care.

She shoves the stupid book back in her bag. It's badly written rubbish, the evidence is thin and the tone is salacious. Margo thinks that Nikki read this stupid book, possibly at a time when she was vulnerable, and it messed with her head. She's not even going to mention it when they meet for a drink tonight. She doesn't know enough about it. She's not going to get involved or do anything. Sometimes people just want you to listen.

14

SUSAN JOGS UP THE outside stairs and gets keys out of her pocket, slips them into the door and goes in.

This is a different house. A big house with lots of ways in. The lights are all off. Empty. She's alone.

Her red Mini is hard to hide, easy to follow, and she's not even trying. Parked on the street last night, after the library and the close call. Just took a couple of hours of waiting behind it in the town for her to come back and drive to a house, not the letter house, another house, one of her punters maybe. Good pay for a full night's work. Must have the cash on her still.

Bitches get everywhere.

This is a big house, front garden hidden behind bushes along the pavement, plenty of dead space between the street and the windows. Good for hiding.

The window frames look loose, can see that from the street. The house is falling down, the doors and windows are peeling, window locks are old or broken or non-existent.

Rev the engine and pull the car away along the street, looking for a place to park, out of sight, somewhere the bitch won't see it.

Have to keep your eye on them, watch them, manage them.

15

JANETTE'S HOUSE IS DUSTY now that no one is moving around in it. A thin film of dry dust settles over everything, clinging to picture rails, skirting boards, on boxes and worktops. Even the toilet seat is dusty.

Margo shuts the front door on the street and braces herself before she turns round. She makes herself look up. There is the stained-glass globe light shade her mother fixed at the kitchen table with Araldite. There is the last scarf Janette ever wore, hanging on the bannister. She leans her back against the door and doesn't want to move. She lets out a sigh and forces herself to step over the boxes and go into the kitchen and put the kettle on. She's trying not to look up because everywhere her eye falls is a job not done.

Janette's house is in Strathbungo, now a 'sought-after area within a vibrant community', according to the estate agents. It wasn't always. Janette bought the crumbling house for a song shortly after Paul Dunlop left them. They needed somewhere cheap. It was only in hindsight that they realised that Janette was clinically depressed for years afterwards.

The house overlooks a sunken railway line that was kept clear of vegetation when they first moved in. Passing trains rattled crockery in the cupboards, made window glass vibrate at a low frequency, almost imperceptibly, just enough to make the outside world seem blurry and uncertain. The house disintegrated around them for the first few years.

They were eating tea in the kitchen one evening, a school night, when they heard a crash in the front room and a cloud of dust billowed through the hall. A ceiling had fallen in. It was a low point, referred to ever after as the Fall of the House of Dunlop.

The villa is early nineteenth century, has grand proportions and lots of original features. Victorian Anaglypta wallpaper runs up to the picture rail, all the fireplaces work, there are butler's bells by the beds and a stained-glass sun room that used to let in the rain. One day, shortly after the Fall of the House of Dunlop, Margo came home to find workmen in the house, replastering the ceiling. Then she found Janette using a palette knife to fit window putty and firm up the glass. Rooms got painted and carpets were pulled up. It was as if Janette had started to admit there would be a future as well as a past. Slowly, she restored the house as she recovered, learned joinery and fixed door frames and bannisters. She painted whole rooms herself and tiled all three bathrooms. She grew a garden from a gravel pit, planted flowers in the small strip of garden that looked out into the street, had the front door painted a jaunty red. The wonder of her hands was everywhere. It wasn't an investment to her. It was emotional signage, a commitment to stay alive.

Then, as if her recovery was contagious, neighbouring houses were bought from the slum landlords who had subdivided and neglected them and the area began to regenerate.

Houses and gardens were restored by gifted amateurs. Neighbours formed committees, helped each other and replaced the cobbles and crumbling walls in the abandoned back lanes. Someone started a book club and an annual barbecue for the street. They campaigned for planting around the railway to dampen the noise and vibrations and the area became more green.

Imperceptibly, the area slid into the second stage of gentrification and became a parody of itself. Professional developers bought houses and fixed them up and sold them to people with money. Soon glass-walled kitchen extensions were being built over gardens, saunas and garden studios were being fitted. Coffee shops opened everywhere. Parking became an issue. They got letters through the door asking if they wanted to sell, first from people who loved the house, then from estate agents. The cars outside got bigger and braggier. Then smaller and sportier and finally electric.

They didn't belong here any more but Janette hadn't noticed because she was busy having strokes. The house was three storeys high and she couldn't manage the stairs, it was completely impractical for her to stay, but she wanted to and she had never asked them for anything before. Margo and Thomas paid for a carer to look after her, for cleaners and bills and the incessant building repairs. They worried about budgeting for the next twenty years, knowing it could only get more expensive. They lived in cramped flats, scrimped on everything and resented it. Thomas went to Saudi chasing money, Margo moved in with Joe, chucked his old flatmate out and took on half his rent. Meanwhile property values rocketed around

Janette. They knew they'd get a good price when it came to what they always referred to as 'the time to sell', but the money was running out. Even between them, they couldn't afford her care. They mortgaged the house and invested but it wouldn't last longer than five years. It was a constant worry.

Abruptly one morning, on her way to work, Margo came in to pick up the shopping list for the day and the carer, Kiki, came down the stairs crying. Janette had died in her sleep. Kiki found her when she went to wake her up. She died without a whimper, twenty years too early. Now Margo would give anything for five more minutes of resentment about the cost of Janette's care. She missed the visits, the strain, resenting Thomas for being away, resenting Janette for being ill. She didn't know what to do with Sundays and Mondays, Kiki's days off, when it fell to her to look after Janette. She missed lifting and washing, she missed sore backs and interminable afternoons. She missed all the bad parts.

Janette wasn't a hoarder but the house is full of stuff. It was a slow accumulation of pleasing things, of ornaments and books and wall hangings and brasses and paintings from art fairs and models of things, none of it intrinsically valuable. Margo has five days to clear the traces of her mum's life from the house before the estate agent comes to take pictures. She's swimming in circles.

She's in the kitchen, looking out of a dirty window at an overgrown hedge and a head bobbing along in the street beyond, wondering why someone is walking down the lane at the back of the house, when her phone rings in her handbag. It's Tracey from the adoption agency.

'Ah, hello again. It's Tracey from the adoption agency, there,' she says, dragging even that sentence out.

'Hi,' Margo says, showing her how quick a greeting can be. The person in the lane seems to have ducked behind a garage a few houses down. She doesn't recognise anyone here any more.

'I was actually calling about that photo of Susan Brodie on the Internet you saw?' Tracey leaves a pause for a response.

'Oh, right?'

'Yeah, so, my husband is actually a computer nerd and he's managed to trace the address of that wee site that you've told me about and they've replied quick-as-you-like and they're saying that they'll take it down. Wouldn't apologise but it turns out they don't have copyright permission. It should be down by late this afternoon.'

The picture is from Robertson's widely available book so Tracey has gone to a lot of trouble for no purpose, but Margo doesn't want to let her down. 'Look, thanks so much for doing that.'

'Aye, no trouble at all. So, there it is … well, I'm here if you need a wee counselling session.' Tracey sounds a bit hurt. 'I can come to you as well.'

'By the way, Tracey, were you at the High Court yesterday?'

'Oh, you *did* go? I never seen you there.'

'So I did spot you on the balcony? Why were you there?''

'Well, yeah. Auch well, it's just down the road from the office and I was on my lunch anyways, like … I was a wee bit worried about you. I felt bad that you'd got only ten minutes with your auntie and then the next day, like, when we spoke … I just popped in to see you were OK …'

'Oh.' It seems a bit intrusive. 'I'd have asked you to come if I wanted you there.'

'Aye, well, it was no problem at all. Did you get to –'

'Look, I have to clear my mum's house out, I'm sorry.'

'Am I catching you at a bad time?'

'Yeah, sorry, Tracey, I really need to go. Thanks very much for going to all the trouble, though.'

'Sure, Margo, you know –' she's super-keen to stay on the phone – 'I's going to say –'

Margo hangs up. She doesn't want to talk to Tracey. She feels guilty about it, Tracey's been nothing but nice to her, a bit annoying but not malicious, but there's something about her Margo finds annoying, she can't quite put her finger on it.

She goes upstairs and stands in the doorway of the big bathroom, paralysed. A brown spider plant droops from the macramé hanger, all its tiny babies brown and wilted, like a sad memory of fireworks.

There's so much stuff in here, all of it dusty and maybe someone would want it. Bath mat and matching toilet surround, a plastic non-slip mat in the bath itself, a green glass jar full of soap jelly, a slimy substance Janette used for laundry, made from all the little bits of old soap bars left in water. A toothbrush in a glass, unused talcum puffs in a fancy red plastic container. A Mabel Lucie Atwell wall hanging with a mildewed corner: *Please remember, don't forget.* So much stuff. She abandons that room and goes into the bedroom.

She looks at the dresser. It is crammed. Half a dozen little Derby shepherdess figurines, all slightly chipped.

Margo takes one in her hand. The little figure smiles softly and has rosy cheeks, a cobalt skirt and a lamb at her feet. Ridiculously romantic view of a hard job: Marie Antoinette at a masked ball. Margo wipes the gritty dust away and runs her finger over a yellowed-glue garrotte on the lamb's neck. Janette liked broken things. She liked to mend.

Despairing, Margo slips it into her pocket, leans forward and looks under the bed. A slipper, an old newspaper folded to the crossword and a thick layer of grey dust over all of it. Her mood is lower than ever.

She gets up and shuts her eyes and visualises herself opening bin bags and sweeping things into them with her arm. She rehearses it over and over and then gets up, goes to the kitchen, finds the bin bags and comes back. She flaps a bag open and empties the top of the dresser into it. It feels great. She opens the top drawer, pulls it out and empties it into the bag. Thermals and long johns. No one wants them but they're in the bag and that's, as Lilah says, a triumph. She takes out the next drawer, underpants, and does the same. Next drawer, thermal vests. Next drawer underskirts and long-sleeved thermals. Next drawer is empty because it was too low down for Janette to reach. The bottom drawer is empty too.

Feeling like a conquering hero, she ties a knot in the bag and takes it out to the hall, lining it up against the wall, leaving room for the many others.

Back in the bedroom she puts the radio on to stop herself from thinking and empties the other set of drawers. She's on such a roll that she doesn't even take that bag out to the hall, she just leaves it by the door and moves on to the wardrobe.

She manages not to press her face to the jackets or smell the scarves or take the pretty brooches off the lapels of jackets. She just shoves them into bags and dumps them by the door.

She strips the bed and puts all of the bedding into another bag, unplugs Janette's beloved electric blanket – the best present they ever bought her – and shoves that in too. She's struggling a little now with thoughts of how wasteful it is to throw all of these things out and how some people don't have lovely coats or electric blankets and would be glad of them. It's Janette's voice in her head and she enjoys it while she can still remember the throaty sound of her.

In the wardrobe there's a shoebox at the back of the top shelf. She pulls over a pouffe to reach it. The lid is dustier than the rest of the house, as if it's been there a very long time. She opens it and finds tiny button-over baby shoes and two black drawstring velvet bags with milk teeth inside.

She takes them down to the kitchen, opens her laptop and Skypes Thomas at work.

'What?' He's eating lunch at his desk.

She shows him what she found.

'What is that?'

'Milk teeth. Tiny shoes. They're ours.'

'Throw them out.'

'Seriously? These have no sentimental value to you whatsoever?'

'I don't remember being a baby, do you?'

He has a point.

'You're the least romantic human being I've ever known.'

Thomas grins as if it's a compliment. 'How's it going?'

He means the house clearing.

'I find it hard. You'd just get a wheelbarrow and tip it into a river, wouldn't you?'

'Yup.' He takes a slurp of energy drink.

'Shall I send you a carefully curated box of sentimental shite?'

'Thank you but no,' says Thomas, giving a small burp. 'I'm looking forward to amassing random crap of my own now.'

They look at each other, for just a moment forgoing the hypnotic draw of their own image.

'This is tough for you, Margo.'

Margo thinks it's nice of him to acknowledge that but it would be nicer if he helped. She can't admit she needs his help though. He's looking carefully at the background now, at the kitchen, and he looks worried.

'Margie?'

'What?' She looks over her shoulder at what he's seeing: it's a mess. Stacks of plates cover the table, and bin bags full of out-of-date dry goods are slumped on the dresser. 'This is all … ah …' she tries to excuse herself, 'you know. Joe and stuff.'

But Thomas has seen the mess and he's worried. 'Margo, have you done *any* clearing out?'

'Excuse me, this is practically the last room, thank you very much.'

Frowning, he sits back from his desk. 'Are you going mental? Should I come home?'

'Tom, shut up. Just, Lilah's doing my head in. Why can't she just stay away from bloody Richard?'

That seems to relax him a little. He takes another slug from the can. 'Richard says she's nicked money from him.'

'Yeah,' says Margo, 'he's hardly going to admit he's hunting her down, is he? He's going to have some complaint against her that justifies what he's doing.'

'True. They don't want it to be over, that's why they won't go to the police.' Thomas won't engage. 'You heard from that aunt woman again?'

'Nah,' she says, avoiding his eye. 'Sort of done with that now. I saved you one of Janette's little statues. The shepherd one you liked as a boy.'

'Call a clearance company, Margo. I need to get on.' He hangs up without saying goodbye.

16

NIKKI MUST HAVE GOT here early because she's standing at the bar, waiting for Margo. She's dressed as herself this time: a pink satin bomber jacket over sky-blue leggings and a big pink T-shirt. She doesn't go for an abortive hug, just nods too much and says hiya too often, but she doesn't seem as nervous or jittery. Margo is wary but not afraid of Nikki. Even if she did send the letter, they're in a public place.

The pub off George Square is a tourist trap. Inside it's all tartan upholstery and claymores on the walls. Soft rock music is playing slightly too loud from tiny white speakers screwed into the ceiling. Giant blackboards show the menu of steak and chips, haggis and whisky-flavoured ice cream. It seems very expensive to Margo but that's probably because it serves visitors to the city who don't know that better food is available two streets away for half the price.

It's quiet. The five o'clock rush is over but the evening hasn't begun. There are only two other customers: men sitting away from each other in the far corners of the L-shaped room, pretending to read newspapers but really just killing themselves with drink. Three members of staff in black slacks and white shirts loiter around the till behind the bar, pointedly keeping their backs to the new arrivals as they chat among themselves. Margo tries to get their attention, leaning this way and that, but they slip her eye expertly.

'HOI!' Nikki shouts over the music. All three turn and look at her. 'Pint o' Coke and whatever my niece here wants.' She thumbs to Margo and repeats it. '*Niece*,' she says and smiles.

One barman breaks away and saunters over. He has a ponderous belly and rosacea. His breathing is nasally restricted. Margo tries not to prognosticate. She orders a tonic.

When the barman delivers their drinks and asks for money, Nikki stands as still as a startled doe. Margo gets her purse out, pays and only then Nikki comes alive again and acts as if nothing happened.

They move over to a table in the elbow crease of the room, as far from the alcoholics as they can get. Nikki takes the seat against the wall and Margo sits across from her.

'I was so glad when I saw you at court. I've been dead upset about what happened. Talked to my pals and they set me right. I've got no business asking you to look up his files. I didn't know it could get you in trouble too. I'm sorry.'

'Well, how could you know? During the lockdown a senior nurse got the sack for looking at his wife's file. He was only checking her medication levels. They take that kind of data breach incredibly seriously.'

'Hmm,' nods Nikki. 'Well, I was at court and thought it would be easy for you to see. We've always thought it was McPhail. Didn't think a wee peek would be – I was having a shit day. I shouldn't have come in and started demanding stuff.'

'Don't worry.' But Margo is pleased she said that. 'I met Jack Robertson yesterday.'

'Loves himself, doesn't he?'

'Yeah.'

Nikki slaps a hand on the table like a judge delivering final judgement. 'Arsehole.'

They laugh together at that.

'Always been famous for it,' says Nikki. 'He doesn't care. Like there's a bit of wiring missing in his head.'

'Well, he told me Susan was clean when she died.'

'Ah, OK, that is true. I lied, I'm sorry, I wanted you to like her, to think she *had* to give you up ... I don't know. We'd just met. You didn't seem very ... You know.'

'Nice?'

'Happy.'

'Gallagher said Susan got clean because she was pregnant with me.'

'Yeah.' Nikki smiles. 'She chucked it for you. Didn't do meetings or methadone or anything so she was fucking mental all the time but she did it. She was getting out of the life as well, just saving up a wee dunt before she did. She was amazing, Susan. She did love you, pet, but she couldn't keep you. She could only give you what we had and that wasn't enough. She was really ambitious. People hated that about her.'

'Did she contact the social work department or did they ask her to give me up?' This is important to Margo, to know if Susan had an active desire to walk away from her.

Nikki says Susan didn't contact them. 'Social work're always around, aren't they?'

'Are they?'

'Well, they were always around us. We grew up in care.'

'I'm sorry.'

'No, no, no.' Nikki flaps a hand in front of her face as if Margo's pity is a cloud of midges. 'No, no, we weren't in care until *later*. We got to twelve and ten before we got taken in, it wasn't like we were in since we were babies. There's, you know, grades. Those baby ones, the ones in care from before they can talk, they don't get much of a chance.'

'Everyone needs someone to look down on?' As soon as it leaves her mouth Margo knows she shouldn't have said that, but Nikki takes it well.

'I suppose. There's a comfort in that, isn't there? Feeling better off than other people. I don't know if it's wrong but you look around and think: yeah, OK ...'

She's nice. Margo is surprised. They smile at each other for the first time, two women who like each other without obligation.

'Before that, where did you two grow up?'

'Oh, we were in the country, all fields and trees and that.' She names a mining town where Margo once did a maternity cover stint. It is in the country but only technically. It was heavily industrialised until the smelter shut down and all the ancillary industries collapsed. Then the shops shut and it became a ghetto. They were treating asbestosis and cancers at the same rate as an inner-city surgery.

Margo says she knows the town quite well so Nikki qualifies her claim: well, it used to be nicer. Their mother, Patsy, moved them to Glasgow when they were wee anyway, to Whiteinch. It's a dockers' area near the river.

'*Patsy*?' asks Margo.

'That's who Susan named you for. Your granny.'

'Is Patsy still alive?'

'No. Patsy died visiting Betty. That's why we got taken into care. She was in an abandoned warehouse in the middle of the night, fell off a broken set of stairs and smashed her head open and died.'

'Why was she in a warehouse building in the middle of the night?'

'Trying to tap money off her sister, Betty. Betty lived at the top of a big deserted warehouse full of rats.' She says it with a certain amount of relish and Margo doesn't know why.

'What was Betty doing there?'

'She had to live far away from other people because she heard the voices of dead people sending messages. That's why the family had to stay away from her.'

'Was she schizophrenic?'

'No, psychic. She did shows and that, travelled with her psychic work. She couldn't look after two weans. Betty was good as well, let me tell you. I know you don't believe but she was eerie. I was terrified of being sent to live with her when Patsy died, but I was only twelve.'

Margo remembers being twelve herself. That was when her dad left them. She remembers it in vivid snapshots: the taste of weak orange squash, white and purple crocuses on the front lawn, listening to Janette having strained arguments on the phone while their dad screamed at the other end.

'Were you ever fostered?'

Nikki wriggles from buttock to buttock. 'Meh, for bits. Back and forth. Always together though. They wanted to split us up once, send her off and not me, and we both says no.'

'I wondered if she had any other children?'

'No. Had an abortion but no other kids. She was young though. About thirteen.'

'Oh. I see.' Grim. A pregnant child. A history of sexual abuse. Predators. No wonder social work were involved. 'Thirteen is terribly young. The pelvis isn't fused yet. The damage can be terrible. Who got her pregnant at thirteen?'

'Barney Keith.'

Margo winces at the mention of his name. 'I found a Barney Keith. He's on Facebook.'

'He's not dead? Jeesh, he was a million years old back then! She was desperate for someone. She met Barney at the four points in town. Know the corner of Union Street and Argyle Street? Had two all-night cafes and that's where the runaways used to hang out. They'd pull a social work van up at two in the morning, load us all in, drive us back to all our houses.' Nikki can see how sad Margo is about it. 'We had nowhere else to go, pet. Barney had a house. Not everyone gets to be young. There was guys in that group home, you know … ?'

Margo doesn't, she's afraid to know what Nikki means by that.

'I mean,' Nikki says, 'you think to yourself: well, why shouldn't I be charging for this? It's happening anyway. Patsy did it. We knew where to go and everything.'

Margo notices that she's finding it hard to even listen to vague hints about everything Nikki's lived through. 'Nikki, I'm sorry if I'm …' She doesn't know what to say. 'I'm sorry.'

'You don't know what I'm talking about,' says Nikki cheerfully.

'I don't,' admits Margo.

'That's what Susan wanted. She wanted that for you. She didn't want you to be involved in any of this and I don't either. It's fine.'

But Margo is involved. Nikki doesn't know it but she is.

'Can you tell me about it though?'

'OK, well.' Nikki sits forward, clears her throat and looks at the table in front of her. 'Patsy made a good living at it. Me and Hairy would be at school wearing all the best, new shoes all the time, new clothes.' She strokes her jacket and smiles to herself. 'Got a taste for good gear. She was actually too drunk to do a washing most of the time so she just bought new stuff – but we got our hair done in hairdressers and that was unheard of for weans in Whiteinch back then.' Nikki's expression softens as she remembers and she gives a long blink. 'We were like wee queens and Patsy was a grafter. She couldn't read or write, couldn't get another job, but when we moved to Glasgow she worked out where to go and what to do. She was out every night, rain or shine.'

'Who looked after you?'

Nikki's eyes roam the room. 'Me and Hairy?'

'If Patsy was out every night?'

'We were in bed.'

'Oh.'

'It was a different time. She'd moved to the city to get away from her man. He was kicking seven colours of shit out of her every night and she just got, like, you know, "fuck this".'

'Your dad?'

Nikki shakes her head as if she's never really thought about it much. 'I suppose he was, really. I mean, he had your hair, Susan's hair and that, so ... yeah. But we were teeny-weeny when we left. I don't remember him much, Hairy didn't know him at all. What I do remember is Patsy's face.' She cups a hand over one eye to show how swollen it was. 'She nearly lost an eye that night so she filled a bin bag and we all got on the bus to Glasgow. That was that. Never went back. Never seen him again.'

'Brave,' says Margo, because she thinks she should say something positive.

'No, just desperate,' counters Nikki.

'But I mean to go out in the streets to provide for her kids, though. She must have cared a lot to put herself through that.'

Nikki gives her a strange look. 'Think so? She was drinking a lot of it.'

'Well, I would imagine it's pretty terrifying being out there, alone in the dark. You don't know who's down there ...'

Nikki's not amused any more. Now she's just annoyed. 'Hm.'

'She must have had quite low self-esteem.'

'"Low self-esteem"?' Nikki tuts. 'Listen: Patsy couldn't read or write but she walked away with a sore face and a bin bag of jumpers because she thought she was due more. She kept her weans and found a way to make a living and be drunk all the fucking time.'

'I just think, you know, probably no one does that job unless they've been traumatised in some way.'

Nikki shuts her eyes. 'POOR,' she says, exasperated.

'What?'

She looks hard at Margo. 'She was *poor*. We were very poor. That's why we did it. We were poor. It's not a mental illness, she didn't have secret daddy issues, it's not about sex for the lassies out there. I mean, you'll tell a punter that if they want to hear it, but it's about money. Getting money because we're poor. Upsets the status quo, doesn't it? That's why it's policed the way it is.' Nikki huffs. 'The cops are there to protect the public. Folk like us, we're not the public. We're a nuisance *to* the public. That's how most cops seen it. They hated us, we hated them.'

'You seemed to like Diane Gallagher.'

'I'll always love her for trying. Don't always agree with her, she's got her opinions, but as a person – yes. She was the only woman in the CID – they used to roll her out as a spokesman. She wasn't in charge then. They were barely investigating the murders before she took over.'

'Why?'

She whispers, 'We didn't matter. That's how they seen us.'

'But people were being murdered.'

Nikki shrugs and holds it, a profound sadness in her eyes. 'See, in New York, back then, when street people got killed the cops used to mark the file NHI: "No Humans Involved". Not even human. When we get killed they call us the "less dead", like we were never really alive to begin with. See, if Susan was a doctor, like you, they'd have brought the fucking army in. You'd be the perfect victim.'

She looks away and Margo wonders if she's just been threatened. It surprises her because it's not something she wonders about very often and she decides that she must be mistaken. She puts her hand over Nikki's.

'Listen, I don't feel that way about Susan. I don't think she's less than human or not important because of what she did for money.'

Nikki snorts and shakes her hand away. 'Don't give me that.'

'But I don't.'

'Why even say it? Would you tell me you don't think she's less than human because she was a teacher? A bus driver?'

Margo is stumped. She's right.

'The other day, I thought McPhail'd be at the High Court, that's why I was in a bit of a state when I met you.'

'What if it wasn't him?'

Nikki is offended. 'It *was*. He's still writing threatening letters to me. The only reason he never got charged was the cops covering up for him.'

'That sounds a bit paranoid.'

'Does it?'

'Yeah, to be honest.'

They are sitting very still now and Nikki is grinding her teeth together.

'Well. See,' sneers Nikki, 'when it comes to family, you get who you get. Who were you expecting – Jacob Rees-Mogg or some posh prick like that?'

'Honestly, that's pretty much the only scenario that could be worse than this.'

Nikki smirks and Margo smiles back. Nikki grins and Margo starts laughing and so does Nikki. Then they can't stop because their laugh is the same: mouths wide, heads back, chests huffing. Nikki slaps the table and Margo copies her and they laugh louder.

The barmen look over. One of them smiles with surprise as if he hasn't heard anyone laugh in a while.

The alcoholics glance over disdainfully, one around the side of his paper, one over the top. They think the women are drunk but they're not. They're just too sad to stop laughing.

Finally, when the tide of hysteria recedes, Nikki says slyly, 'I've got those letters if you want to have a look.'

'On you?' says Margo, wondering if Nikki wrote the abusive letters as a set, if this is the trap she's been setting up all along.

'Keep them at my pal's, a wee walk down the road from here.'

'Why don't you keep them in your own house?'

'In case he breaks in and kills me and steals them. Want to see them?'

17

THEY'RE COMING OUT OF the pub together. The Susan in front and then Nikki-fucking-Brodie in that pink jacket. They're not drunk, they're steady on their feet, but that's a mistake, they've missed a trick by not getting a skinful, it'll make their shift much harder down by the cold river in the dark sucking off guys for fivers.

She got the letter, seems nervous. That's good, she'll be jittery and easier to get into the car.

Nikki leads the way, training their weans like they always do. She's a dried-up sack. She's a pig who couldn't give it away. Just as well she retired. Nobody would touch that.

They have to be young to be teachable. Have to get them young and teach them what they are. Can't teach an old whore new tricks. To get them really working they need to get broken young.

It's when they make their money, when they're young. She's younger but not that young. She'd do well though.

They're walking down towards the Green where they be-long, crossing streets, walking fast, down to get their hole ripped up for money.

The smell of her. Is it a memory? A memory of a smell? Disgusting. Filthy. Meat gone bad. Must be a memory but it lingers on the nose. It's a dirt smell, the kind that makes you turn away and shut your eyes. Contamination. Needs cleaned away.

Their kind give it off, it comes from the blood. They can look down on you, they can have qualifications coming out of their ears, but you can always tell where the rot is, where the smell of rotting is.

Dirt.

18

THE SALTMARKET IS SLOWLY going upmarket but it still has pockets of the old rough city. There are dead ends and dark corners, beggars and fighting drunks, but Margo feels comfortable there. Nearby there are streets of cool restaurants and independent photography galleries and a bar full of retro arcade games, frequented by bearded hipsters.

It's seven o'clock on a quiet Wednesday evening in the city centre. The temperature has dropped, frost is creeping white along the pavement, sparkling in the air under street lights. Occasional buses trundle past, windows dripping with condensation, passengers shifting around inside like fish in dirty tanks. Taxis patrol the main streets, prowling for customers, but they're not taking a taxi, they're walking.

Despite being clean and sober Nikki still has an addict's distinctive walk. She's fast, lifts her knees high like an antelope, never looking to see if her companion is beside her, eyes dead ahead, on a mission. Margo sees underweight people in ones and twos walking like that through busy streets all the time. She envies their singleness of purpose, the certainty that they're walking towards something that, if they can only get it, is guaranteed to make them feel better.

Nikki walks fast taking a route that Margo wouldn't and Margo trails her, hurrying to keep up.

They skirt waste ground, go down an alley stacked with mattresses that stink of piss, cross a car park pitted with broken tarmac. Nikki doesn't take the streets lined with arty venues. That's not what the area looks like to her.

They pass under a low railway bridge and slip between a gathering of smokers outside a pub. Margo steels herself for personal comments, insinuations, insults, but none of the smokers even look up. They all seem glum, intent on their cigarettes or vapes. It's so cold now that thick frosted breath is almost indistinguishable from sweet-smelling vape clouds.

Nikki stops suddenly at the edge of the pavement and looks across the broad street, up to a brightly lit window on the second floor. Her face softens.

She looks left and right on the empty street, down to the bridge to the Gorbals, up to the Trongate tower where witches used to be burned. 'Mon.' She darts across the road and Margo follows her.

They reach the door of a high tenement and Nikki presses the buzzer. The door falls open. She pushes it wide and holds it for Margo. Margo hesitates: this seems unsafe. She has no idea what is in there or who Nikki really is.

Still holding the heavy door, Nikki smiles. 'Text a pal this address. Tell them to call the polis if they don't hear from you.'

Margo is slightly stunned. That's exactly what she should do and precisely what she was thinking her way towards. She doesn't even have to disguise what she's doing because Nikki told her to do it.

Nikki waits, holding the door open with her back, watching patiently as Margo texts Lilah and puts her phone away, realising that it's probably what a sex worker does when she goes into a building she doesn't know. She steps into the close and Nikki lets the door go.

'Would people do that if they're ...' She doesn't know the word. She points to the street. 'Out there?'

'Yes.'

'Would you send it to your pimp?'

Nikki barks a high-pitched, ridiculing laugh. It's gorgeous and honest. 'We didn't do pimps, not in Glasgow, we needed every penny.' But she waves a hand and corrects herself. 'Nah, that's the old days. It's all cam work and indoors now, they're all paying cuts. But we never.'

Margo likes Nikki more the longer she's in her company. She doesn't trust her but she likes her. She hopes she has her grace, a disjointed way of moving: pelvis then legs, shoulders then spine, wrists then fingers. In the meantime she's enjoying being near to Nikki and the frankness of her.

The door falls gently shut on the street, slowing as it closes, giving out a loud click that sounds like a finale.

It's a plain close, no fancy tiles or flooring, just painted green gloss up to shoulder level and cream above.

The bitter edge of the cold evening is tempered in here. Margo can smell bacon cooking. Nikki leads her up to the second floor and an open door behind a worn rainbow flag doormat. She pushes it open and they go in.

It's a square hall, higher than it is wide. The walls are hung with clip frames crammed with jumbled family photos, some have slipped and fallen over other photos. None of the pictures look staged, they're all snaps of parties and faces and people sitting on settees holding babies. The sound of a television comes from a dark room on their left.

Nikki calls, 'Hiya?'

'Nikki, that you?' The voice is so gruff it's hard to gender. It's coming from the direction of the television.

Nikki goes into the room and Margo follows her.

A middle-aged person as small as a child is sitting in the lone armchair, their back to them, greying hair in a mannish cut.

She only knows it's a woman because Nikki says, 'Lizzie,' and touches the hair gently.

Lizzie is watching football on a gigantic flat-screen TV bracketed to the wall. The room is warm and cosy, the TV the only light source. A hospital bed table is swung over her seat and on it sits a packet of cigarettes and an ashtray, a lighter and a giant mug with '*I love the boaby*' printed on it. Lizzie is so engrossed in the football that she doesn't turn round to look at them.

'Go all right, honey?' she asks the screen.

'Aye.' Now Nikki is watching the football too. She has crossed her arms. 'Brought her over to show her the letters. OK to just take them?'

'Aye, aye,' Lizzie tells the television. 'Look at this shower of donkeys.'

'Pile of halfwits,' says Nikki fondly.

A young footballer fumbles a pass. The screen is so big and clear it's almost half life-size. Another player gets possession and the first player, apropos of nothing, falls over and his face crumples in pain.

Nikki and Lizzie laugh disparagingly. Their eyes never stray from the screen.

'Dear oh dear,' says Nikki. 'Three hundred grand a week or something.'

'I mean –' Lizzie's tiny hand comes out in entreaty towards the telly – 'for that money: take some acting lessons.'

They huff their knowing laughs again and Nikki turns and pushes past Margo. 'Mon.'

She leads her through to a small kitchen, muttering excuses about the mess in a shamed undertone. Packets of cheap biscuits line the worktops and the sink is full of dirty plates and pots. She reaches up to a high wall cupboard and opens it to a jumble of mugs. A fat brown envelope is tucked into the side, flush to the wall. She takes it out. It's battered and ripped and almost full. At the table she uses her forearm to sweep letters and flyers to the side and clear a space. She puts the envelope down and they sit next to each other and look at it.

Bracing herself, Nikki reaches into the envelope and pulls out a bundle of ten or twelve clear food bags, fanning them out on the table like a set of playing cards.

Inside each is a handwritten letter, the paper size and type variable, sometimes A4, sometimes proper letter-writing paper, sometimes it's a page ripped from a jotter.

It's all in the same handwriting as the letter Margo found in her hallway yesterday morning.

The words slant forward distinctively and the 't's and 'f's are all small and straight, just like the letter she gave Robertson. They're written by the same person.

Margo suddenly feels cold and small. She forces herself to take a deep breath and nods calmly at Nikki. 'Why are they in plastic bags?'

Nikki looks down at them, puzzled. 'I thought we might get DNA off them or hairs or something, if I kept them good. Put them in there a couple of years ago.' She glances up at Margo, as if she might know. Margo thinks Nikki was copying actors in TV cop shows.

'DNA has to be preserved at the time, Nikki.'

'So … ? These bags are pointless?'

'Sorry.'

Nikki looks at them sadly. 'I just thought it might be worth a shot, you know?'

'I know.'

'I'm doing my best for her.'

'I know.'

Margo looks down at the letters. One letter has a clump of dark frizzy hair stuck to the inside of the plastic. It could be her own hair if she didn't oil it. It's held together with a rotting blue elastic hairband. Another one has a dirty scrap of tartan blanket with the same pattern as the crime-scene photo: red shot through with yellow.

Nikki points at the hair but baulks at touching it. 'Hair,' she says, as if that needed pointing out. '*Her* hair. He knew she was nicknamed Hairy and it was all wiry like that. And the bobble? That's hers.' She rubs her forehead sadly, moving her lips as she reads lines of the text. 'Well, this one here is the second one. I got it a year after Susan was found dead.'

Margo reads:

To Nikki Brodie: I'm the boy who murdered your hoor of a sister. I stabbed it and washed it and pissed on her as it died. She was a peece of shit. I fund her in Wellington Lane & brung her to mine. I had [scored-out word] her sex many times but this was the sweetest.

I enjoyed it. My work isn't done yet neither.

The Ram

Margo reads it again. Same handwriting, same grammar, same syntax as her letter. She thinks of gender-ambivalent Lizzie watching the football in the living room and, probably just because of that, notices how insistent this letter writer is that they're male. It makes her wonder how often anonymous letter writers mention their gender. It makes her wonder if the author is a woman insisting that she's a man to deflect suspicion. Nikki could have written these herself. 'Pathetic,' she says, for something to say.

'Yeah.' Nikki clears her throat. 'But I've had worse said to me in the street, that's not what bothers me —' her voice is shaking and breathy — 'it's the things inside with the letters. He knew her. He did. I think he was with her when she died.'

Margo watches Nikki blinking quickly, trying not to cry. The letter is quite creepy.

'Nikki, how old were you when you got this?'

'Twenty-two?' she whispers, rubbing her index finger hard between her eyebrows as if she wants to cover her eyes. She nods and keeps her hand there. 'Stopped when McPhail was in prison. Last one was two months ago.'

'Why didn't Gallagher do something about these? Warn him off or something?'

'She said they could be from anyone. But I know it's him and I know he killed Susan. He was known for pissing on lassies. Sometimes he'd pay and then piss on you after. He had these black eyes, the pupils, deep, kind of ... hard to describe.' She sucks her teeth. 'Anyway, there's details in the letters, about what she was wearing, where he grabbed her. Only the cops knew that stuff so it was definitely from him. Cops were interested at one point, they took the letters from me and examined them, but said it was nothing. I had to make her give them back to me.'

'Gallagher?'

'Yeah. The guy before her wouldn't even look at them.'

'And the letters had details only the police knew?'

'Aye. Genuinely. I'm not making that up. Stuff I didn't know but *they* knew. About the peeing on her. Gallagher said the letters were right about that stuff.'

'If McPhail was a police officer couldn't he get that information from other cops and put it in a letter? The bits of rug and hair, maybe he got those things from an evidence locker? Doesn't mean he killed her but he could have written these letters to warn you off telling people he did. Maybe the police even know that and that's why they didn't want to take it any further?'

'God, that's possible!' Nikki seems pleased at that and nods respectfully at Margo. 'That makes sense. He was angry at me saying I thought he was involved.'

'Robertson said he was nasty.'

'Oh aye, nasty just about sums him up.'

The door opens into the kitchen and Lizzie is standing there. It's half-time. They can hear adverts from the TV. Lizzie has a functional haircut and large bifocals with clear frames. She's even smaller than she seemed when she was swamped by the armchair, less than five foot tall. She's dressed like a man in straight jeans, grey socks and a boxy sweatshirt. She tips her head back to use the bottom half of her lenses to see Margo, magnifying and warping her grey eyes.

19

'This her?' asks Lizzie, staring at Margo with saucer eyes.

Nikki rests her hand on Margo's forearm. 'Aye,' she says. She looks proud and shy at the same time.

Lizzie comes over and looks closely at Margo, a smile flickering in her eyes. 'Awful nice to see that wee face again.' She breaks off to sob, covering her face with both hands, crying like a child. Nikki laughs fondly at her reaction and comforts and coaxes her to sit with them.

They sit her down in Margo's seat as Nikki laughs at her and rubs her back.

Lizzie shakes her head and mumbles through her hands, 'It's a happy ... I'm happy.' Breathing unevenly, Lizzie dries her face on her sleeve and asks Nikki, 'Is she fucking mental like Hairy?'

Nikki rubs her back again, hard this time. 'No. She's pretty sedate.'

Margo asks, 'What do you mean by "fucking mental"?'

'No, no.' Lizzie waves a hand, 'I don't mean she was mentally ill. Just – Susan was scared of nothing. God knows she had plenty of reasons to be scared, enough had happened to her, she was just one of those lassies who didn't have that in her.'

'Ah, well, that's not true.' Nikki smiles ruefully at the table. 'Hairy *did* get scared. She told me once that she was scared all the time, even when she was sleeping, and she just realised one day that she couldn't get more scared, that it wasn't going away, and after that she just did what she wanted. She said she had nothing left to lose so she could try anything.'

Lizzie tells Margo in an awed whisper, 'She carried a *knife*.'

'Really?' says Margo, not sure what to say.

Lizzie looks at her critically, taking in her flattened down hair, her bland Marks and Spencer coat and her cream cashmere crew neck.

'Is it OK? Does she know what we are? Because I'm not lying about myself in my own house.'

'She's a grown-up, Lizzie,' says Nikki nervously, 'I told her.'

Lizzie tilts her head, abruptly aggressive. 'You know, do you?'

Margo isn't sure what's going on now.

Lizzie's eyes harden. 'We're *prostitutes*.' She hisses the word and waits for a reaction, relishing the tension.

Nikki says flatly, 'Lizzie, she already knows. I already told her.'

Lizzie doesn't break Margo's gaze. '*Whoors*. D'you know what I mean by that?'

'Sex for money?' says Margo, careful and not wanting to offend.

'Aye. Most people think we should lie about that, call ourselves something else, lie about it, but I won't. We're whoors. Can't say it, can ye?'

Big wet owl eyes bore into her. Margo doesn't know how to be right in this situation. 'Is that the word? I don't know what's OK and what's offensive.'

'Oh, words.' Lizzie folds her arms and draws her lips tight, nodding smugly. 'Fucking words. Give me a fucking break. The City Mission wouldn't let them call us prostitutes or sex workers for a year, for a whole year they couldn't call us anything. We're out there getting killed and these politics twats are having fucking arguments about words.'

Nikki looks nervous and mutters, 'She's not interested in that, Lizzie.'

'Well, she should be! We can't all be Tanya fucking Williams! She should be interested in it! She should!' But the more Lizzie insists the less convinced she sounds.

'What was different about Tanya Williams?' asks Margo, a bit scared of Lizzie.

'Oh, she was completely different from the rest of us.' Lizzie's furious. '*Completely* different. Had a family. Sat on a horse once.'

'Come on, Lizzie, Tanya Williams was a poor wee soul like the rest of us,' says Nikki but she turns to Margo. '*That* was different. The cops investigated and witnesses came forward and everything. No one came forward when it was us getting attacked.'

'Why?'

Lizzie gives her a hard stare. 'You tell me. *You're* the public. You tell me.'

Nikki doesn't want to talk about that. 'Look, Tanya's folks were lovely people. They made TV appeals. She was young, she'd had a sad life. That's why they did a proper investigation.'

Margo can't believe that. 'You shouldn't have to be *nice* for the police to investigate a murder, surely?'

'Yes.' Lizzie nods slowly, 'You *do*.'

'But that's what the police are there for.'

Nikki pats her hand. 'They're there for you. For Tanya. They're not there for us.'

'In fairness to the cops –' Lizzie waves a hand at Margo – 'the public don't give a shit either. When it's us they pretend it didn't happen. They'd step over you in the street. *You'd* step over us in the street.'

'She wouldn't,' says Nikki quietly.

'Aye, she would.'

'She wouldn't,' says Nikki, half smiling. 'She's a doctor.'

'Is that right?'

'Aye. An actual doctor in the family.'

'God, she is like her, isn't she? And she's a doctor,' says Lizzie admiringly. 'Amazing.'

'I know,' nods Nikki proudly.

Nikki and Lizzie smile and look at Margo as if she is a very pleasing breed of dog. Margo speaks, almost just to show she can. 'Did the police think McPhail did the Tanya Williams murder?'

Lizzie and Nikki chuckle at each other.

'No, we shouldn't laugh about that – it's not funny,' says Nikki. 'She was a young nice lassie and what happened was terrible.'

'You're right,' says Lizzie. 'Her poor wee mother.' She turns to Margo. 'We're not laughing at what happened to the wee soul, it's the cops … just, they're fucking idiots.'

'And you know,' says Lizzie, 'if they had investigated the other ones, the rapes and assaults and the other murders, they could have done a better job when Tanya was killed, couldn't they? But they fucked it up *royal*.'

Nikki tuts and turns to Margo to explain. 'See what happened was that the cops decided it was these Turkish guys. Bugged their cafe for two years. Charged them all. Said they caught them talking about it. Then, when the defence lawyers got these two years of incriminating tapes, it turns out there was nothing there, just muffled sounds and them playing a Turkish card game called "Hide the Lady". Cost millions. Case collapsed. Police put a big fund aside to investigate what went wrong in the investigation. Turns out they spent it all trying to find out who told the press they'd fucked it up. They were illegally tapping the phone of the cops who'd told on them.'

'Fucking hell.'

'Fucking hell, indeed,' says Lizzie, serious as a newsreader. 'And that's what happens when they do care.' She shoves her glasses back up her nose and looks at the letters, pawing through them until she hits the one with the scrap of dirty tartan material in it. 'Whoever he is, he's a fucking arsehole. Susan's murder broke us, so it did.' She gets agitated at some memory, reddening. Nikki rubs her shoulders roughly, telling her to shake it off. 'Even Betty. She was never the same.'

'*Psychic* Betty?' asks Margo. 'Did you know her?'

'Since she lived down in Washington Street,' says Lizzie. 'She lived above a warehouse. Building was full of rats.'

'It sounds horrendous. Why live there of all places?'

Lizzie raises her eyebrows and defers to Nikki.

'Those voices in her head,' says Nikki. 'Too loud for her if she lived with other people. She had to be alone.'

Lizzie catches a stern look from Nikki and suppresses a grin. 'Well, I don't know, maybe she was hearing dead folk saying stuff, not just avoiding her mental family.' She gets up and steps away.

'She *was* psychic,' Nikki says firmly. 'Wasn't she, Lizzie?'

'Well –' Lizzie slaps her mini hands on her tiny tummy and shifts her weight onto the foot nearest the door – 'if she wasn't psychic she certainly did a very good job of appearing to be.' And then she winks at Margo behind Nikki's back and excuses herself from the kitchen. They can hear the football resuming on the TV.

Nikki shakes her head. 'Betty lost the sight the night Susan died.'

Margo looks at the envelopes. 'Same postmark on all of them?'

'All Easterhouse, where her wee body was found.' Nikki sighs and shakes her head as if she's had this conversation many times. 'You don't believe me.'

Margo doesn't want to tell her about her own letter. If Nikki sent it she'll be expecting her to and if she didn't Margo knows it will frighten her, so she doesn't say anything.

Nikki speaks quietly. 'McPhail killed Susan. No one believes me.'

'Jack Robertson believes you.'

'No, I believe *him*. That's when I realised it was McPhail, when his book came out. Can't believe McPhail is still out there.'

If she isn't writing these letters herself, Margo thinks Nikki is vulnerable, that someone is messing with her. She thinks Nikki probably knows the person who is, that it's someone close by, that they see her getting upset and it excites them.

Could be Lizzie. Could be the boyfriend who smashed her teeth out. But they've made a mistake in picking on Margo because she has a degree and a car. She doesn't believe in psychics or magic or genius serial killers. Margo can call the police and they'll listen to her. She's not Nikki.

Nikki gathers up the letters and carefully puts them back into the brown envelope, pats the fat package and lets her hand rest on it.

'Susan,' she says sadly.

Margo wants to say something helpful. 'I'm sorry, Nikki,' she says. 'Look: what can I do?'

It's a line she uses on patients in the surgery to move them on to the next part of the ten-minute consultation, after they've described their complaints and had a cry. She regrets saying it now because it sounds clinical, almost adversarial.

But Nikki loves that she said that. She straightens up. '*Care* about what happened to your mum. No one cares. When I'm gone it'll be as if she was never even here. Then he'll really have killed her.'

20

MARGO IS LEAVING. THEY'VE been together for two hours but it feels like a month. She can hardly wait to be alone and comb through everything.

Nikki gets a Post-it notepad and a tiny Ikea pencil out of the drawer and writes down her home address, an email and mobile number and her landline. She gives it to Margo and hands her the pencil and pad. Margo feels trapped, she's got enough going on, but Nikki is staring at her, at the pad, at the pencil, so she writes. She puts her mobile number down but changes the last three digits. She gives a home address to the north of the city, in the opposite direction of her real address on the Southside. She gives an email address that's just a jumble of letters and numbers.

Nikki takes it, reads it and smiles, she folds it very carefully. She puts it into the pocket of her jeans and pats it, smiling at Margo who feels like a duplicitous cow. Then Nikki says she'll stay on at Lizzie's to watch the end of the game but insists on escorting Margo down to the outside door to say goodbye there.

Margo would really rather say their goodbyes in the flat, where it's private, in case Nikki cries again, but Nikki is in- dignant about that, she comes from a culture with different customs and says not escorting Margo down to the street would be very rude. Out in the hallway she puts on slippers and a blue dressing gown, both of which are too big for Lizzie. Margo wonders if the women are a couple.

They leave the flat and trip down to the mouth of the close, get to the outside door and Nikki opens it to the cold night.

'I can't thank you enough for coming to meet me, Nikki.'

Nikki hugs her awkwardly and lets go. She says maybe they can meet again, in a few weeks, now Margo's got all her contact numbers and her home address. Margo says yes, lovely, and you've got mine.

They don't know how to end their meeting. Margo steps out of the close and turns back to see the door shutting and Nikki watching through the narrow mesh window. Margo waves bye-bye and turns away. She is alone and relief sweeps over her.

She's finally alone.

She glances back and sees Nikki still peering out at her through the narrow slit of glass, smiling. She nods and smiles too and Nikki waves but doesn't leave. Margo turns away and performs looking for a taxi. She looks down to the river and the bridge but there's nothing coming. She looks up, past the railway bridge, to the bright Trongate. Few cars, no taxis, but she sees movement in the dark under the bridge.

Two hundred yards away, in the shadows, a group of drunk men are walking towards her. Three men walk in a row but the fourth is an advance scout. He's the smallest, the drunkest. They're hanging back from him. He is unaware of this, out in front of the group, waving his arms and shouting. He emerges from the dark under the bridge and his heel skids on the icy pavement. He catches himself from falling and shouts a swear word. He is wearing a white tracksuit with a streak of mud up the backside. He has already fallen over.

He spots Margo standing alone on the edge of the pavement and shouts, 'HAA HO! FUCKING GORGEOUS!'

He barrels towards her, straight arms rising like a baby demanding to be picked up. His friends hang back, embarrassed, letting him go. He's shouting but she can't understand what he's saying so she smiles at no one in particular, feeling awkward, not knowing what to do. She looks away down the road for the orange eye of a saviour taxi but can't see any. He's closing in on her. She hurries across the empty road to get away, pretending to look for taxis that aren't coming.

He changes his trajectory, he's crossing too and he's shouting something. She glances back and finds that he's alarmingly close, twenty yards, moving fast. His friends have stopped under the bridge and are pretending not to know him. One of them turns back the way they came and then the others do the same.

The drunk is closing in, gathering speed, running on his tiptoes as if he's going to fall on her. He's so near that Margo can see a raised red rash on one side of his mouth and a burst capillary in his left eye. His eyes shut as he closes in, fifty yards, hands up, falling at her. Margo has never been jumped in the street before. She is aware, with a sudden dawning horror, of how close and dark Glasgow Green is. The entrance to the park is a hundred yards away. He could drag her in there, into the dark.

Fantasy Margo would punch him, hit him with her bag, kick him in the balls, she has always imagined herself quite able and angry, but this is real life. She freezes, shuts her eyes and holds her breath.

A high, loud crack fills the street, bright and clear in the cold air. The sound ricochets back and forth across the stone valley of the tenements.

Margo looks.

A sprinkle of shattered glass skitters across the tarmac behind him. Lizzie is hanging out of the second-floor window and shouts, 'Fuck off!' The man is frozen, just ten feet or so away from Margo, his dirty fingernails aimed at her face. His mouth hangs open and Margo can see cracks in the yellow fur on his tongue.

Lizzie leans further out of the window and drops something. It's metal, heavy and falls straight down to the pavement in front of the close where it clatters like a scaffolding pole. She lifts another bottle and holds it high, aiming straight at him.

The close door flies open, banging against the inside wall, and Nikki runs at them, screaming: 'LEHERALANE! LEHERALANE!'

A second bottle from Lizzie hits the man on the shoulder. It bounces off him and shatters on the road.

He backs away, surprised, his hands up, calling, 'Ho! Ho! Gir-als!' his feet crunching glass. 'Bit of fun! Come on!'

Nikki brandishes a metal baseball bat over her head and the fluffy blue dressing gown billows out behind her. Her lips are curled tight into her false teeth and she screams again,

'LEHERALANE!' She's working her way between Margo and the man, shouting and swinging the bat in a figure of eight to separate them.

Margo looks to Nikki but sees her looking past her, her eyes open crazy-wide. The man jumps at Margo, his fingernail scores her cheek, but Nikki swings at him, hits his knee at the side and knocks him down. He lands heavily on his shoulder, on his back and he howls.

Nikki swings at his forehead. The metal bat makes an oddly comedic *thunk* as it hits his skull. She tells him he's an arsehole.

He looks up, brow low, eyes cold and angry and shouts: 'YA BUNCH OF LESBIAN COWS YE.' He runs out of breath and whines back to his friends. 'She's burst my fucking knee!'

Margo is pretty sure he hasn't broken anything but his knee will be very painful. Now he's rolling around in bits of glass which can't be good either.

Nikki raises the bat and slams it hard on his hand. He screams. That is definitely broken. Margo can see it from here. She wonders who's on at the A&E in the Royal tonight, who'll get him.

'NO! NO! NO!' He scrambles away cradling his hand, grinding his hip along the glass.

Nikki follows him slowly, the tip of the bat scumbling noisily along the ground. He stops and she steps over to him and spits on his face. A thick gob of saliva hits his chin and drips off. Lizzie laughs loudly at the window.

'Youse!' Nikki shouts to his pals hiding under the bridge. 'Get thon wee prick OUT o' here!' She is speaking with her real accent now, mellifluous and guttural, consonants swooping into vowels. 'Mon, get him! He's wi' you. Aye, we seen yees. You there, the baldie arsehole –'

The baldie arsehole does not enjoy being singled out. He affects surprise, touching his chest.

'Aye, you. Baldie. M'ere and get him. Don't leave it to me and my wee pal up there. No our fucking problem, is he? You're out wi' him.'

Reluctantly, Baldie does come over and lifts the small man roughly by the arm, keeping his gaze averted from Nikki as he pulls him back to the other men, who hurry away and disappear round the corner. Margo notices that the small man is putting weight on the leg. She calls after them, 'He needs to go to hospital with that hand.'

He has spots of blood on his hip and leg from rolling in the glass. None of the cuts are deep. He isn't losing much blood. They watch the men fast-walk away.

Nikki is embarrassed. 'Pet lamb, I'm so sorry. I'm sorry that happened to you.'

Margo can hear her own blood pumping in the quiet street. She's terrified but in awe of Nikki because she didn't freeze. She acted. A window opens across from them and an angry man appears. He looks over to Lizzie at her window. 'Were you watching that there?'

Lizzie grins. 'That penalty.'

'Fucksake!'

He looks down and asks Nikki if she's OK. She says she's fine and asks him to call a taxi for her niece. He says aye, no problem, goes back inside and shuts the window.

The metal bat catches the street light and blinds Margo for a moment.

'Nikki, you were amazing,' she says.

'Nah.'

Margo couldn't have done that.

'I don't know what I did to make him come over.'

'Get that crap out your head. Ye did nothing.'

'I should have called a cab from the flat.'

'Oh aye: coulda shoulda woulda.' Nikki looks up the road to the corner where the men disappeared. 'That wee prick'd go home and batter his poor wife or ma now. That's why I hit his hand. That's what they do when someone stands up to them.'

They hear a window slam and look up to see that Lizzie has gone back inside. They're alone in the road. Nikki grinds the tip of the bat in the glass on the ground.

Margo shouldn't have come here, she shouldn't have gone to the adoption agency in the first place. It's grief-avoidance. She vows not to see Nikki again but she feels bad about it. She wants to leave her with good memories of their meeting.

'I's just saying to Lizzie there that meeting you, Margo, well, your wee mum would be blown away.' She looks up through damp eyes and Margo knows that Nikki hasn't tried to threaten her. She didn't write the letter. Nikki's just a casualty. 'You're just a wee lady,' says Nikki, as if that's the nicest thing she can think of to say to any woman.

'Thank you.'

'Genuine,' she says shyly. 'I hope you don't mind us, what we are.'

'Not one bit. I think you're both amazing women.'

'A lot of people do mind, but you get tired lying. Me and Lizzie, we're too old to keep fucking pretending to be someone else now.'

'Nor should you have to.'

'It's not a choice. You just fall into it and then it's hard to get out and it's something you can't just shake off.'

'I can imagine.'

'The things that happened to us, you never really get over them things. You see ... you need –' she nods up to Lizzie's window – 'you need other folk so you can just be yourself and to talk to. Those politics people she's talking about back there: they never want us to just be. They don't want us to know each other. They keeps us all apart. But you need it because the shame'll kill you.'

'Lizzie's a good friend.'

'She is that. She's a good friend.' She looks at Margo and seems suddenly young and shy. 'You're nice to talk to. You don't seem all that judgey way. Lot of people you can't say these things to, you know, because they'll have you down as lowlife but, you're different.'

'They train doctors to listen. Say the right thing.'

Nikki blinks at that. She doesn't know if she's being insulted. 'Well, I like it.'

An orange light hits the corner of Margo's eye and she turns to see a black cab pulling up to take her away. She's so relieved that she gives Nikki a sincere hug, chest to chest. Nikki whispers, 'Wee baby Patsy' into her ear.

Margo says she'll call Nikki and see her again really soon and gives the driver her address through his open window before she gets in.

Nikki retreats to the pavement as the cab turns a tight circle in the empty street and straightens up to take the bridge south. They pass Nikki. Her hand is resting on the metal bat, her head tilted at an odd angle, her mouth open. Margo raises a hand to wave but Nikki doesn't wave back. Her expressionless face follows Margo at the window of the cab.

It's a flicker, a moment, only noticeable when the street light catches her cheeks in a certain way. Tears are rolling down Nikki's withered cheeks. Steam is creeping from her mouth.

Nikki is heartbroken.

21

THE TAXI DRAWS THROUGH the Gorbals as Margo tries to fathom what just happened. She can't understand why Nikki's mood changed so abruptly or why she was crying.

Maybe she found the hug overwhelming. It could be generalised emotional liability. Maybe Nikki regretted having a fight in front of her, wishes it hadn't happened and is ashamed of using her real accent. Maybe she didn't want Margo knowing that side of her and thinks she's let herself down. But none of that feels right because Nikki's not that fragile.

She is a bit mad but well-functioning. She has delusions about a serial killer but, at the same time, she maintains friendships over long periods of time, she has overcome innumerable adverse childhood experiences, several violent deaths in her family and a heroin addiction. These are the disasters Margo knows about. There are bound to be others. The violent partner who broke her teeth. They didn't even get around to talking about Nikki's life since Susan died.

But something happened that made her cry like a lost child.

Sitting in the back of the rattling cab Margo replays their final moments and startles when she realises: it wasn't something Nikki did that made her cry. It was something Margo did.

Nikki heard Margo tell the taxi driver to take her to Holly Road instead of the address she had written down. Nikki knew her contact details were bullshit. Nikki knew Margo smiled and looked her in the eyes, said all the right things to get away from her. She knows Margo doesn't ever want to see her again.

Margo feels sick. She said those things, *I don't mind one bit, Lizzie is a good friend, you are both amazing*, to get away, because she's a snob and she thinks Nikki and Susan and Lizzie are scum. She'd step over them in the street. She thinks they're less than.

Margo sinks forward and covers her face with her hands. No more. She can't face any more hard truths about herself today. Nikki was kind and was on time and took Margo to her girlfriend/friend's house. She saved her from a drunk man.

She's scared of going back to Holly Road alone. She texts Lilah and asks her to meet her there but Lilah doesn't reply. Maybe her phone is off again, which is very annoying, but then Margo remembers what Tracey said: everyone's entitled to boundaries. Lilah's right to do that sometimes and Margo shouldn't feel this bad for not wanting to be swamped by Nikki. If they meet again she's going to say that.

She sits up and imagines defending herself to Nikki, drafting plausible excuses: she wasn't actually going home in this taxi. She rehearses a conversation she will never have with Nikki. She was going to visit a friend. A sick friend on the Southside. Nikki says, oh! Lucky you're a doctor! Hahaha!

If she ever meets Nikki again, if they bump into each other in the street, that's what she'll say. She'll laugh off the suggestion that she was deliberately lying because she's a snobby patronising bitch. Hahahaha, she'll say, as if! She didn't get in touch again simply because life got in the way and that's all. And Nikki will reply: I understand fully because I also have been simply very busy with my life. And they'll part on good terms. It doesn't sound convincing because Margo can't write dialogue.

But when Nikki tries to call her the phone line will be unobtainable, the email will bounce back. Nikki knows Margo lied. Nikki knows why she lied. Margo humiliated her. Could she drop a card over to Nikki's house with her proper contact details? Would that make it all right?

She googles the address Nikki gave her and reads down through the results. That can't be right. Nikki can't be living in a bungalow in a posh area out in the east of the city. She isn't living in a bungalow that recently sold for three hundred thousand pounds. Margo looks at the listing: it has brand-new double glazing and a rockery. It has an alarm system and a wheelchair-accessible bathroom.

That's when she realises: Nikki lied too.

22

LILAH IS WAITING OUTSIDE her house, sitting perched on a brick wall across the street. Judging from her pink silk dress and green fake-fur jacket she's been on a night out. She opens the taxi door for her and hollers into the cab, 'YOOHOO!' She's a bit tipsy.

'I'm not much of a bodyguard,' she tells the driver who remains unmoved. 'But I saw your text and legged it over.'

'I thought your phone was off.'

Lilah doesn't say anything. Margo thinks she just can't be bothered picking up.

Margo pays and gets out. They cross the street to the door.

Lilah explains that she's been out drinking with Deborah, trying to cheer her up. Deborah copped off with a guy in the bar. Started winching him right there in the bar. Margo is shocked. 'We're a bit old for that.'

'We're far too old for that. They were all over each other – he was dipping her dress for Godsake. In the Blythswood! It's disgusting.' Lilah smiles. 'She says she's met him in there before.'

'Paul won't appreciate that.'

'Well, she's miserable, what can I do?'

'It's nice of you to come here just because I'm scared.'

'I was in a cab on my way home anyway. Richard turned up at the Blythswood and I bolted.'

'How is he finding you? Are you posting your location?'

'Hardly.'

But Margo can tell she's excited by being the centre of a drama.

'He'll hurt you one day, Lilah. You should report him.'

'I was watching your door for murderers while I waited: nothing to report.'

'Well, that's a boon.'

Through the security door. Lilah says, 'God, I hate these flats.'

Margo's flat is on the top floor. As they walk up the stairs they can hear a radio through someone's front door and a cat mewling softly inside another.

Lilah walks in front of her, trying to cheer her up by telling her that Deborah was quite a good laugh tonight, actually: she has a cousin in Hong Kong with a sebaceous cyst on his back that's the shape of a tiny can of Coke. Showed her a photo and everything. Margo keeps her head down, focusing on Lilah's nonsense and forcing one foot in front of the other. She doesn't want to go back up there.

Lilah stops one step from the top. 'Oh fuck.'

Margo's front door has been broken open. They step up to the landing and stare at the splintered door frame, shocked at the degree of violence. The lock has been crowbarred open, the wood is fractured and hanging off.

'Could it just be a burglar?' says Margo.

'Bit noisy ...'

They look at each other and realise at the same time that the person who did it might still be inside. Lilah grabs her arm and they tiptoe-run down to the lobby where they stand, frozen to the wall, staring up, not having the first clue what to do.

They both listen acutely to the noises in the stairwell: the cat has gone quiet. The radio is still playing. They can't hear anyone else.

'No one up there,' whispers Lilah, but neither of them moves.

Margo slowly comes to life. She takes out her phone.

'What are you doing?'

'Calling the police.'

'That'll take hours,' Lilah says. She jogs back upstairs as the cat-miaow door opens. A woman in yellow pyjamas is standing there, holding her cat and waiting for them.

Margo slows and says, 'Did you hear noise from up there?'

'Yes. About a half an hour ago, it was.' The woman looks upstairs. 'I heard an almighty crack. I thought it was that bloke's computer game but the cat hid behind the washing machine for twenty minutes. I just got her out.'

But Margo is trying to keep up with Lilah and calls back, 'Could you call the police for us, please?'

Lilah takes the last flight of stairs and Margo hurriedly follows. They step into the hall and turn on every light. The flat has been ransacked but it looks staged. Books have been thrown to the floor, the sofa is upended, files and lamps have been shoved around but nothing seems stolen. The telly is still there. The radio and an old-fashioned CD player. Even the CDs are scattered but not taken.

'Is it just vandalised?'

'Maybe they were looking for something?' says Lilah. 'Is something missing?'

Margo looks around the flat, in the kitchen and living room and bathroom. Nothing is gone. They're standing in the hall when Margo says, 'You know, if you want to leave before the police get here, that's OK.'

'I don't.'

'I know you're dodging them after Emma's baby shower. You don't have to wait with me.'

'I'm not dodging them. It's just boring, that's all.'

Margo looks over Lilah's shoulder and notices that her bedroom door is shut.

'You need them anyway,' says Lilah. 'To get the insurance to pay for the front door.'

Margo leaves the bedroom door open because the sun shines in through the window and the room gets too hot. She's sure she left that door open.

'I'm not scared of the cops,' witters Lilah. 'I'm just embarrassed about Richard. It's mortifying, you know? I don't want my name coming up in two police reports in one week.'

Margo reaches for the bedroom door and opens it. The duvet is on the floor and has been trampled on, the bed sheet pulled half off. A bottle of Chanel No 5 has been poured out on the mattress, emptied and dumped on the floor. Janette gave her that bottle. It was too old for her. She had never worn it. But whoever did this hasn't stolen anything: her laptop is sitting on the bedside table.

'What even is this?'

'Fucker's been in your bedroom.' Lilah is behind her in the doorway. 'That's creepy. Call the cops, Margo.'

Margo fumbles her mobile out of her pocket and calls, gets transferred from place to place because it's not an emergency and there's no threat or anything.

She has to wait on the line for quite some time and while she does she stands in the doorway looking at her bed.

She finally gets connected and explains what has happened to a constable.

'Just a break-in then?'

'Yes, and sort of threw stuff about.'

'Nothing stolen?'

'No. I think it was done as a threat. I got a threatening letter through the door this morning as well. I'm sorry to be so vague but I don't know what's going on.'

She is asked to wait in for officers to come and take a report. She asks how long it will be but they hang up on her.

'Can we open a window at least?' says Lilah and only then does Margo realise that the smell is clinging to her face and clothes.

They open all the windows and sit down, perching un-comfortably on the edge of the sofa in the living room, waiting and jumpy. Lilah suggests packing up Margo's stuff while they're hanging around but Margo says it's probably better not to touch anything.

'What the fuck is this about?' says Lilah.

'Susan Brodie? The threatening letters?'

'I know an unusual amount about this and my review would be: quite shit threats, a completely substandard ran-sacking. This is very stupid. I mean, if they did murder someone thirty years ago and got away with it, why flinch at stealing a laptop?'

'And how did they find me?'

'How is Richard finding me? Is he following me around?'

'You'd have spotted him.'

They both know that's true. Richard is tall and beefy, looks distinctly like a wealthy Londoner, and he's not exactly discreet.

The sweet high notes of a half-bottle of Chanel hit their noses and Lilah shakes her head a little. 'Fuck this. This is un-glam, squared.'

They sit together for a while, currents of cold air sweeping across their ankles from the open windows.

Lilah takes Margo's hand. 'OK, not Iceland, but let's just fuck off until this is all sorted out? Can we go away, go up north or something? We can stay in a hotel, Gleneagles or somewhere with heavy-duty security.'

'What about Muttley and Pitstop?'

'Take them with us. Come on.'

Margo is too tired to tell a face-saving lie to Lilah. 'Look, Janette's care was so expensive and I'm basically paying for three houses. I just don't have money for that at the moment.'

'Ooh, right?' Lilah is startled that she said that because they're rarely so honest with each other. She fumbles in her handbag and presses a brick of notes into Margo's hand. 'Look here, see? That's five grand. Take it. You take it. For me.'

Margo looks down at the bundle of fifty-quid notes, held together with a paper band. 'Where's this from?'

Lilah shrugs. 'Where's any money from? My account. Why?'

'How much money did you take from Richard?'

Lilah smiles. 'I've always got a stash on me. Bet you're glad now.'

Margo doesn't feel right taking the money. She feels she's being implicated in something, somehow. 'Why doesn't Richard want the police involved?'

'Well, maybe he's not snowy white either. Antiques dealers don't like the cops much.' Lilah looks around the living room. 'You need to tell the police everything, OK? Don't be brave or downplay it, it's OK to be scared and ask for help. Remember: they've killed before.'

But Margo knows whoever killed Susan didn't break in. 'Let's go and wait in the car. It smells like Elizabeth Taylor exploded in here.'

23

THEY'RE SITTING IN MARGO's Mini. They've been there for an hour and ten minutes, waiting, and now they're speculating about who could have done it.

'It could have been the auntie.' Lilah gasps and grabs her sleeve. 'Oh my God! She did it!'

'No, wasn't her. I was with the aunt tonight. I just left her at her friend's house. I've been with her for hours.'

'You saw her again? If I could move my forehead, my eyebrows would be in my hairline right now.'

They watch the street for a moment. A young drunk couple sway and giggle past the car door. A street light blinks frantically at the far end of the road. Margo can hear the bass-heavy thunder soundtrack from her neighbour's computer game even here, out in the street.

They see them at the same time: two uniformed police officers walk up Margo's street, a man and a woman. Both officers wear bulky hi-vis vests and carry a lot of equipment on their shoulders and belts. They look around for Margo's block of flats and find it, approach the door and ring her buzzer. She opens the car door and Lilah offers to come up with her, to show she isn't avoiding the police, but Margo can't deal with navigating Lilah and police officers at the same time.

She leaves her in the car and hurries over, explaining to the cops that she was waiting in a car over there with a friend because it's quite creepy up there, and then, just because they seem so humourless, she giggles.

The male and female officers glance at one another. She knows she seems suspicious. The man is doughy and the woman short and slender, her dark hair is pulled up in a tight bun. They're both wearing stab vests which seems pre-emptively accusing. They ask her for her name and whether she called them, talking in a strange language, their grammar alien and strangled. She thinks they're being filmed or recorded.

'We would like,' says the man, 'to take a statement from yourself about the course of events.'

Margo wants to reply in a nasal voice, to say that she, herself, will be willing to cooperate in the giving of such a statement on the course of events, but realises just in time that taking the piss out of the police is probably a really bad move.

'Of course,' she says. 'Indeed ...'

She keys the code into the security pad and points out how unsafe this whole keypad thing is. She goes on too long about it, which makes her nervous, which makes her go on even longer about it. They follow her upstairs. When they see the broken front door, the female officer says, 'Top marks for effort anyway.'

They examine the deadlock. The wood is compressed where an instrument was used.

'Brought tools with them,' says the man.

It's not a heavy door and wouldn't have been hard to smash open. It doesn't look as violent on a second viewing. When they get inside the flat the smell has dissipated because of the open windows. She feels a bit silly and melodramatic and tries to excuse herself. 'I got a fright, to be honest. I just wanted to get out of there. I don't know why anyone would do that and not take anything.' She takes them around and shows them all the items of value that they might have stolen.

'So I don't know why they did it,' she concludes.

The female officer holds Margo's eye and nods as if she has said something very profound. Then she says, 'Yes.'

Margo knows that she is doing that to validate her feelings. She has been on an engage-with-the-public course too.

They follow her into the bedroom and stand in a solemn line at the foot of the bed looking at what, quite suddenly, looks like a bed someone accidently spilled perfume on. Margo feels stupid but she knows why she finds it so alarming. It has distinct, deliberate echoes of Susan's crime-scene photo.

'Could a cat have knocked the bottle over?' suggests the woman officer.

'No, I think it was poured there to look like something else. I didn't call you because I spilled my perfume,' says Margo. 'The bottle is nowhere near the bed.'

She points out the empty bottle on the floor, wondering if the officer thinks this is just how her bedroom always smells. She tells her that she also got a threatening letter yesterday, hand-delivered through the door, and explains the context, about meeting Nikki and finding out about Susan. She shows them the crime-scene photo in Robertson's book and points out the similarities to the bedroom. By the end of it she feels like a fool.

'Oh, yeah, I've heard of this,' says the female cop, showing it to the man, 'I've heard of this book.'

He mutters to her, 'That's who that ex-CID guy is suing, isn't it?'

The officers glance at each other but change the subject. He addresses Margo formally, 'Might we see the threatening letter?'

She explains that she gave it to the guy who wrote the book, he wanted to check it out in case it was from the ex-CID guy. They look at each other again, more wary of Margo now.

'Well,' he says, 'can you get it back and bring it in to show us?'

'Yes, I will.'

Margo sounds like a panicky idiot who watches too much telly. She wants to tell them she's a doctor but doesn't know how to slip it in without sounding like a grandiose, panicky idiot.

The male officer takes photos of the bed on a phone. He takes them from several angles.

'It is horrible, being broken into,' says the policewoman, a rare moment of informality breaking through her professional mask.

'Isn't it?' says Margo, glad of the human contact.

'Have you got somewhere else you can stay?'

'Yeah,' and she gives them Janette's address and her mobile number. She can tell from the amount of nodding they're doing that they're assessing her, wondering if she's a mad-woman who smashed her own door in and trashed her own bed. It all sounds overly elaborate and unlikely, especially when she tells them about the court case. As she's telling the story she imagines a splinter Margo whose mum just died, a broken woman who went into the High Court and saw all the drama around the murder case and thought she'd like some of that and then came home and pretended to get a letter. She looks up and sees the cops nodding at her, taking notes, their eyes a little bit glazed as they have private, reflective thoughts about her. She thinks about Nikki and Lizzie and wonders how the police would react if they called them over a trifle like this.

'Those other letters you've got there.' The female cop is looking into her handbag. 'What are they?'

They're Nikki's letters to the adoption agency. She feels stupid enough already.

'They're just letters from my mum. She died recently. I like to keep them with me.'

They both nod and take that in: recently bereaved, going slightly mad.

'I'm sorry for your troubles,' says the female cop, eye-contacting her half to death with training-course empathy.

'Thank you for saying that,' says Margo, doing it back.

Once she's finished telling them everything, they ask: can Margo think of anyone who would want to hurt her?

No one.

They ask about the neighbours, they know there were protests outside during the building of these flats. Have there been any incidents since she moved in? No, she says, and she doesn't know the neighbours well enough to have a dispute with them. She's only been here for a month.

Is there any CCTV in the building?

No, everything here has been done on the cheap.

They ask about ex-boyfriends. She explains about Joe, that they split up a few months ago and she moved out. They're interested in that but she says no, no, Joe is a nice person and he would never, ever do that, not to her, not to anyone. They nod and say OK then. Can they have his address and phone number so they can rule him out? She gives it to them and they tell her not to worry, they'll just have a word. Margo doesn't want Joe being bothered with this. He's a good guy and is very busy with his bike shop. She herself is a doctor, actually. There, she got it in and she looks up and sees from their expressions that they think she's either making it up or mentioning it as a status grab, which she is. But the male officer writes it down and the female officer holds her eye and nods kindly.

At the end of the interview the police ask her if she wants to say anything else. They stare at her, hoping, perhaps, for a revelation about Joe's violent past, or that she'll laugh and admit she spilled an expensive bottle of perfume and called them so she can claim it on her house insurance.

Margo smiles as sanely as she can, which makes her feel as if she looks crazy, and says no, not really. Just the break-in and the letter. Sorry.

'No,' says the man, standing up and adjusting his stab vest, 'there's no need for you to apologise. This is exactly what we're here for.' And they glance at each other again.

Margo doesn't think they trained as police officers to search for spillers of Chanel No 5 but it's nice of them to pretend.

They're leaving. The woman tells Margo she should get the door fixed asap because her insurance won't cover the contents of her flat if she leaves it. An open door is an invitation to some. Then they leave her standing in the hall, listening to their receding footsteps on the clangy stairs. Thunder emanates from the floor. The cat downstairs starts whining. They open the outside door and a current of cold air streams up from the street, swirling around the flat, whipping up the smell. The outside door falls slowly shut.

High notes from the perfume have burned off and the flat smells heavy but sweet. She feels like a fool.

She's standing in the hall, noticing this, when two things happen at exactly the same moment: her front door falls off completely, thudding to the ground with a great ear-slapping clatter, and the door buzzer goes. It takes her a moment to work out which noise belongs to which.

It's Lilah on the buzzer. 'Let me in.'

She comes up and helps Margo get her stuff out of there, goes around the flat with open boxes scooping everything in and carrying them down to the car.

Several trips later her flat is empty of everything but the big furniture. She's glad to get out of there.

'You don't ever have to come back here,' promises Lilah. 'Give me the keys. I'll get the door fixed.'

Intensely grateful, she gives her the keys and Lilah hugs her and tells her not to worry, OK? Get some sleep and don't worry. 'Phone if anything happens, OK?'

'I will.'

'OK.' Lilah can see that her mind is elsewhere. 'OK?'

'I will. Will you be OK in here?'

'I'll be fine. Just don't tell anyone I'm here, OK?'

'OK.'

Margo walks down to the Mini. When she gets to the bottom of the stairs she looks back up at the window, worried about leaving Lilah up there alone.

24

SHE'S BACK AT THIS house. It's like a palace. There's big bushes of flowers in the garden and a bit of grass. The house is old, solid, stone. The front door is painted bright red. The steps up have matching blue pots on the top step. Posh as fuck. And a worthless bitch like that in there.

Called the cops back there. It was exciting. She must be terrified. Couldn't believe she did that. The letter must have scared her.

She's read it and cried and called the cops. As if they're going to give a fuck about a letter. They never did before.

Moved out because of the letter, too scared to stay there. Just a letter, not a knife or a punch to the side of the head, nothing real. It's thrilling.

Born scared like her mother. She's an easy mark, she shat herself when the guy tried to grab her at the Saltmarket. Easily frightened. Needs someone else to take control and tell her what to do.

This new street is narrow and that's a problem. There's parking regs everywhere. Have to keep moving around. Can't afford to get a ticket so have to keep moving, watching the house, watching the street, moving sometimes when a new space opens up so that no one gets too used to the car being in the same space.

She's alone in there.

Park up for a minute. Out the car and slip through a gap in the hedge. A low window into the kitchen.

She's alone.

See her through the window, moving around, making tea, sitting. She looks upset. Crying at the table. Got no one to tell her what to do. She's all over the place.

Back to the car and start the engine, pull it around to the main street and back for one last turn.

There's a shape, someone going in.

The gate shrieks as the metal scratches along the concrete path. It's a man, a thin bloke, wiry, tall, with a bike hanging on his shoulder and a cycle helmet on. A fucking bloke.

Shit.

25

'AM I THREATENING YOU?'

'Joe, it's two in the morning.'

He's standing on the top step, his bike resting on his shoulder. She feels her pupils dilating as she drinks him in. He looks half mad in his cycling tights, hi-vis cagoule and white helmet. He only buys cycle gear in sales because he says it's overpriced and, because he only buys in sales, his clothes are often the wrong size and always mismatched. Tonight he's wearing black tights and a fitted cycle jacket with pockets on the back hem that are crammed with cotton hankies, packets of crisps, chewing gum and house keys. His thighs are over-developed and his leggings so tight that she can make out his shin bone.

'I just want to know. The police came over to ask me if I was behaving in a threatening manner to you. Am I?'

'No. Holly Road got burgled and they asked me if I had a boyfriend, that's all.'

'Burgled?' He nods. 'Have you been crying?'

'No.'

'Is it OK, me being here?'

'Why wouldn't it be?'

'Can I come in?'

'What are you, a vampire? Of course it's OK.' She pushes the door open wide. 'Come in.'

He looks in the hall for somewhere to put his bike down. 'Bloody hell, lot of boxes. What is all this?'

'It's boxes of things from Holly Road and the stuff from all the rooms upstairs,' she lies, 'Janette's things.'

He shuffles in and props his bike against a dune of bin bags.

She invites him into the kitchen. As she leads him down the hallway she's so aware of his presence that it feels like a blazing three-bar fire at her back.

'Did you hear about the Blythswood? Richard got lifted by the police again.'

'Oh fuck, no.'

'He's being held overnight. Tried to fight the bouncer. His face is a mess.'

Joe could be crowing about Richard's fall from grace. He is the disappointing hippy and Richard was their parents' pride and joy. He was a capitalist firebrand, making big money travelling around the world to buy rare antiques and wanted them all to know. He paid for meals for everyone and took fancy suites in boutique hotels whenever they came home to visit. He rented a bungalow in St Lucia for a month so that Lilah could invite her friends and family.

When Joe moved up to Glasgow after they first met he wasn't pursuing Margo, he just liked the sound of the low rent prices in the rougher areas. As if he was trying to let everyone down, he opened a bike shop and barely scraped a living. His passion is racing and teaching adults to ride bikes. Margo kept bumping into him in Queen's Park when she took Janette out in her chair. They got to know each other slowly over the course of a year. Margo pursued him. She would go and sit in the freezing cold shop, talking to him while he worked, drinking tea and listening to the radio together.

He's eccentric, she knows that. He means well, she knows that too. She used to find it all cute and had never looked to a man to support her anyway. The split over Lilah and Richard would probably have healed in time but the moment she realised that she was pregnant everything shifted. Joe's eccentricity went from being charming to seeming really quite mental. He disappeared for weeks at a time, following his racing team around the circuit, lived hand to mouth, refused to buy a house or even contemplate a mortgage. She was pondering all of this when a woman came into her surgery with three kids, all of whom were screaming with painful ear infections. The husband was dressed in a full Celtic football strip. He looked rested and took the only chair. He didn't speak during the whole fraught consultation but just sat there, smiling affably while the frazzled mother comforted their kids and explained that the Calpol wasn't helping and she'd been up for days.

Margo does love Joe but everything feels so difficult. She thinks she might manage better on her own.

'Oh,' says Joe, looking around the kitchen at the boxes and still-full cupboards sitting open.

Margo sighs. 'I know. I've hardly started in here. So much stuff.'

'Thomas thinks you should call a house clearance company.'

'I should,' she says. 'I should do that.'

Joe sits at the kitchen table and peers over inch-high tidy piles of things that need sorting out, correspondence from banks and Janette's lawyers and friends who only-just-heard.

'So what happened? The police said someone broke in and vandalised your bed.'

'I think someone was trying to frighten me.'

'Can I stay?'

'Joe ...'

'Let me stay with you.' He's speaking calmly but his eyes are tracing the line of her neck, her hairline, his eyes are saying he loves her, that he's thinking about touching her. Her eyes are saying that she remembers that too and the sight of Joe is balm to her, that she loves the smell of his coal tar shampoo. She can't remember why they're not together but knows it's important.

They look at each other.

'Are you seeing anyone?'

'No.'

'Good.'

'Are you?'

'No.'

'Good.'

The clock ticks loudly and Margo's defences are up. They sit in the dusty kitchen as the gritty spirit of Janette swirls around them and reminds Margo that finding someone adorable doesn't mean it's a good idea to raise children with them.

'Are you worried about Richard's mental health?'

'Yeah,' he says. 'And I'm worried about you. So is Thomas.'

'I'm fine,' she says but sounds really angry.

He looks around the cluttered room, nodding to himself. He looks at his watch. 'It's two fifteen. I could stay?'

She can't let him see upstairs, how little she has done, admit that the hall stuff isn't all there is and she has completely failed to cope with this one small task. So she says no and it feels final.

At the door he wrestles his bike onto his shoulder, struggling to turn among the boxes in the hallway. She opens the door to a cold night and doesn't want him to go. He passes her, edging out awkwardly, because of the bike, the boxes and the narrowness of the hall.

'Why did you finish with me?' he says. 'Reporting Richard doesn't feel like enough of a reason. Is it because Lilah's back in Glasgow?'

'No.'

'Will you ever tell me?'

Margo shrugs. She's really tired. Janette died and her flat was ransacked. Her eyes are burning.

'It is Lilah. I know it is.'

He doesn't like flashy, bitchy Lilah, he thinks she's an arse, but Margo thinks about Lilah coming to the flat with her, bravely jogging back up the stairs to the broken-into flat even though they didn't know it was safe. She thinks about Lilah looking after Pitstop and Muttley and packing her things up and looking after her.

'Bye.'

'Bye, Joe.'

She stands quite still in the hall until his shadow is gone from the frosted glass. Then she puts the light out and stands there until she's too tired to stand at all.

26

SHE WAKES UP IN the bed of her childhood, momentarily comforted by the familiar sounds of the house and shape of the room. The ceiling is high and slopes to a bright curtainless window. An old sycamore tree sways outside. The bed is small with a spring mattress that bounces when she moves. But when she opens her mouth she finds her tongue is dry and her fingertips are puckered from dust.

On her bedside table Margo sees the mended shepherdess figurine she found in Janette's room. The lamb looks up adoringly at the fey shepherdess, its eyes two little dots denoting love and trust because of the angle of its neck. But the neck has been broken, mended but still the yellowed-glue remains of the injury are there. She remembers that Janette is dead and she's hiding here, that this house is full of urgency and chores. Even this room has a massive bookcase full of books and diaries and tin toys that don't work. She's basically lying on top of a three-storey to-do list.

She promises herself a coffee if she gets up, if she just gets up now and gets through the next hour or so. She throws her legs over the side of the bed, trying not to look up at the room full of reproaches, when she hears the faint doorbell ping-ping down in the hall.

It's got to be Lilah or Joe. No one else knows she's here. Pulling a jumper on, she walks to the head of the stairs.

Bright morning glows behind the frosted-glass front door. The hall is stacked with boxes and shopping bags.

She freezes, because there, sitting in a pool of light, a blue envelope is lying, face down like a drowning victim. Margo steadies herself on the bannister, her breathing shallow.

She blinks fast, trying to wipe the image clean. The hallway is bright and busy, a big aspidistra that won't die, all the boxes from Holly Road, a hatstand festooned with hats for all weathers and some for holidays, the frosty white light coming through the glass on the door and checkerboard tiles on the floor. She blinks but every time she opens her eyes the letter is still there. She drops down on stiff legs, holding tight to the bannister.

It's just an envelope.

She makes herself take a deep breath, drops another step down, but her hand is sweating and sticks to the wooden handrail, dragging on the skin.

She looks up at the door and takes each step with both feet, being careful, until she's at the bottom of the stairs. The envelope is in front of her.

She looks down at it, daring it to bite but nothing happens.

Suddenly angry, she picks it up and turns it over and finds it addressed to 'fucking bitch Brodie, Marywood Sq'. Same handwriting: small, straight 't' and 'f's with a hurried forward slant to the letters.

This envelope is heavier than the last one. It feels spongy. Something is in there, something flat and heavy.

She opens it roughly, ripping the top edge, and pulls out a single sheet of writing paper. Something sandwiched between the folded page drops on the floor.

It's a scrap of red tartan rug, heavy with age and grease, old and rotting and dirty, as if it has been fingered and rubbed at for three decades. It's on Janette's tiles.

Margo leaves it on the floor and reads the letter. Same fucking bullshit. Threat, taunt, insults, know where you live, posh bitch, call the cops if you want, you better get ready. Move house as often as you like, you cannot get away.

Margo looks at the glass window on the door. She steps towards it, picking up a heavy knotted wooden walking stick from the hatstand and raising it over her head.

She throws the door open and stands, ready to attack.

The street is still.

A magpie screams in a distant tree. The wind ruffles the bushes by the door. She looks up and down the street but sees no one.

Dropping the walking stick to her shoulder, she goes back inside.

The bit of tartan rug sits on Janette's restored tile floor. Janette used earbuds and paint stripper to get the grime off them. She did each one individually. It took her months and now this rotting thing is touching them.

Margo picks it up.

She can see the vibrant yellow weft through the greyness of age. It's a match for Nikki's little chopped-off square, it's from the rug that was under Susan's body. Susan, saving up and brimming with potential. Susan, who was never given a chance but took one anyway.

Her terror subsides slowly and she turns cold.

She reads the letter again and again, standing in the hall, and she notices one thing: there's no mention of the break-in at Holly Road.

She goes upstairs and throws clothes on, pins her hair back tight.

Down in the kitchen she grabs her car keys and handbag and takes the heavy walking stick from the hallway to her car.

She sets the GPS for Nairn Drive, High Blantyre.

27

THE STREET IS WET but the rain has stopped, replaced by blinding sun that flashes off wet cars and pavements.

Margo is in her car, watching Martin McPhail's house. She is sitting with the walking stick on her knee, holding it tight. She can see someone moving in McPhail's front room.

The window is dirty; the yellowing net curtains hang heavy and grey in the window. Even from here she can tell it's a heavy smoker's house.

This is a four in a block, good council stock building with bad tenants. She can read the road. It's as far from the local school as it can be, next to no swing parks or shops. CCTV cameras are prominently displayed on all of the street lights with signs declaring what they are and warning passers-by that they're being watched. It's one of those odd, child-free areas that only make sense when you know. It's where sex offenders get rehoused.

There are few cars and no movement in the street. A cat ambles from a concrete front garden to a lamp post and disappears round the back of one of the houses.

As she's watching she sees McPhail's door open a little, shut again and then open wide. She holds her breath but no one comes out. Two metal handles stick out of the doorway, a hand grabs the outside of the door frame and McPhail pulls himself out of the house. He's in a wheelchair.

Laboriously, he backs his chair out of the door, stepping his feet and pushing the chair with his heels. He lifts a crutch resting on his lap and hooks it through the handle of the door trying to pull the door shut but it's an awkward manoeuvre – she can see he's cursing. He can't get it to close. Holding the wall, he leans forward in his chair reaching for the handle. The wheels lift at the back as the chair tips forward and he pulls the door shut. He checks it twice. Then he sits back, fits the crutch on the back of the chair, uses the wheel rims to change direction towards the street and slowly walks himself forward to the kerb. He stops, pulls on the chair handbrake and looks up the street. He's waiting for someone.

Martin McPhail is a spent man. Margo has seen men like this lined up outside hospitals, tanned fingers and missing limbs, keeping each other company as they die. These are the inveterate smokers, the ones who will never give up, men and women with an unbreakable addiction that is eating them from the inside. It doesn't take everyone like that. Some smokers go on for years, some die of unrelated illnesses, but not these ones. It's a special look.

Martin is a grey husk. The meat of him is gone and she knows that the photo Robertson showed her was not a release photograph. Maybe his police friends told him it was but the man in front of her is half the man in that picture. He has grown a silver-and-gold beard but it's discoloured, brown and dirty around the chasmic mouth. He spots her car, sees her waiting, and a grey, cracked tongue sneaks out of the hole in his face to lick at the side of his mouth.

Margo gets out of the car and takes her walking stick with her.

'Are you Martin McPhail?'

He peers up at her. 'Who the fuck are you?'

'Are you Martin McPhail?'

'You social work? She's not even been here.'

Margo is thrown by the comment. 'Who's not even been here?'

But McPhail is looking at her heavy walking stick, he's looking at her – a tall, healthy woman, looming over him in an empty street, clearly angry. He thinks she's going to hit him. She's not sure he's wrong.

'Ne'mind.' He knows he's said the wrong thing and looks away. His hand half rises and he points at a pole with a sign on it warning residents that they are being watched. His hand is trembling. He's terrified of her.

Then she notices the thighs of his joggers. They are covered in drips and spills, crumbs fill the creases. McPhail couldn't make it up Janette's front steps. He isn't getting up when no one is looking. He's not travelling across the city in the middle of the night and sneaking into flats to leave threatening letters. The letters are not from him.

A small electric bus turns the corner at the end of the street and makes its way silently towards them. McPhail looks back at her. His cheeks are wet with frightened tears.

'Who in the fuck are you anyway?' he says as the bus pulls up.

She watches the driver get out and go round the back, open the doors and use the button to lower the electric ramp.

McPhail shoves the handbrake off and gives her one last glance. 'Don't even fucking know who you are,' he says and turns away, using his feet to walk the chair away from her towards the back of the bus.

'I'm Susan Brodie's daughter.'

McPhail stops. He slumps forward as if he's been kicked in the stomach.

The driver has the ramp down and looks around the side of the bus, eager to get going. 'Mon, Marty, I haven't got all day.'

McPhail rears up, takes a breath so deep that his body arcs backwards. He turns round and looks Margo in the eye and he says:

'Wasnae me.'

28

SHE TAKES THE WALKING stick from the well of the passenger seat when she gets out of the car. She would have hit him. She would have gone for the side of his head if he came for her. She knows she would and it frightens her. She didn't think she was like that.

She locks the car and goes through the gate, noticing only when she's fitting the key in the lock on the front door that the gate is open. She shut it on the way out.

The front door swings open into the house and she knows that someone has been in there.

It takes a moment for her to register why she knows. It's the smell. A smell of piss.

She backs out to the front step, hoping, somehow, that her senses are awry. But she can smell it out here now. Strong, concentrated. She leaves the door open and goes back to the car.

Armed with the walking stick, Margo approaches the open door again. She steps into the hallway and listens. She knows this soundscape so well, deep in her bones she knows the crack of wooden stairs on a summer evening, the soft groan of the plaster, the deflected coo of wood pigeons resting on the chimney stack.

The house is empty.

She reads the hallway. Nothing different. She holds the walking stick high as she walks into the kitchen. Nothing moved from the table, no stacks of plates touched on the worktops.

It's in front of the sink. A puddle of stinking yellow piss, half absorbed by the spongy plastic floor tiles Janette never got around to replacing. Two footprints next to it and they're alone: no companion walk-in prints from the hall or the back door, no walk-out footprints. And a fresh strip of filthy tartan rug sitting in it.

Margo knows that no man over thirty pisses as fluently as that and no one can come into a room to piss without touching the ground.

She gets Robertson's book out and turns to Susan's crime-scene photo, looking at the rug under her body. She thought the edge was folded over on itself but she can see now that it has been cut off.

A sudden hammering on the front door makes her drop the book. She lifts the heavy walking stick high and slides along the wall to the hall.

A shadow in the frosted-glass grows as the person outside approaches the door again. Margo steels herself but a hand comes up and knocks three times. The first knock wasn't a hammering at all, she's just scared.

'Yoohoo!' It's Lilah.

Margo hides the stick and opens the door a crack.

Lilah is holding a greasy bag of rolls. 'Yoohoo?'

'Anyone out there when you came up the path?'

Lilah looks behind her. 'No.' She looks at Margo. 'Still weirded out about last night?'

'No. Got another letter and someone broke in here this morning.'

They go into the kitchen and look at the pee.

'Fucking hell,' says Lilah. 'We can't call the police again, can we?'

'I don't think so,' says Margo. 'They'll think we're a two-woman time-wasting tag team.'

Lilah takes charge. She sits Margo down and orders her to eat one of the rolls while she cleans the piss up with kitchen paper. It's no bother, she says, because she has to do this for the dogs all the time and you get used to it. Honestly.

She throws away the bit of rug but can't get the smell out with Flash and the tiles are kind of peeling up at the edges anyway so she pulls them up and puts them in a bin bag and scrubs the floor underneath with a Brillo pad and a scourer sponge. Then she dabs Dettol on the floorboards.

'Disgusting fucker,' she says as they stand and look down at the result of her hard work.

Now the floorboards have bits of piss-soaked sponge stuck to them and are swollen with Dettol.

'That's almost worse,' says Margo and they stand and laugh at the mess until she starts crying. 'How in almighty fuck am I going to get this place organised?'

Lilah sits her down again and says look: things are getting done. A man has come to fit a new door in Holly Road. She propped the door shut last night and went back this morning to let him in. So things are getting done, it just feels as if nothing is happening. She picked up Margo's mail from Holly Road and gives it to her.

It's a bank statement. Margo doesn't open it because she's had enough bad news. There's also a fresh brown envelope with her name and address handwritten in black pen.

She opens it and finds a letter from Jack Robertson on embossed paper. The threatening letter from the Ram is folded and tucked inside. Jack thanks her for dinner and for lending him this horrific threatening letter (enclosed). He hopes she doesn't mind but he has informally notified the police out of concern for her well-being and personal safety. Please be sure to let the police know if anything else happens and if he can be of any help his details are at the top here, just let him know.

'Piece of shit,' says Margo and tells Lilah about him. 'That's where that crime-scene picture on the Internet came from. It was in his trashy fucking book.'

She shows her *Terror on the Streets* and Lilah snorts at the vulgar cover design and is appalled by the crime-scene photo. But then she looks at the author portrait on the back cover.

Jack is smiling wryly. His hair is voluminous. His Rolex is prominently on display. She is aghast.

'Is this him?'

'Yeah.'

'You're joking.'

'I know he's quite good-looking, but believe me, he, he's a total shit —'

'No, no, no, Margo, he was there last night. At your flat. I saw him come out of your building while I was waiting. I saw him there. I spoke to him.'

'In Holly Road?'

'I was waiting and I saw him come out and, honestly, I thought he was a bit of a ride and I wondered if he was a neighbour.' She looks embarrassed. 'Because of the hair, I noticed him. You know?'

Lilah would have noticed him. He's just her type: tall, slim and a total arsehole.

'He asked me if I was lost because I was waiting for you.'

'What did you say?'

She rolls a shoulder. 'Just sort of, you know, hello, sailor.'

'What was he doing there?' Margo picks up the envelope his letter was in. 'Was he delivering this?'

'No, that came in the mail this morning. It came with the bank statement while I was waiting for the door man to measure up. What was he doing there?'

Margo explains that Jack stands to lose a fortune in the defamation case whether he wins or loses. He was annoyed she hadn't phoned the police about the letter and probably ransacked the flat so she would call them.

'Maybe he wrote the nasty letter in the first place?'

But when Margo compares Jack's writing with the writing on the threatening one, the script is completely different.

'Couldn't he just have used his other hand or something?'

'I don't know. Could he?'

'Look it up.'

Lilah looks up 'forensic' and 'handwriting' on her phone and finds a ten-minute TV interview from the eighties on YouTube. They sit close, heads touching, and watch.

The expert document examiner has huge blonde helmety hair and a yellow kitten-bow blouse, like a sexy version of Margaret Thatcher with a thick New Jersey accent. She did the analysis of the Zodiac letters, which could be a recommendation or a damning indictment, depending on your view.

She explains that the Zodiac letters were printed, meaning the letters were not joined together, as opposed to cursive which means all joined up. The handwriting was also 'fluent', meaning that it was written quickly. They can tell this because of the 'flying finishes' in individual letters, where the pen lifts from the page at the end of a letter. This shows a speeding hand and that the writer was using their everyday writing. It's very difficult to disguise handwriting, she says. If it was disguised there wouldn't be any flying finishes and the size of individual letters would be inconsistent throughout the document. When handwriting is disguised it looks more like a drawing, takes a lot of effort, and the pen moves differently on the page.

Margo checks both abusive letters and Robertson's and they both have flying finishes, are both written fluently in the authors' natural hand.

Margo concludes, 'Wasn't him but he's still a massive piece of shit.'

Lilah holds up Robertson's letter. 'His address is on this. Let's go and tell him he's a wanker.'

This seems like a good idea, mostly because Margo is desperate to get out of here, they're both angry and Margo knows she can change her mind at the last minute. They grab their coats and bags and lock up the house, heading out to the car.

They get in, Lilah puts the address into her phone GPS and Margo pulls out.

'Oh fuck.' Lilah slides down in her seat. 'Fucking Richard.'

Richard is standing four garden gates down from Janette's, frowning at his phone as Margo's Mini glides past him. His jaw is very swollen and he has a black eye.

Clammy but very calm, Margo takes the turn into heavy traffic and stops at the lights. 'How the hell did he find us?'

Lilah is clutching her phone.

'Is that your old work phone? Are you still using the phone he gave you?'

'Well, why not?'

Margo pulls over and makes Lilah show her the phone settings. The tracker is on.

'That's how he keeps finding you.'

'Ooh, shit. He knows where I'm staying, doesn't he?'

'He'll know everywhere you go. Lilah, Richard is not well.'

'I agree, I know, I do know that, yes.'

'You need to keep that tracker off. You need to stay away from him. You can't go back to Deborah's house either.'

'OK.'

'He wants to hurt you.'

'OK.'

'He will hurt you. I can't believe you didn't tell me how bad this was, how ill he was.'

'Well, I knew what you'd say.'

Margo tuts. 'No, you didn't.'

'I did. You'd tell me to stay away from him and I wasn't going to.'

'I'm a baddie because I don't want you to stay in an abusive relationship?'

'No, but it means I can't talk to you unless I'm ready to leave. And I wasn't.'

Margo doesn't know what to say about that because she's got a point.

29

JACK ROBERTSON'S HOUSE IS in the leafy suburb of Newton Mearns. The houses are big here, set in large gardens with driveways and massive extensions.

The GPS directs them to a whitewashed two-storey square art deco house with big horizontally leaded windows. Mature trees screen it from the street but they can see through the driveway to a big front garden. It's overgrown now, run to seed, and the lawns are long and windswept. A huge white rhododendron bush flourishes in the middle of a white gravel drive.

A huge Ford Ranger truck, bright orange and gleaming, is parked in front of the house. It's too big and clean to be useful.

A garage that looks like a miniature of the house is tucked around the side and they can see directly down an alley between it and the house into a large garden at the back. It seems to go on for miles. A rusted swing set faces the house and the grass is knee-deep.

'Not bad at all,' mutters Lilah.

On closer inspection the house is very rundown. Paint peels from the wooden window frames. The white gravel has spread thin in parts, the muddy brown earth peeks out.

Lilah explains that gravel like that needs to be raked regularly. 'He's got rid of his gardener. Only a few months ago, by the looks of it.'

They hesitate in Margo's car for a few minutes because they can't quite agree what to do.

Lilah wants to go up and knock on the door and tell him they know he broke in and messed the house up and to fuck off or they will smash his face in and then tell the cops.

Margo doesn't know if that's a good idea. She thinks they should just tell him Lilah saw him last night and tell him to fuck off. She hasn't told Lilah about meeting McPhail but it has made her wary. They don't know anything about Robertson. They don't know what they're walking into and the garden seems quite enclosed. They could be walking into a trap.

'He won't be violent or anything,' says Lilah. 'He's a writer.'

'Writers can be violent. Norman Mailer stabbed his wife. William Burroughs shot his wife. That Dutch writer killed his wife, denied it and then wrote a book about it.'

'Well, let's not get married to him then.'

They get out of the car. As they approach the house Margo wishes she had her walking stick with her. It had a good cudgelly weight to it. She hasn't got anything with her if this goes wrong.

The street has the creepy dead feeling of suburbia in the middle of the day. Margo looks at all the dark windows peering out across lawns and tarmacked driveways and feels watched, as if she's being filmed on CCTV.

They crunch up to the front door, feet slipping on unexpected puddles of gravel as they cut around the Ranger.

Margo is still considering backing out but Lilah rings the bell immediately.

'I wasn't ready.'

'Well fuck it,' she says and straightens her hair.

Silence. There's no one in.

Lilah whispers, 'Why don't we break in and smash *his* house up?'

Just then they hear movement inside, a door opening, footsteps coming down the hall towards the door. It swings wide and the sound of 'What Up Gangsta' by 50 Cent filters up from the basement.

Jack Robertson is red-faced and panting, covered in a sheen of sweat, his T-shirt and jogging trousers are dark and wet and heavy.

'Oh!' he says. 'Hello? Margo, is it? Hello again.' He looks at Lilah.

Lilah sucks her cheeks in.

'Well, OK.' He turns back to Margo, smothering a smile. 'You're here? I'm sorry, I did post the letter back to you. It should come tomorrow if you haven't already —'

'It came this morning,' says Margo, 'but I wasn't there. My flat got broken into last night. I had to stay somewhere else.'

'Oh God. How awful. That's very upsetting. God!'

'You'd think it would be, wouldn't you?'

'God, yeah. Was it him, do you think?'

'Who?'

'McPhail? After that letter I had a feeling he'd try something else.'

'Have you seen McPhail recently?'

'Me? No.'

'I met him this morning.'

'Did they arrest him? Did you have to identify him?'

'No, I went to his house. In High Blantyre.'

'To identify him?'

'He's in a wheelchair.'

'Oh.' Robertson didn't know. 'Full-time?'

'Yeah. He really is. He was waiting for the mobility bus.'

'Oh?'

He turns his attention to Lilah. 'Who's this?'

Lilah smooths her hair. 'Don't you remember me?'

Robertson very clearly does remember her. He raises his eyebrows slowly, waiting for her to call him out.

'We spoke last night in Holly Road.'

'Sorry – where?'

'In Holly Road. I was sitting on a wall, waiting for her, and you came out and asked me if I was lost.'

'Oh.'

'And I said, "Why, do I look lost?" and you said, "No, you look perfect." Remember that?'

They're smiling at each other, flirting. This is not the fuck-you confrontation Margo is hyped for.

'I think I would remember meeting you.'

'I think you would too. Most people do remember meeting me.'

Robertson lifts the hem of his T-shirt to wipe the sweat from his face. Margo can see he's smiling and trying to hide it. She glances at Lilah but she's reading his abs.

'Look, things seem to have gotten out of hand. Would you ladies like to come in?'

'Listen, you old fucker,' says Lilah, sounding aggressive but drawling sexily, 'we know it was you who broke in.'

'I have no idea what you're talking about.' He's awful at lying. His face toggles between genuine glee and cardboard shock. 'Why would you think that?'

Lilah tuts. 'We're going to call the police right now.'

'I can call the police if you like,' he says. 'I have a lot of friends in the police.'

But they can't call the police because Lilah has been involved in two Richard incidents this week and may have stolen a lot of money and Margo still feels stupid about last night.

They all stand there for a minute until Lilah says, 'Why are you all sweaty?'

Sheepish at being called out, Robertson points back into the house. 'I've got a treadmill ...'

Lilah looks down the hall. 'You've got a gym?'

'... in the basement.'

'Oh.' Lilah and Robertson lock eyes.

'Is it big?'

'Lilah, for fucksake!'

'Sorry.'

'Look –' Margo points at Robertson's damp nose – 'Leave me alone, you sharky prick. I'm not a prop in your stupid defamation case. I hope he wins, I hope you lose your house.'

He's smirking now and so is Lilah.

'You broke my fucking door.'

'I didn't. And I didn't pour perfume on your bed.'

Lilah snorts. '*We haven't even mentioned that yet!*'

They start to laugh conspiratorially and Lilah slaps Robertson's arm. He's enchanted by her and a little bit embarrassed.

'God,' he smiles, 'look, I'm just desperate – he's going to ruin me. He's a rapist, he deserves to – I'm so sorry. I didn't break anything, I didn't take anything, I just thought if I made a mess you'd call the police and file a complaint against him and it would help us prove he's a shit. It didn't seem that bad while I was doing it. I'm so sorry if I frightened you.'

But he doesn't sound sorry.

'It *did* frighten me.'

'You're a fucking idiot.' Lilah says it as if it's a compliment.

'Come in and I'll make us all coffee or something? I'll re-place the perfume, I can make it up to you.' Jack's not even talking to Margo now, just to Lilah.

'No!' Margo grabs Lilah's arm and drags her away. 'No. Not another fucking nutter, Lilah, no.'

She keeps hold of her arm as they slide and crunch grace-lessly through the gravel and get back into the car.

'Fat lot of fucking use you were,' she says.

Lilah giggles. 'I'm so sorry.'

'You're no more sorry than he is.'

She pulls her seat belt on and sees that Robertson is standing at his open door, leaning on the door frame. He and Lilah are watching each other.

'Christ, Lilah, you're unsalvageable. That man is about to go bankrupt, he vandalised my flat to support a legal claim against a man whose life he ruined. Read the fucking signs.

I'm not watching you jump from one burning bucket of shit straight into another.'

Lilah is quiet for a moment as they draw away, looks out of the side window and mumbles to herself:

'Fit though.'

30

No alarm system on the house.

Watching a house is nice. It's calm, making plans and watching. This is a good bit.

This house will be easy. There's a loose window at the back. The whole house is big so that sounds downstairs might not be heard everywhere. You could get in and walk around before anyone knew it.

The window, the one that's loose, is next to a door that has been broken and fixed up with tape but it's easy enough to push it in.

Anyone could get in during the night, sneak upstairs to the bedrooms. Her light goes on in the corner room.

Anyone could see that light and know where she was sleeping. Anyone could get in.

No neighbours through the walls. No one to hear a bitch squeal. Not with a hand on her mouth. Not with a hand on her mouth and a wee combat knife stuck in her tit.

So undefended, the door might as well be left lying open to the street. Anyone could get in there. Anyone with a mind.

Why even bother breaking in when you could walk up to the door and blow it open?

31

SHE'S CRYING IN THE living room when her phone rings.

'Oh, hi there, I was just giving you a wee ring there to see how you're feeling today –'

'Tracey?'

'Yeah, hi there, it's Tracey from the adoption agency, I was just calling up to –'

'Look,' she says, 'I'm so sorry, but all this contact, support, this is too much for me.'

What she actually wants to say is fuck off.

'OK: Margo?' says Tracey quietly. 'Listen, I'm outside right now. I know you're on your own. Can I come and talk to you? It'll take two minutes.'

'Oh, well, I'm not in Holly Road, I'm afraid, I'm –'

'In Marywood Square, yeah. That's the address we had in the office, remember?'

'Oh.'

'I'm walking up to the door.'

The phone clicks and the line goes dead.

Margo hangs up. She gets up and steps out into the hall, trying to breathe, her stomach tightening with dread as she sees a grey Tracey-shape beyond the glass. A tentative knock raps on the glass.

She keeps her eyes on Tracey's shadow, seeing her turning to look out into the street, back at the door, fixing her hair, straightening her clothes.

She half opens it and Tracey slips into the hall and starts talking immediately. Oh, thanks for letting her come in! She has arthritis actually so it's good to get out of that cold out there, so it is. She looks around the hall, stepping further into the house and says Wow, what a big house, lucky you, very full, isn't it? That's a nice wee light up there with the stained glass and all that. Yes, so, thanks for seeing her, that's kind of her. Grand. Yes.

They've somehow worked their way into the kitchen and Tracey's eyes are on the tea caddy and the kettle.

Margo crosses her arms. 'What can I do for you, Tracey? I'm pretty busy.'

'Oh, aye. Yep.'

They stand in silence. Tracey takes a deep breath and stalls.

'What do you want?' says Margo.

'Aye.' Tracey is suddenly coy and wringing her hands. 'So, you may have noticed that I've been kind of hanging around you a wee bit more than was maybe appropriate and I want to apologise for doing that. I know from my own experience as an adoptee that this is a fairly difficult time in your life and so on. Um. My own, um, contact with my birth mother wasn't a happy ...' She's looking at the window. 'Is that dry rot there?'

Margo turns and looks at a grey shadow above the lintel. It's coming from upstairs. 'I don't think so. That's always been there.'

'You been here a long time, yeah?'

'In this house?'

'Yeah.'

She's looking at the fine cornicing around the ceiling and the range cooker.

'Tracey?'

'Sorry, yeah, so. I live nearby, as I says, lived here for ten years and so on. Up near the petrol station? You know that wee bit up there, yeah, by the park, and, well, what I'm here to ask is: can I buy your house?'

Margo is so surprised she laughs.

'I know,' says Tracey, almost crying. 'It's inappropriate for me to be here but as soon as I saw your address on the form and that, well, we've been around here putting leaflets in people's doors asking if they want to sell but they're all done up to top spec and we don't need that, we just need a family home in this area because our kids are at the primary school just round there and the landlord is trying to put us out of our flat and it's so expensive. I didn't come to the court case for this house, I came because I was worried she'd thump ye. She's kind of a scary person, your auntie, and the minute I saw her I thought to myself "she's going to eat that woman whole" but it seems to have been OK in the end. Is it OK?'

'It is, so far, yeah.'

'I'm sorry for even asking about the house. Just say no to me, that's OK, but I'd have kicked myself if I didn't ask, I've been working up to it. That's the only reason I'm here, so I don't kick myself later on, when I'm walking the weans to school and this is two luxury duplexes with a craft studio out the back.'

Margo smiles.

'D'you want a wee cup of tea, Tracey?'

They sit for a while at the grand old table and Margo doesn't promise her anything but she likes her very much. Tracey, outside of work and without a secret agenda, is lovely.

She tells Margo about meeting her own birth mother, how the woman told her she'd been in prison for fifteen years for being an active member of the IRA. Tracey was quite impressed by that until she read a book about Dolours Price and realised she'd stolen her story. Turned out her birth mother had beaten her boyfriend to death with a saucepan when she was blackout drunk. She covered him in blankets and left him lying in the kitchen. Cooked for the lodgers, stepping over him, until someone called the police on her weeks later.

'But that was in London, right enough,' she says, as if such things were common there.

Margo tells her that she can't empty the house. She can't even call in a clearance company because she knows they'd sell off all Janette's stuff to junk shops and she keeps imagining patients coming in to surgeries she's taking, wearing Janette's brooches or carrying one of her plastic handbags. She's scared that she'll be walking past second-hand shops and glance in and see their best china service yellowing in the window, that she'd be broadcasting the seeds of Janette over the city, leaving them to flourish, setting up ambushes for herself in the future.

'No,' says Tracey, looking around, 'that just means you're not ready to do it yet. Sometimes you just have to sit and feel things for them to pass. It won't always be this bad. Give it a month or so.'

'I don't have a month. My brother thinks it'll be done by next week.'

'Did you tell him how hard it is?'

She hasn't.

'Tell him,' says Tracey. 'You take your time.'

She gets up to go and Margo says she'll think about selling her the house but Thomas'll have a say.

'Listen,' says Tracey on the top step, 'you know, I'm only here because I'd kick myself if I didn't ask. There's no rush now, just take your time and think about it. Whatever you decide is grand.'

They hug on the step and Tracey hurries off to get her kids from afterschool. Margo waves from the top step.

Tracey wants a nicer house. Margo thought her motives were sinister but they're banal as milk.

She has a long bath, watches TV for a while, then gets ready for bed. She tries to call Lilah but she's turned her phone off.

She texts her:

Again with the phone off? Or is it off? Where are you?

Margo stares at her phone but gets nothing back. While she's waiting she texts Diane Gallagher, asking to meet up, thinking she might reply in a few days but she gets an immediate answer:

Are you free tomorrow?

A little bit surprised, Margo says yes thanks, that would be great and Diane texts her a time and an address.

Margo goes to bed, glad to see the back of the day, and falls asleep listening to a podcast about the invention of rayon.

While she's asleep, deep in the middle of the night, the person who stabbed Susan to death creeps up the creaky stairs in Janette's house. They come into Margo's room and slide along the wall to the very darkest spot and they watch her.

32

It's late afternoon as she takes a turn for the steep valley between Maryhill and Cranstonhill. Margo knows that she must have been background-checked fairly thoroughly before being invited here, that maybe Gallagher knows someone she knows or worked with. Scotland is a small place and all you need to do is listen. Either way, she knows she has been vouched for, because ex-DCI Diane Gallagher has invited Margo to visit Gallagher in her own home.

The entire estate is new. It's so new that the red-brick roads aren't even dirty yet. Margo follows the GPS to the address at the end of a long, downhill sweep past houses built of cheerful yellow brick.

The houses are small and pretty, all designed with minor differences from their neighbours to mimic the organic development of a proper village but the fiction doesn't take: they're all built of the same materials and have the same windows and doors.

Margo finds the address. The newly laid lawn is so perfect that it looks like AstroTurf, and white hellebores flourish in pots around the porch. She parks, undoes her seat belt and lifts the box of biscuits from the passenger seat, turning to find the front door being opened by Diane Gallagher. She's wearing a pale lavender sweater and cream skirt and she's smiling.

Margo suddenly wonders if she should text this address to Lilah for safety but Gallagher's not going to strangle her. The address is in her car's GPS and Gallagher texted it to her.

Gallagher welcomes Margo to her home with a firm handshake and a warm smile, takes the box of biscuits, thanks her and leads her into a warm, bright kitchen where a pot of tea is already made and shortbread biscuits are fanned out on a plate. Large grey clip files are sitting at one end of the table. Two cups and saucers and side plates are set on the table. Gallagher is so ready it's a little intimidating. She's a careful person, a strategic thinker, still very much a police officer. Gallagher seems sure. After her stint in Accident and Emergency Margo didn't have much to do with police officers but she recognises as familiar Gallagher's delicious certainty, her military grooming. She looks tidy and has a tidy home and a tidy mind. Everything is in its place: good guys, bad guys, impropriety. Joe would have made a good cop if he didn't have such a problem with authority.

'Do tell me all about being a doctor,' she says, pouring milk into a jug at an open fridge. 'What an interesting job.'

They're not going to talk about Susan straight away, it's clearly further down the chat-agenda.

'Not compared to being a police officer,' says Margo.

'Still,' says Diane. 'Still – a doctor!' She nods at Margo and her eyes stray to Margo's hair, to her eyes, to her eyebrows. She's seeing Susan in her and Margo loves that. She hopes she's going to say nice things about Susan, the way she did to Jason. She doesn't care if they're hollow, she just needs something to hang on to.

So she sits down in the kitchen chair she has been assigned and then realises that she is facing a blank wall. This is an informal meeting with all of the props and flummery of two women having tea and biscuits together but she's still facing a blank wall and sitting in an assigned chair. It's probably an interview technique, to make her concentrate. She thinks Diane must have been a very good police officer.

'I might just sit over here.' Margo moves to the other side of the table opposite the window. 'So I can see your garden. It's so pretty.'

Diane sees her taking charge and shifting the power in the room. A smile flits across her eyes. 'Do you garden?'

'No. My mum was a gardener. She died quite recently.'

'Oh, I'm so sorry. How old was she?'

'Sixty-eight.'

'Young.'

'It was.'

'Did that prompt you to contact Nikki?'

'Sort of.'

Diane looks at her a couple of times as she pours the tea. 'What do you know about the Brodies?'

'The family? Just that Patsy died in a fall, and Betty – is it Betty?'

Diane smiles. 'Yes.'

'That Betty was a stage psychic?'

Diane titters to herself. 'She was good! I heard – I never saw her show but she was very popular. The Brodies were

241

kind of famous. Tough nuts. Clever – criminal but clever. Scary people. Patsy couldn't even read and now you're a doctor. Imagine what she could have achieved if she'd been given a chance. You look very like Susan, you know.'

'I'm glad you knew her.'

Diane nods at the table, remembering. Margo gets the impression that she is struggling to find something nice to say. 'She was a very strong character. Took no nonsense from anyone, I'll say that. I was looking forward to seeing what happened to her but then ... well, you know ... she was a force to be reckoned with.'

She's struggling to say anything positive about Susan. She's a police officer who has comforted devastated people many times and must have a ready collection of soothing bullshit. But she's Diane Gallagher and she won't lie. She has integrity.

'You didn't like her?'

'Well, it's a strange relationship, cop to crim. It's not a rounded look at anybody. I'm sure there was more to her than I saw. Let me think now ...'

'It's OK, you don't have to lie. I'm sad that she wasn't very nice, not the, you ... you know ...' She takes a bite of a biscuit that she doesn't want.

Diane sips her tea.

'You know, people often ask sex workers why they do it. The answer each woman gives is very telling. It's like a little personality test. Some say "I like it", they're defiant. Some say "I have to", they're fatalistic. Susan used to say "I'm saving up to buy a house". She was in control, or that's what she wanted people to think.' Gallagher smiles to herself. 'People hated her for that. Officers hated her for that. I did a bit. But the older I get the more I think about her and why she made us all angry. We were trying to save people, you know? Some of us. It's a mission for some of us. Not the ones who do well, they're politicians, but you have to feel you're reaching down to save people and Susan was always – you know, so *proud*. She was in getting booked one night and she asked the arresting officer what he earned. Told him she made twice his salary every week and she was right. That makes people angry.'

Margo thinks of Lizzie and tries not to smile.

'Because most of them were in a bad way and did need our help,' says Diane, 'Susan was unusual. Most of them had to take drugs to be able to do it.'

'I thought they did it to buy drugs?'

Gallagher shrugs. 'Chicken and egg.'

The ghost of Susan sits between them, fitting into no one else's story, not trying to be likeable, making wrong choices and refusing to be sad or sorry about them.

'Nikki says they did it because they were poor and addicted and that was all.'

'Yeah, takes a special kind of person though, special mindset. Lots of addicts don't do it. They were the toughest, most resilient human beings you could ever meet. They could ignore the cold, their bodies, the violence, the way they were treated and the dangers.'

'Did McPhail kill her?'

'No. Look, I know you're interested because she was your mum but those were strange times and you might be better leaving –'

'I'd like to but I can't. Since I met Nikki two houses I've been staying in have been broken into. I've been sent anonymous threatening letters. Was it McPhail?'

'No. He had an alibi. Have you reported these things to the police?'

'I have. Robertson thinks McPhail's alibi is fake.'

'Robertson.' She nods slowly. 'Why does he think we'd give McPhail a fake alibi?'

'Because McPhail was a police officer at the time. Because the police would be liable.'

'For what?'

Margo hasn't really thought about that. 'I don't know.'

'We're not liable for anything. McPhail was already on suspension. He got his books shortly afterwards. But if the alibi isn't fake then what? That means Robertson wrote and published a book slandering a man who maybe deserved it. He's a bad man. He's been convicted of rape, might be overturned on appeal, we'll see, but trust me, when Susan Brodie died he was in hospital with a collapsed lung. He had a bad drug problem. McPhail was a pathetic specimen but he wasn't a murderer.'

'I met him. He's in a wheelchair.'

'Oh?' Diane can't look at her.

'Did he have a stroke or something?'

'No. I believe he was attacked several times. Assailant unknown. Brain injury. Just awful. Whatever you think of him.'

She busies herself pouring more tea. Milk? Help yourself. Everyone likes their tea different, don't they?

'This is lovely of you to have me over,' says Margo. 'Thank you. I really appreciate it.'

'You're very welcome,' says Diane, looking her in the eye. She snaps a biscuit between her teeth.

'You must have known Robertson back in the day then?'

She chews and sighs. 'Yes. He was young then but just the same ...'

'I think he's a weapons-grade shit.'

Diane laughs unexpectedly, blowing biscuit crumbs across the table. She chortles and wipes them up and puts them in a saucer. 'Well, I couldn't agree more. That book.' She shakes her head. 'That book ...'

'It has a picture of the crime scene in it. It must be a police photo. How did he get that?'

She's embarrassed as she says, 'He's in with a few of the, you know –' she points up to the gods – '*them*. They must have given him access to files. They shouldn't have. Unprofessional. And then he writes *that*. Making an entertainment out of what those poor families went through. Darkest days of their lives.'

'Maybe he thought it would make people care, if it was an entertaining story.'

'Some of us already cared.'

'Not enough of us though, some people caring isn't enough. Those stories will be forgotten otherwise.'

Diane doesn't agree. It's not proper, she says, to write it like a story. It's not respectful. It's different if you actually know the people. It's not an entertaining story. It's their lives. And they're always written by idiots who get basic things wrong.

Well, says Margo, she's a doctor but she quite likes medical dramas even though they're all rubbish, thinks they have educational value, but Diane says this is policing and policing is different. Anyway, Robertson accused a man of murder in print. The reason he could publish those things was because he self-published. A real publisher would have said no.

'And now he's being sued,' says Margo. 'He thinks he'll lose his house.'

'Publish and be damned. Well, he'll be damned.'

Margo thinks he probably will.

'You know, Susan grew up in a hellish situation. The children's home they were in was shut down after an inquiry. She was one tough lady.'

'She was pregnant at thirteen, I know that much.'

'Didn't know that. By Barney?'

'Nikki thinks so.'

'Barney said she was his carer more than his girlfriend towards the end. He said she helped him. He didn't know she was actually saving up to leave him.'

'How could he not know that?'

'Barney didn't know much. We brought him in for questioning and he was asleep most of the time. I've never met a more pathetic individual, and I was a Glasgow copper.'

'Nikki said he might be my father.'

Gallagher looks at her face, reading her features. 'Hm. I don't know. I can only see Susan in you.'

Margo thinks Diane can probably see traces of Barney in her but she doesn't want to say so.

'You never suspected him?'

'Barney? No, I don't think we did.'

'Did he have an alibi?'

'Yeah. He was out of the country, Holland, I think. We had to pour him into a car to get him in for questioning, I remember that vividly. You'd have to meet him to know why he was never in the frame. Anyway, I don't think he'd turn up at the High Court like he did the other day if he was guilty.'

'Barney was there?'

'Yes. I was surprised he's still alive.' She puts her cup down and sits forward. 'So,' she says, 'tell me about these letters. What did the police say?'

'I really only told them about the break-in. I've brought the letters with me, actually.' Margo takes them both out and puts them on the table. 'I'll be honest, Robertson is so keen for the police to know about these I have wondered if he wrote them.'

Gallagher isn't worried about contaminating DNA or traces of fibres. She opens them, flattens the paper with the edge of her hand and reads. She nods as she reaches the end. 'Uh-huh. Well, that seems consistent, from what I remember. Same writing as Nikki's letters, same bad grammar. See here: "brung"? Yeah, that's consistent. I remember because it was the first time I had even seen that word written down.' She shrugs. 'I don't know what to say about these. I doubt Robertson's responsible. He's not that good a writer.'

'Did you test Nikki's ones for DNA?'

Diane tries not to smile. 'No. DNA wasn't a thing then and we didn't think they were related to the killer. They were nasty but they didn't seem to know much about the other murders at all. I see this one mentions the bleach.'

'Does that suggest that it's from the murderer to you?'

'A more likely explanation is that the information was leaked.'

'I got that one yesterday morning. Had a bit of red tartan rug in it.'

'An escalation ... ?'

Margo doesn't really know what she means by that so she takes out the greasy scrap of material and shows it to Gallagher in her hand. She doesn't want to put it on the nice clean table.

Gallagher nods at it. 'Didn't Nikki get one of them in her letters?'

'Yeah. She also got bits of Susan's clothing from the night she was killed.'

'No. We didn't know what Susan was wearing that night. She was found naked. There was nothing to compare. Barney wasn't in the country but he told everyone what he *thought* she might be wearing, it was in the papers and everything. The letter writer could have read it there. You get a lot of false confessions in these things – we had a very credible confession in that case. A woman came in a month after Susan was found and claimed it was her. Took us a week to realise that it was mince and she'd been in the locked ward at Woodilee Psychiatric Hospital at the time of the incident. What I'm saying is that a confession didn't necessarily mean the letter writer was the killer.'

'Who would write those horrible letters to Nikki?'

'Honestly –' Diane throws her hands up in surrender – 'we don't know.'

'Why didn't you investigate?'

'Look, we had no evidence that the letters were related to the murders. It was ten years after the Yorkshire Ripper. We didn't want to make the same mistakes as West Yorkshire because they'd squandered half of their resources finding the author of hoax letters and cassettes. They interviewed Sutcliffe nine times but let him go because he didn't have the same accent as the man on the tape. Three more women were killed by Sutcliffe after they decided to let him go. It was disgraceful, it was inept, there was *nothing* to link the correspondence to the murders. We were determined not to do that. People write these sorts of letters.' She opens her hands helplessly. 'We don't know why but they just do.'

'I wondered: could the letters have come from another cop?'

'No.'

'How could you know that?'

'I just do.'

Diane gives her a reprimanding stare and Margo buckles and hides her face in her tea.

'You know,' says Diane, 'when I started there were very few women officers. Rapes and assaults of street women were almost never prosecuted. Once, very early in my career, I was on my beat, just starting my shift, and I stumbled on a woman who'd been badly assaulted, lying in a lane. Her face was beaten to a pulp and her leg was broken. She told me that she'd managed to flag down a cop car three hours before I arrived, but they told her that she'd got no more than she deserved. A cop said that to her. They drove off and just left her there. The old guard, they called those women "street furniture". Getting them to care, it was like turning a tanker around. It was never going to be instantaneous and the drug aspect made everything harder. It was rough on the Drag before but now it was chaotic and busy and really messy. Intravenous ... A lot of blood and needles. Heroin can make you –' She winces and makes a vomit gesture with her hand. 'Very intense, physically challenging for men who were still shocked if a woman burped in public.'

They smile at each other about that.

'It's important to be ambitious in policing but,' she says, 'we mustn't let perfection get in the way of a lot better.'

'Robertson sent me McPhail's current address.'

'Yes, the one in High Blantyre.' Gallagher gives her a long stare that says she's keeping an eye on him too.

Margo wonders how many women are watching McPhail, tracking him, waiting for him to die before they breathe out.

'OK. The letters could have been from a cop. Susan was washed with bleach,' says Gallagher, 'that was a detail we didn't release to the press. She smelled very strongly of it when we found her. That was mentioned in one letter to Nikki, I remember, but I don't want you to think McPhail could have killed her because he was in hospital at the time. But, I must admit, the letters *could* have been from him or another officer. We're people too.'

'Why didn't you tell the press that?'

'Help us sieve out those false confessions.'

'Was Barney angry that she was planning to leave him?'

'He didn't know until after she died. He actually found her savings hidden in the house and brought it into the station. Thought it was a clue, God help him. Load of greasy fivers and tenners in a Presto's poly bag. He thought she was blackmailing a punter and he killed her, but we'd heard from other women that she had plans. No one wanted to tell him, he was so broken already. We drew lots and the loser had to go in and tell him Susan had been saving up to leave him. Had to make him take the money back. Poor Barney. I swear he was two inches shorter when he left the station that night. He was obsessed with solving her murder. It was Barney who came up with the idea that it was a serial killer, then he decided it had to be a cop, that's where Jack Robertson got it from.'

She glances at her watch and Margo apologises for taking up so much of her time.

'Not at all. Some things are just too painful to accept. Those women were killed by lots of different men: fathers, brothers, husbands, neighbours, and we didn't get most of them. They're still out there. I saw one suspect on telly the other day in a football crowd, holding up a Palestinian flag. They're still out there. That's on me.'

'I saw you in the papers, threatening to turn up at people's doors. Did you really know who was around that night?'

'Yes, we knew. We were down there night after night, recording car registrations and faces. We knew it would happen again. But once we weeded out the sex offenders, the gawkers and the family, what you're left with is a cast of fairly ordinary men.'

'The *family*?'

Diane hums. 'Family members would come down and visit the women during their shifts. You can't walk around with money on you, not there.'

'What do you mean by *family* though?'

'Husbands, kids, mums.'

'*Mums?*'

Gallagher nods. 'Addiction is intergenerational. One boy I knew, an addict, he used to come to the Drag and get his cash twice a night from his mum. She was an addict and felt responsible – didn't want her boy having to do sex work. He OD'd, that boy. So did she, a few months later. I think of her often. It's a kind of heroism. I couldn't do that for my children.

'That case the other day: we never even had Moorov in the frame at the time. His name never came up. He wasn't in trouble for twenty years afterwards and then got DNA-tested for something else. Serious Crime database matched him to that murder and only that one. He'd been married in the meantime and had three kids. He's a good dad. You surprised by that?'

'Yes.'

'I'm not.'

As Diane talks the weight of it all seems to suck the colour from her.

The tea is finished and Gallagher isn't going to offer any more. She glances at the clock, signalling that she wants Margo to leave.

'I'd better go,' says Margo, 'I've taken up enough of your time.'

'No,' says Gallagher, getting to her feet to show Margo out, 'not at all.'

At the door on the way out Diane holds Margo by the shoulders and says nice things about Susan. She uses some of the very phrases she said to Jason: not the manner of her passing, given a difficult hand. And although it's a repetition, and Margo thinks Diane has said these things many times to many different families, they touch her very much.

She gets into her car, starts the engine and drives away.

The sun is setting as she crests the hill. She imagines, for a moment, the multitude of mourners, all the friends and children and family and social workers and cops, lives ruined by the loss of those women. She thinks of the men who inflicted it, men blind to the worth of the people they hurt and killed.

And she thinks about how many of them there are like Moorov, how many of them did those things and then got married, became fathers, uncles and co-workers. She realises that they're everywhere.

33

SHE'S PULLING INTO MARYWOOD Square, slowing down to park, when a car drawing into the street behind her catches her eye. It's old for the area: a boxy Honda saloon in green. It's not old in a cool retro car way, it's just old. It doesn't fit here. It looks as if someone is in the front seat and they're facing Janette's house. It looks like the car from the Mitchell. She can see the driver is a slim figure, sitting in the shadows of the deep, boxy cabin.

The likeness makes her uneasy enough to pull in and let the car cruise past her, watching from the corner of her eye to see who's driving but the sun visor is down again just like it was outside the library. She can see the shadow of a face and hands on the wheel. The old car passes quickly and then draws in eight parked cars ahead.

Margo pulls out and drives up to it, acting normal, keeping her speed steady as she passes. It might be innocent, it might mean nothing at all. She keeps her eyes forward, playing the part of an ordinary person who forgot something at the shop, maybe, and realised just as she pulled in and – my goodness! She'd better just pop back to the supermarket and get that thing. But just as she passes, and her shoulder eclipses the driver, the head turns to look straight at her. She speeds up, turns at the corner and follows the one-way system to the main road. She doubles back to Janette's street but the weird old car is gone.

Margo draws into the space the green car was parked in. What the fuck is going on? It feels threatening but she doesn't even know how she would describe that to someone. A car was parked? A car moved? A driver looked at her?

The sun is setting and Janette's house looms, dark and cold. Someone is in there, she's sure of it. She steps out of the car, tries to call Lilah but her phone is turned off.

Suddenly convinced the green car is behind her, Margo startles and swivels on her heels, sees that no one is there. It's dark, the street lights are bright on the main road but not on in this street yet.

In a panic she gallops up the steps and opens the front door, turning on the lights before she gets inside. She doesn't know whether to shut the door or leave it open. She can't decide. She stands looking at the door, trying to do nothing but she can't do nothing. Doing nothing is leaving the door open, doing nothing is doing something.

She stands still and the smell of Dettol hits her.

She doesn't know how they got in. She doesn't know if they're in here now. But she can't move. She's too frightened of doing the wrong thing.

The terror rises up through the floorboards, she's powerless. It comes in heavy black waves that stun and drown her, dragging her down to a frozen place.

She stands by the open door for a long time, unable to move. Twice she tries to sit down but her body doesn't obey.

Time stretches, the seconds drag out so far that the end of each is lost to view. She stands there until her ankles ache and the night falls in through the open door.

Her uterus twinges, as if someone is poking her side. Even as she stands here, frozen, life is growing.

It makes her think of Susan, who was afraid when she was asleep, who couldn't get any more scared so she did what she wanted.

Then Margo moves.

Moving like a stranger in her own body, she packs a bag and gets into the car, starts the engine, pulls on her seat belt and pulls out.

It takes her a while to even notice that the Honda is following her.

34

THE JUNCTION TO THE main road is busy with traffic. Margo is driving strangely, she needs to take her time because she's finding it hard to concentrate. All she can think about is Janette, the absence of her, how wrong that feels. She glances in her rear-view to see if anyone is waiting behind her, hoping there isn't anyone so that she can be careful and take her time without making them angry.

A windscreen fills her mirror, a car is right behind her, too close to see. The pine tree air-freshener swings from the mirror slowly: they haven't just zoomed up behind her. They're in no hurry and it's an old car, probably an old person's car. She pulls out cautiously, taking a right turn towards Shawlands.

She stops at a set of lights on Pollokshaws Road, pulls right at the lights, forgets where she's going and why, turns left into a quiet side street to remember, slowing and glancing up to check her mirror.

Isn't it the same car? A car that looks the same is still behind her which is weird. The mood starts to lift. It's getting easier to breathe again. She takes a left into another narrow street of parked cars and that's when she concentrates and sees that it's the Honda. It's following her, hanging back, trying not to draw her attention.

Margo slows down. The Honda stops. Margo takes another right to the junction with a busy road. She stops and watches the Honda crawl slowly round the corner, stopping when it finds her waiting. Then it starts to crawl towards her, gathering speed.

Margo shoots forward, taking an uncharacteristically reckless turn into fast traffic, scraping into a space between two cars. She's barely thinking about Janette at all now and doesn't care how this ends. She speeds up and pulls out, overtaking a bus pulling into a stop. The Honda is still there, quite far behind but still there.

She gets onto a broad, straight road leading to the motorway and speeds up, driving fast, checking her mirror so often that she's basically trusting the traffic ahead to take care of itself. The Honda follows. She can't see the driver's face, just slim hands and a slim chin, because it's dark and the car is well behind but it is there. She stops at the lights and sees it pull in four cars behind.

She knows that speed and swerving are not the answer – she's seen enough crash trauma victims to know that. She should drive somewhere busy, get among a lot of people and stay visible until she can work out what is going on.

The lights change. Cars in front draw languidly onto the motorway. Margo is trembling but breathes deep, holding her breath to stop herself hyperventilating. She's tailgating the car in front of her, symbolically nudging it down the slip road to the motorway. Traffic is light but steady: four lanes of cars and trucks weaving gracefully in and out of one another, anticipating the fork up ahead.

Margo stays in the second lane from the left. The Honda follows, staying back, straddling the first and second lanes uncertainly, watching for a cue from her.

Margo has done this drive many times. She knows that the fork up ahead bifurcates the motorway: two lanes slope left onto the M74, two head right over the river on the Kingston Bridge. She stays to the left and the Honda copies her, Margo on the second lane, the Honda on the inside. At the very last moment Margo ducks across the chevrons, changing to the cut-off for Kingston, ducking between two lorries. The Honda glides past her on her left, slowing, knowing it has lost her.

She drives over the Kingston Bridge, breathing deep, her heart in her throat.

They have been waiting, watching, coming into the house. Questions tumble over each other in her racing mind, her heartbeat pounds in her neck and sweat prickles her forehead.

The M8 slip road to the city rises from the bridge, rising like a stunt driver's ramp and then sweeps right. She is driving with her arms locked straight, wired and terrified and aware of her limitations, talking herself down like a passenger-hero left to land a plane. Brake-brake-brake, she stops at the lights. Check mirror, change gear, thank you, ground control.

She needs somewhere she can defend, somewhere that she can get out of quickly. She drives down to the Squinty Bridge. There are hotels here, lots of hotels.

This hotel is new and shiny and it seems safe. It's free-standing in the middle of an enormous car park, has cameras everywhere and is surrounded by roads that lead to the motorway, to the town, across the river.

She calls Lilah and leaves a voicemail: 'I'm at the Radisson Red. I'm about to ruin my career. Can you come?'

35

SHE PARKS THE MINI round the back of the building in a private car park that isn't attached to the hotel. It's out of sight of the road and, even if they find her car, it won't automatically lead them to this hotel.

She hurries inside.

Maybe someone famous is staying here because excited teenagers are standing out in front and a photographer is loitering inside. Everyone in the foyer seems mildly startled and a bit pleased. On the right of the foyer a casual restaurant is screened off by a giant white plastic room divider but she can see in. The tables and bar stools are full of drunk people. Everyone is animated and talking and laughing too loudly.

At the desk Margo asks for a room and the receptionist explains that it's very busy tonight: someone she's never heard of is playing at the Hydro, but he can offer her a half-price discount on a suite below the SkyBar because of the possibility of unbearable noise. The after-party is there. It's still three hundred pounds more than she can afford.

Margo takes it. No, she says, she won't be getting room service, she doesn't want to give him her credit card.

He hands her a key card for the door and the Wi-Fi password. She takes the lift up to the seventh floor.

It's a disorientating design. The corridor is red, the walls, ceiling and carpet the same shade of crimson. Only the doors are white.

Margo finds her room door and swipes herself in. It's a corner suite with a corner of glass and a view of the river and the city.

She lets her coat drop from her shoulders to the floor, takes out her laptop and does something she would never have done a week ago. She signs into the NHS Electronic Health Records database and accesses Martin McPhail's patient file. It takes her a while to find it. She has to use his address to narrow down the search. The system gives her the chance to do the right thing: asks her several times if she is entitled to access these files.

She lies, scrolls through until it asks if she is 'giving support and advice to a current professional who is involved with this care'. She says yes, knowing that a senior nurse was sacked for doing this very thing three months ago. Anyway, she's in.

What she finds is an enormous file. McPhail has been in fights and had a lot of illnesses and accidents, often broken bones, and had several concussions.

Most recently he's been going to hospital a lot, taking his medications well, attending outpatient appointments. He has Parkinson's, diagnosed four years ago, glaucoma and COPD caused by smoking.

In his newer notes there's a handwritten Statement of Lasting Care, instructions about how McPhail wants to be cared for if he's unconscious and admitted to hospital. He does not want to be resuscitated. He wants all the drugs they can give him. When he dies he wants his ex-wife to look after his dog. It's handwritten, scanned in and his writing is big and tremorous, jagged. He didn't write the letters. She searches through the files, going way, way back, and finds an admission slip to Hairmyres Hospital. Patient admitted with collapsed lung. It's dated four months after she was born.

She stands in the dark at the floor-length windows. Lights in the windows of the flats directly across the road illuminate snapshots of lives: eating alone, watching TV, working at a dining table while someone plays video games in the next room. Behind her the bed is stay-puft huge and white; the smell of a jasmine air-freshener creeps from the bathroom. Night hangs softly over the river. She watches a slow stream of red tail lights on the high Kingston Bridge and realises that this is the old dockland, the roughest part of the old town. She can see the Drag from here. Just beyond the Kingston Bridge is Washington Street, where Susan was taken, where nine women lost their lives.

The city is building luxury flats and restaurants and music venues over all of that, and over all of them. Susan is being buried and forgotten once again, without fanfare, just covered over with dirt as the city moves on.

Margo pulls on her coat, takes her car keys and heads down to the Drag.

36

IT'S LIKE A DREAM, seeing her here, Susan back in this place. This stinking place, where so much happened, so many nights.

It's quiet now, they don't come here like they used to. Some do, the desperate ones, the new bitches in town who don't know where to go to sell it inside. A girl had to be clean to get indoor work then, presentable. They had to have it together enough to turn up and stay all night but not now.

They'll take anyone now but there's still a few left stumbling about in the dark and the cold. Hopeless. Desperate. Beggars during the day, looking at the ground and accepting Costa coffees and sandwiches that don't scratch their itch. What they need is cash, not another fucking latte. They need cash and, when they can't beg it, they come down here in their anoraks and jeans, dirty fingers and missing teeth, and they'll do anything for a tenner because they're desperate not to feel the way they're feeling. Just for a few hours off from how it feels to be them. They'll fuck for a bed and a bag of chips. That's how low they are. Worthless. Nothings.

She smells stronger already, that smell: vinegar and ulcerated track marks. Something bad, nature's signal that something is wrong. How can they stand themselves? This is where they belong, those girls, the Susans.

Susan strides across the road, takes the steep hill and follows it down to the Drag.

Worthless, lower than shit, lower than dog.

Watching her walk down a dark street of shut-up offices, walking Susan's walk, the sway and swagger, looking left and right, seeing who's about and what's happening the night.

She's going to try it down there and once they're broken they never go back. She'll never come back from this.

37

THE DARKNESS DOWN HERE feels sharp and brittle. It cowers in corners, slices suddenly across pavements, cutting the feet from her. The lanes where business is conducted are so dark that Margo feels she could be swallowed by it. There are women there, down in the dark, she can hear shuffling and see movement, but there are no faces, no voices, no life.

She parked downhill and has been walking for forty minutes, up to Blythswood, around the old bus station. She's walking back down on West Campbell Street, a steep hill running straight down to the river, full of dark-windowed office buildings with smart brass door plaques and impressive entrances. The office buildings are high and it's this height that creates the deep darkness in the lanes intersecting them.

She imagines Susan, nineteen, still tender from giving birth, walking here, being cold and standing in the dark lanes to get enough money to start her young life over again.

The wind whips up from the river, making her shiver and hunch. For generations these have been the streets where the women came to do this. Where men came to buy this. She wonders what the men saw when they looked at these skinny women in dire need, standing in the cold, ready to do anything for money. How could they choose to fuck them and hurt them even more and then go back to their lives and their wives and their jobs the next day?

She walks down to Waterloo Lane, steps into the dark, tries to imagine Susan standing against a damp wall but she can't conjure her at all. Margo's just standing in a stinking alley feeling sorry for herself. She needs to walk.

By the time she gets to the Waterloo pub she feels as if she's missed the Drag by a mile or a block, she doesn't know where it went, but she crosses Argyle Street, bright and busy with traffic, the luminous glass over the Central Station bridge glowing white into the night, and realises that this is all that's left of it: a small group of two or three women standing to-gether in a dark lane, huddled around the light from a phone as if for warmth.

Margo stares at the women. She doesn't know how to start talking to them.

One of the women looks up at her and catches her eye. She nods as if she recognises her and gives a polite little wave. Margo gives an uncertain wave back. The woman raises her eyebrows, asking Margo what she's doing there. They can see that she doesn't belong.

She scurries to her car, gets in quickly and drives away.

She's waiting at the lights on George Street, a quiet office area, deserted because it's ten o'clock at night.

A car is stopped on the cross street, fifteen feet away and around the corner. A woman gets out of the passenger side. It catches Margo's attention because of the strange dynamic: the woman gets out quickly. Turned away, she slams the car door and doesn't look back at the person inside to say goodbye.

The driver's eyes are hidden in the shadows but the bottom half of his face is clear in the street lights. It reminds her of the Honda driver and she can see that this man is young, that his teeth are good, that his mouth is slack, as if he's just about to say something or smile. It turns her stomach, she finds that disgusting but doesn't really know why. He's in his mid-twenties, dressed in a grey hoodie. He could be anyone. As soon as the door shuts the car speeds away down the empty road.

Left alone in the street, the woman reaches under her pink anorak to her waistband and pulls her jeans up. She's dressed as if she's going hill walking, in a waterproof jacket, a big lumpy jumper, jeans and dirty trainers.

She slowly scans the street, sees nothing and then heads straight for Margo's car, tripping on her tiptoes, leading with her face, a little unsteady. She's on something and has to concentrate to walk.

Margo reaches down to the door panel and locks all the doors. But the woman isn't coming for her, she's just crossing the road. She swims through the bright white headlights and looks in at Margo, making eye contact, slow blinking.

It's Susan. It's Tanya Williams.

She holds Margo's eye as she trips past the bonnet, turning her head, connecting and then breaking away to look forward to where she's going. Margo panics at the loss of contact. She presses a button and the woman hears the window coming down and turns. She stops. She comes over to the car.

'Are ye, aye?' she says, as if they're in the middle of a conversation.

Margo doesn't know what to say.

'Will I get in, aye?'

Again, she doesn't know what to say so she nods. The woman nods back.

''K.' Then she nods again and puts her hand on the bonnet, feeling her way around to the passenger side. She tries the door but finds it locked. Margo, not sure why she's doing this, unlocks it. The woman gets in and sits, staring forwards, as if this was somehow fated, as if they were always going to take this drive together.

The car begins its warning song because her seat belt is not done up. She nods at the dashboard, 'Aye, OK,' and reaches over with chapped and swollen hands to pull it down and clip it on.

The lights change and Margo drives on with a strange woman in her car.

She has brought the cold of the night in with her. It halos around her, coming off in gusts when she moves in her noisy anorak. She sits upright, looking around the car, working out where she is and what could happen to her here. Margo realises that the woman has no idea who she is, where she's taking her, or what she's taking her to. It must be frightening. She must be desperate.

'Ken prices, d'ye, aye?'

They are climbing a very steep hill. Margo changes gear and says, 'I'd like to talk to you, if that's OK.'

'Aye. Five quid.'

'Twenty,' says Margo, feeling bad that anyone would get into a stranger's car for a fiver.

She huffs a dismissive laugh. ''K.' And then she thinks of a catch. 'How? Where is it we're going, like?'

'Well, where d'you want to go? Have you got a flat?'

'Naw. 'M in a hostel. I'm not going intae any fucking house anyway. I've did that ...'

She's staring at Margo, reading her for threats, not sure what's going on, a bit scared of the possibilities. Margo can't stand it any more. She draws the nose of the car into a space on Blythswood Square and pulls the handbrake on. 'Is this OK?'

Suspicious, the woman looks out to the street. 'Aye.'

'Or would you rather go somewhere for a cup of tea or something?'

'Naw.' She notices that there is an empty parking space next to them and jolts forward, seeing another one on the other side. 'You got someb'dy coming?'

'No.'

'I'm not – I dunno what you're for.'

Margo has scared her and doesn't know how to fix it. 'I just wanted to talk to you –'

'MONEY,' she barks and looks away out of the passenger window. Her nose is fine and long and she has scraped her hair back and up so tight that slices of her moon-white scalp are visible. It looks painful. She could be any age between eighteen and forty.

Margo feels inside her pocket and peels a hundred quid.

The woman takes the money and looks at Margo as if she's seeing her for the first time. 'What's this?'

'I was adopted,' says Margo. 'I just found out my real mum did this job. Can I ask you about it?'

She looks at the money. She looks at Margo. 'It's not a job.'

'What is it then?'

'A way of getting money.' She flaps the notes at Margo. 'Different than a job.'

Margo feels her reassessing the situation and realising that she isn't a threat. Now she's a bit scared of the woman because she can see how weak and needy Margo is. 'What's it like?'

'What?'

'This. Doing this. What's it like?'

The woman laughs, loud and bitter, a rat-tat-tat bark, and gives her a hard stare. Then she laughs again, straight into Margo's face. It's a threat of a laugh. Margo wants to cry. She's so stupid. What did she let this mental woman into her car for?

The woman reaches forward, slowly putting her hand flat on the dashboard. Her fingers curl slowly into a fist and she pulls her hood up over her head with the other hand, looking away.

Margo's expecting the fist to swing around and hit her but then hears the woman whispering, 'This life is no life. What you're asking ... This life. I take drugs tae no think that. What it's like. What it does tae ye.'

Margo can see now that she's really young and frightened. She's suddenly afraid the woman is going to go into details of sexual encounters, of brutal nights and sore days that she'll never get out of her head. 'Look, I don't want to pry –'

'NO!' she shouts at her knees. Then she drops her voice. 'I've got weans. In care, like. Mibbe one day they'll come and ask somed'y.'

Margo takes this to mean that she's not going to rob or hit her but she's sorry, because what she has asked is so intrusive. She asked her to think about the one thing she doesn't want to think about, about what she's doing and how she feels about it.

'I'm sorry,' she says, 'I didn't think, I'm so sorry.'

The woman looks at Margo, her chin convulsing, and she whispers, '*This is a dying life*.' Then she starts to cry.

'Ah no,' says Margo, suddenly crying too, 'I am so sorry, I shouldn't ask that.'

The woman hides her face and wilts towards Margo, ashamed of the only thing she has left to be ashamed of, that she cares about what is happening to her.

They hold each other and cry.

They're both afraid to let go of the stranger next to them so they just hang on tight, arms entangled, faces tucked tight into one another's necks. Whenever she can manage to breathe in Margo smells her hair. It smells of coconut. Margo says she's sorry over and over and the woman tells her no, nonono. No. No no no. No.

The woman pulls away. Margo gives her an unopened packet of hankies from her handbag. She rips the plastic off and pulls the bundle of paper hankies out, using them to cover her face, pushing them into her eyes as if she's trying to press the tears back in.

'Fuck.' She says it like a sigh.

Margo would quite like one of the hankies to dry her own face but she's scared of reaching over and taking one. She just wipes her face dry with her hand.

'My mum and auntie did it,' says Margo. 'Just found out.'

The woman nods. 'Maybe goes way back. Who knows.'

'Is that usual? For it to go down the generations?'

'I don't know. Didnae ken my ma. Did they get out of this?'

Margo can't tell her that Susan was murdered and then let her get out of the car. She thinks about Nikki. 'Yes. They did. She's been clean four years.'

'Your ma?'

'No, my auntie. I think my mum did this *clean*.'

'Fucking hell. Tough bird. She'd have been fucking minted but. There is money but not many can stand to do it.' She grins at her knees and nods up at Margo. Her teeth are rotten. 'How'd she get clean?'

'I don't know. She just did.'

'Well done, anyway.'

'Do any of the other women have kids?'

'We don't really talk or nothin'.'

'Aren't the other women friendly?'

'Naw.'

'You're just out here on your own?'

'Aye.' She blows her nose. 'On your own.'

'Not safe, getting in and out of cars, is it?'

'Well,' she brightens, 'if I feel unsafe, what I do is –' she pulls at her hair – 'I pull out a wee bit and tuck it –' she puts the imagined hairs under her seat and looks quite pleased. 'Then if you go missing there's … you know. They can find ye.'

It's so bleak that Margo doesn't know what to say. 'Have you got other family? A partner, or … ?'

'Nah, some of them've got men at home, like.'

'What do they do, those men?' Margo wonders. 'Just sit at home? Are they pimps?'

'Naw, they get together wi' ye. Support ye one way, you support them another, ye know ...'

'I don't really. How does it work? I'm asking because I wonder if she had a man sitting at home while she was out here, you know?'

'Ask her, like.'

Margo forgot she'd resurrected Susan. 'I'm embarrassed to.'

'Aye. Yeah. Guys, they just stay home and the lassie gaes them the money and buys gear for both of them. Doesn't always start out like that, but it's a lonely life. Be nice, coming in to somebody, know? But they'll arrest the partner for taking money. Say they're pimping. It's fucking lonely.'

Margo doesn't know what else she can ask without upsetting her again. She reaches into her pocket and lifts out the rest of Lilah's brick of cash. She gives it to her, glad to be rid of it. She's expecting gratitude or surprise or delight but the woman doesn't react at all. She just takes it and her eyebrows rise as she slips the money into her inside pocket. Then she zips her anorak up and looks away. She thinks Margo made a mistake, gave her the wrong money and she's expecting her to ask for it back.

When Margo doesn't, she glances at her, wondering, perhaps, if she's got any more.

'Aye. Is that it?'

Margo says it is because she can't think what else to ask. She doesn't want it to be the end though because she is overcome with a need to help, to save this woman, whoever she is. Get her somewhere safe and off the streets, out of this life. Realistically that would mean denying her the right to make terrible choices. Realistically that would mean taking her hostage.

'I'm sorry I made you cry.'

'Aye.'

'Do you get any support out there?'

'City Mission. Gae ye tea and biscuits and that.'

'Where is it?'

'Down there.' She thumbs over her shoulder. 'Crimea Street.'

'Can I drop you somewhere?'

'Crimea Street.'

Margo pulls out.

The woman is still afraid, unsure if she's going to be asked to do something for the money or to give it back.

'Look,' says Margo, 'I know that's a lot of money but I want you to have it.'

'How?'

'I just want you to have it. For my mum's sake.'

'Aye,' she says, but she's shaken by Margo's gesture. She can't even look at her now. She pulls the peak of her hood further over her face, titters, and crosses her arms over the bump of cash and sniffs and laughs.

Then she starts talking.

She came here from Dundee to get away from something or someone, it's not clear. She was in a flat up there, maybe, with a person or people. Her storytelling is confusing because she's not using any nouns. She's substituting 'hingmy' for a lot of other words and using fillers, 'like that' and 'like know'. Margo stops interrupting or asking her to clarify and just lets her talk and somehow the story becomes clearer that way.

She was doing this in Dundee but it is very small. A'bdy kens a'bdy. She has a drug problem and it is difficult to pay for. She came to Glasgow to try to address these issues but slipped back into street sex work. A girl in the hostel was always bringing in McDonald's takeout and coming in at strange hours and she just knew that she was working the streets. She asked her and the girl took her out and now she's here again. She has two children in care, they're back in Dundee, she thinks.

Margo says care isn't the worst thing that can happen to a child and her companion says yeah it could be *a lot* worse. They're getting fed, got their own space and they get to school and everything. Margo says *and* they're warm and care is a lot better than it used to be.

'It's when ye leave care,' says the woman, 'that it all falls apart.'

Her voice is gorgeous, deep and velvety, and she tells Margo it got like that from smoking and singing too loud. She likes singing.

Margo pulls in to Crimea Street. It's an unloved part of the waterfront, a wasteland of demolished buildings and giant Victorian warehouses with bars on the windows and steel girdles holding them true. This is where the riches of the Empire were sorted and stored, straight off the cargo boats from Jamaica and Ceylon. Now the great storehouses' highest ambition is to not melt into the street.

She parks outside the City Mission. It doesn't advertise itself. It's a free-standing glass building, plain, with long windows onto the street. Inside Margo can see tired people in outdoor clothes, mostly men, eating from plastic plates at trestle tables. Security cameras are trained on the door.

'At's it there,' she says. 'They'll be shutting up for the night soon.' But she doesn't move to get out. She pats the money in her pocket.

'Will I sing ye a tune?' She pats her chest. 'For the money, like?'

Margo says that would be nice.

She sings for her: 'Die In Your Arms', a Justin Bieber song with lots of step-runs and scales. Her voice is strong and warm, filling the car. She raises her hands to conduct herself, doing a symbolic sidestep with her shoulders to keep time. Her voice makes Margo's scalp prickle and her face split into a grin. And then it's over.

She turns to Margo. 'What d'ye hink o'that?'

'You gave me goosebumps.'

She gives a loud 'HA!', claps her hands together with delight. 'My first paying gig!' Then she throws the door open and gets out grinning. She crosses in front of the car, doesn't look back at Margo, but slaps the bonnet twice as a goodbye.

Margo sits in the car, the sweet song and metallic slaps resonating long after the woman has disappeared through the door.

Margo didn't give her the cash because she's a good person or because she pities her. She gave it to her because of Susan, to give her a night off.

She draws the car out into the street and notices that she doesn't feel sorry for her any more. She remembers the song and the woman's gorgeous gusty voice, thinks about Susan sitting with a patronising policeman, batting his pity back to him by boasting that she made twice what he did, being so cheeky she was remembered for it thirty years later. Susan, who did what she wanted because she couldn't feel any worse.

Being Susan Brodie's daughter, it might be a gift.

38

SHE'S HUNGRY. HER STOMACH is churning as she pulls in next to the hotel. The concert at the Hydro has started. The hotel has resident only parking but outside of that the cars are parked as far as the eye can see, lined up on pavements and abandoned in loading bays. The lights on the Hydro are bright and changing, a fluid bleed from pink to purple, and when she gets out of the car she can feel the thrum of the bass pulse through the soles of her shoes.

Standing on the steps of the hotel she takes out her phone and calls Joe.

'I'm pregnant.'

'You're pregnant?' He's stunned. 'Where are you? Can I come over? I'm coming over.'

'No, Joe, I'm not home. I'm starving, I'm just going to have something to eat and then I'll come over to you.'

She can hear another man's voice mumbling in the background. 'Who's that? Who's there with you?'

'Thomas is here.'

'Thomas?'

'He's here, he's come home.'

'Why's Thomas home? Why didn't he tell me he was coming?'

'He's …' Joe speaks away from the phone – 'Why are you home?'

Thomas mutters something.

'He doesn't trust me to clear the house, does he?'

'No. He thinks you need a hand.'

Thomas has taken Joe's phone. 'I don't trust you and I've been round there so don't try to bullshit me. Why does it smell of Dettol? Are you going nuts?'

'Are you *worried* about me, Tom?'

'Fuck off.' She can hear that he's smiling. 'I'm going to be an uncle?'

'Yes.'

'To a baby!' He sounds very excited.

'I don't want to go into details at this stage but yes, it will be a baby at the beginning.'

'OK.'

She's delighted and only now realises that she thought Thomas was tired of her, that he found her boring and worthy and dull. Joe takes the phone back and he's so excited she can't get him off the phone, but her stomach feels as if it's folding in on itself.

'I have got to get something to eat.'

'Have you told Lilah?' asks Joe. 'Please tell me you told me first.'

'I haven't said anything but I can't actually find Lilah. She's not picking up.'

'I don't know where she is but Richard's gone all quiet as well,' says Joe. 'I hope they're not back together.'

'Shit.'

'Look, let's just have a night off.' She can hear his grin. 'Let's just forget them tonight and be happy.'

'OK.' She can't stop smiling. The wind coming off the river is drying her lips. 'I'm very happy.'

'I am too.'

They listen to each other breathing for a moment and she knows it won't be perfect but she's willing to take a chance. 'Anyway,' she says, 'I'll be there in an hour.'

'OK.'

As she walks to the entrance, a cigarette falls from a nearby balcony, the red tip helicoptering to its death. She stands and watches it fall, elation fluttering in her chest, and vows to find out who sent those letters to her, to Nikki, to find out who killed her mum.

Inside she catches the eye of the receptionist. He calls her over and gives her a message in an envelope. It's a hand-written message from Lilah: 'Yoohoo. Popped in to see you. Call tomorrow.'

Typical obscure Lilah. She can't be reached and it isn't clear whether she will call or Margo should. But Margo is too happy to be annoyed. Thomas is home and she's told Joe she's pregnant. She hums the Justin Bieber song to herself as she walks across the lobby to the restaurant entrance, waiting by the service desk inside the restaurant.

She smells faint hints of vinegar and grilling meat and starts to salivate.

Across the room a waitress raises a finger in acknowledge-ment. She plucks a menu from a waiting station as she makes her way between the tables, smiling politely. Margo smiles back but, as the waitress approaches, she sees a man at the far end of the room standing up to greet her. He's wearing jeans, a white shirt and a suit jacket. He's looking at her expectantly, as if they had arranged this. It's Richard. His black eye is yellowing at the edges, the swelling is down on his chin. He looks dishevelled.

He nods over to Margo as if he's been waiting for her.

'Table for one?' asks the waitress.

'I've, um, just seen a friend,' says Margo, stepping awkwardly around her and walking over to the table.

Richard dabs his mouth with the napkin in his hand and steps out from behind the table to greet her. Even fifty yards away she can see that he is agitated.

'Hello Richard. What are you doing here? Joe is looking for you.'

'Oh yeah, hi.' He kisses her on each cheek, though they don't really know each other well enough for that.

He doesn't seem able to focus. She finds herself checking his pupils. 'Are you staying here? In the hotel?'

'Is Lilah?' He looks at Margo, startles a little, as if he's surprised it's her there again. 'I thought she was here. Is she?'

'I don't think so. I don't know.'

'Is she staying here? Burgers.' He laughs abruptly and sits down. 'It's amazing! Taste.' He holds the plate up to her. 'Honestly, taste it. So good.'

Margo shakes her head. He looks at her expectantly.

There's something really wrong with Richard.

'Yeah.' He looks behind her. 'Is she with you?'

'No, she's not with me. Why did you think she'd be here?'

His breathing is shallow. He smells unkempt and doesn't look mentally well. His eyes are wide and red, his face is pale and taut. 'Is she here?'

'Richard,' she says carefully, touching his arm, 'did you track Lilah here?'

'No.' He knows he shouldn't be here. He knows it's a giveaway.

'She's not here.'

'I think she is here. I do think that she is and I think you're lying for her because she won't see me.'

'She was here.' She hands him the message left behind the desk. 'But she's gone now. Her phone is turned off. I think you're tracking her phone and scaring her a bit.'

'D'you know she stole money from me?'

The waitress with the megawatt smile is coming over with a menu held high in the air. 'So what are we doing then?' she sing-songs. 'Eating together? Eating apart? Eating at all?'

Margo orders what Richard is having. The waitress confiscates the menu and leaves them alone. 'Richard?'

He takes a big bite of burger and widens his eyes, chewing and gesturing that his mouth is full. He laughs – haha – and a shred of mayo-heavy lettuce drops from his mouth, landing on the table with a small splat. She waits for him to swallow.

'Richard? Are you feeling well?'

He shakes his head as if he hasn't heard her. 'What?'

'You don't look well.'

'How do I look?'

'As if you've been under a lot of strain.'

He laughs bitterly, takes another bite and then something strange happens. Richard's shoulders rise, his gaze hardens and all the giggly confusion that hangs around his eyes drops away. He is a different person. Margo suddenly can't quite draw a deep breath. She notices a scar on his knuckles, the broadness of his shoulders, the cold fury of his demeanour.

'You know Lilah stole money from me.' His eyes narrow with malice.

'You should call the police.'

'Where is she now?'

She'll be round at Pitstop and Muttley's taking them for their final amble of the day. If he has been tracking her movements for the past week he'll have noticed the pattern. It's a matter of time before he accepts that she isn't upstairs.

'It's a yes/no question, just nod. Is Lilah upstairs?'

Margo nods.

'Are you in the same room?'

'She's in the room next to mine.' She reaches into her bag for her phone and shows it to him. 'Shall I call her?'

'No, don't call her. Is she there?'

'Yes.'

They lock eyes. Richard smiles. 'No, she's not.'

'She is, she is upstairs just now.' The phone is on her lap. Without looking down at it she stabs in the security code but can see it refuse her. 'I'll call her down for you.'

'Don't call her down.'

'I'll ask her to come down and see you right now.'

She tries the security code again and gets it right this time. She goes to recent calls and presses the last number.

Richard sees the phone in her hand. 'She's not upstairs. She's walking those dogs.'

'No, she's not, she's upstairs.' She brings the phone up to the table but fumbles it and Richard sees that she has called Joe.

'HANG UP.' He lashes out at her, grabbing her left wrist, twisting the skin. He's halfway across the table, spilling plates. 'HANG THE FUCKING THING UP.' He's screaming at her, his free hand is scrabbling for her phone but it falls into her lap.

'Hello?' Joe's voice sounds small and distant, a thousand miles away. 'Margo? Where are you? Is that Richard?'

Richard has her by the wrists and twists her to her feet, bringing her close until his nose is inches from hers. Margo grabs her phone as it slithers down her thigh and holds it high and shouts: 'Joe, Richard's here and he's hurting me.'

'Margie? I can't hear you.'

Richard holds her wrist high, burning the skin and using his other hand to peel her fingers open and take the phone.

'Margo? Are you there? Are you OK?'

Richard looms over her, he's not going to let go and she understands Lilah for the first time, the desire to pacify and normalise and dodge, because he's really scary.

'Richard?'

'What?'

'Fuck you.'

Richard raises his hand up high as Margo shouts into the phone 'CALL THE POLICE.'

He brings down the closed fist, smacking her hard across the temple with the phone.

A loud chorus of dismay rises in the restaurant as the phone drops and shatters, glass skittering across the floor. Margo is knocked back into her chair, dazed and half blinded.

Richard stands over her, the stomach of his white shirt smeared with ketchup and mustard and lettuce. Margo cowers, arms over her head, giving him her back to hit, leaning into the table to protect her belly and the baby.

'Margo? Margo!' Joe calls to her from the floor. The smashed phone is still working, as Richard slides from his seat.

'Bastard!' shouts a woman from across the room.

'Ho!' shouts a man and runs towards Margo. She thinks he's coming to protect her, but this is Glasgow, and he runs past her, going after Richard to start a fight.

He's small and tubby and he's catching up with Richard who is calmly leaving the restaurant. Margo drops her arms and watches as the short man leaps high onto Richard's back, wrapping his arms around his throat. But Richard is huge. He shucks him to the ground as if he was a heavy scarf without even looking at him. Then, as if nothing at all has happened, Richard turns and walks out of the hotel.

Margo drops to her knees and shouts into her phone, 'Joe, call Lilah! Warn her! She's with the dogs. Richard knows. He's coming!'

But the screen is black and Joe is gone. Blood runs in a sudden warm sheet into her eye. She's cut. She needs to save Lilah.

39

MARGO RUNS TO HER car and gets in. She is bleeding pro-
fusely from the temple, keeps having to wipe the blood from
her eyes and forehead, smearing it away with her sleeve. The
cut isn't deep, it hasn't hit anything, but head wounds bleed
heavily. She's reversing out of the parking space when she
catches sight of herself in the mirror. She's wild-eyed, her hair
matted with blood.

She gets outside the hotel car park barrier and finds the road
flooded with people. They're leaving the concert, trying to get
back to their cars and they're excited and happy, sweeping
down to the river from the bright mouth of the Hydro. They
don't care that Margo has to go and save her friend, they're
reliving their night, dancing and weaving through the parked
cars, spilling from pavement to roads, blocking taxis and buses
and cars who honk their horns and try to weave around them.
They surround the car, someone bangs on the roof. A woman
in a tight dress falls against Margo's window, laughing when
she catches herself.

Margo inches forward in a fug of horns, wiping blood
from her head, ignoring the shocked looks of concert goers
who see her bloodied face through the windows as she pulls
carefully through the crowd. Suddenly she's free and clear.

The lights of the night city flash past as she speeds through the West End to Pitstop and Muttley's flat. She knows she's too late when she sees the close. The door is open, a street bin has been smashed through the glass window. Richard is upstairs.

Margo stops her car in the middle of the street and gets out, leaves her hazards on, pulls off her jacket to wipe the blood from her face as she bolts upstairs.

The front door lies open to the dark hall.

As Margo steps into the dark she hears something fall deep inside the flat.

A woman's voice. Lilah is crying somewhere in the back hall.

'Lilah?'

Lilah is keening softly, repetitively, like a shocked animal.

For a moment Margo looks for a weapon, a vase or a statue or a plate, but that's too complicated and she still has blood in her eyes so she just stumbles on towards the voice.

'Lilah?'

Margo steps into the low corridor and is swallowed by the dark. She hears a sound behind her, nails pattering on a wooden floor and spins to see Muttley in the hall, panting, ears erect, watching.

'Help me.' Lilah's voice is closer, coming from the bedroom on the left.

'I'm here, Lilah, it's OK.'

She rounds the door frame looking into an even darker room. It takes her eyes a moment to adjust. A foot in a black leather brogue is lying just inside the door on a threadbare rug. Margo flattens herself to the wall and slides along to the open door, her field of vision widening to show a second foot. They are not moving. A man's feet on the floor. Richard's feet.

'Lilah?'

'Margo?' Her muffled voice comes from behind the door.

'Where are you?'

'In here.'

'With Richard?'

'Yes!'

'Can I put a light on?'

'NO! NO! DON'T DO THAT!'

'OK, Lilah, OK, it's OK.'

'I CAN'T LOOK. I CAN'T STAND TO SEE IT.'

'OK, it's OK.'

Margo takes a step into the room. Richard is on his back. His face is pale but freckled red, scarlet speckles are scattered across his forehead and his mustard-smeared shirt. Then she sees the dark, black pool on the floor.

She falls to her knees beside him, feels for a pulse but his neck is slick with blood. She feels through all the cold wet. There is nothing. Like a diver going down again, she takes a deep breath and feels again, trying to concentrate this time, as if she can conjure him up from the dead if she tries hard enough, but her knees are slipping on the wet floor, her fingers are numb and she knows it's hopeless. She tries the wrist. He's gone. Richard is dead.

She sits back on her haunches and looks at him. His carotid artery has been severed. It would have taken just a few minutes for him to bleed to death.

It takes a moment for her to hear keening from just feet away and she turns to see Lilah crouched in the corner, her back pressed up against the wall, knees tucked high. She's naked, covered in bloody spray, her eyes wild in the dark.

'Lilah?'

Her mouth hangs open and she cries silently, looking at Margo, staring at Richard, at the deep pool of blood around him.

'Lilah?' she reaches out to comfort her.

'WHAT THE FUCK IS WRONG WITH YOU?'

She raises a horrified finger to Margo. Margo realises, too late, that she's covered in blood too and must look terrifying.

'My head got cut. Did you stab Richard?'

'Is he dead?'

'He is. Did you kill him?'

'Not me.' Lilah shakes her head. 'He did.'

That is when Margo notices the bedclothes are pulled back, the bed has been occupied. Suddenly she hears another sound, a gasping, rasping breath and sudden retching. It's coming from across the corridor. She looks to Lilah for an explanation but Lilah can't talk or move. Her eyes swivel to the door, horrified.

'Please …' A man's voice is coming from the bathroom. He sounds as if he's drowning. He's in trouble.

Margo stands up, slides sideways in the viscous blood, catches herself from falling and steps out into the narrow hall.

'… Help me.'

Now she sees what she didn't notice on the way into the room: bloody footprints and smeared red hands on the walls trailing along the corridor to the bathroom, fading as they move away from the room.

Margo steps clumsily to the bathroom door, uncertain of her body. The lights are on and it's green inside, light bouncing off the pale green wall tiles. It's a long thin room with a big white bath. At the far end is a toilet behind a modesty screen of mottled glass.

A shadow moves behind it, a bloody hand on the glass.

'Fuck –'

It's a man. He bends down and rises again, bends and rises as if he's bowing. Loud, dry retching.

He throws his head back violently, staggering from behind the partition. He's naked, his hair and face so drenched in blood it takes her a moment to recognise him.

Jack Robertson is not hurt. She hurries to him but he sees that she is covered in blood and is shocked and bats her away just as he jack-knives over the toilet again. She checks him for injuries while he's dry-heaving: he's not cut. He's just shrouded in Richard's blood.

40

SHE IS MADE TO stand still for what feels like three hours but is actually nearer twenty minutes. The police keep telling her not to move while they wait for the scene-of-crime photographer.

Margo is frenziedly compliant: sure, sure, of course, not a problem, not a problem at all.

They're working around her, trying to understand how she could have arrived at a murder scene covered in blood. Margo is trying to calm herself down by focusing on Joe and Thomas. They're standing out in the close, watching and waiting for her, holding Pitstop and Muttley's leads. The dogs have been removed from the flat because they were licking Richard's blood off the floor and interfering with the investigation.

'Margo,' Joe calls at one point, 'are you OK?'

'I'm fine.' Stupid thing to say. 'Are *you* OK?'

He nods but he's looking over her shoulder. ''Scuse me, officer? I'm sorry to bother you, I can see you're very busy, but that lady is pregnant and is in shock.'

'I'm perfectly fine,' she says. 'Officer, that is the man on the floor's brother. His younger brother. The other man out there with him is my brother.'

'I see,' says a cop, neither writing any of it down nor really listening.

'I think,' calls Joe, 'she might be in shock.'

The cop thinks so too. He goes off to get permission and then comes back and tells her to go and sit in the front room.

It's not until Margo tries to move that she finds that she's covered in dried blood, has a huge scab forming on her temple, that her knees aren't working properly and she might fall over. The officer lifts her with one arm around her waist and sits her down on the sofa, telling her to put her head between her knees and do some deep breathing. Everyone is very kind.

She's so faint that she doesn't notice when they make Thomas take Joe away from the crime scene. He's just suddenly not there any more.

She's in the living room. Flash photographs are being taken all around the flat, blinding her at first until they move away into the bedroom.

The atmosphere changes when four men in suits arrive. They're not kind. They make her give up her shoes in case there's anything on them and bark at her to show them how she came into the flat, what she touched, where her feet went. Then two of them walk her downstairs.

'I'm so sorry,' says Margo, hoping that will make them like her.

It's raining outside and her car is gone. She doesn't have any shoes on but can't remember why. She walks through the wet, through puddles, making her feet cold and clean, bringing her back from the foggy shock, to a police car where they sit her in the back seat and shut the door.

'I have a car,' she says as the two men get into the front. What she means is *where is my car?*

'Do you?' says one of them and holds her eye in the mirror, waiting perhaps for her to confess.

This does not feel as if it is going very well at all.

They drive through rain that falls so hard she can't see out of the window. They could be anywhere at any time, except that Richard is dead. She startles every time she remembers the sight of him. She remembers it every five seconds.

Then they're driving down through the town, empty as a bottle on New Year's Day, past Glasgow Green and the river, through wide empty roads bordered by wasteland until they arrive at a big glass building with the police logo stuck to the front.

They are buzzed in through doors and walk down corridors. They climb stairs and report to people. Margo gives them her coat, anything to help.

Is Lilah OK? Where is Joe?

Lilah is in hospital, they tell her, she has been sedated. Joe is being questioned in another room.

Then she's in a windowless room with a high ceiling, two armchairs and, bizarrely, the same Ikea sofa as the adoption agency reconciliation room. She stares at it for a long time wondering what it means, why it's the same. Is she imagining that? But it is. It's the exact same one. Why? She has washed her face and her skin feels very dry. The cut on her temple is tiny, less than a centimetre long, hardly worthy of the two butterfly plasters she put on it. Then someone has given her a blanket to help with the shivering. She's wearing a pair of clunky pink trainers that don't belong to her.

Two men are in the armchairs, talking to her. She is on the sofa. These are different men from the men who brought her here, not uniformed, but their clothes are pressed and neat, one a blue shirt, one a grey T-shirt. Their haircuts and demeanour say they are policemen as much as a uniform would. One has blue eyes and a rugby player's nose. The other one is small and oddly nondescript. He looks like a photofit picture because his face is so featureless, his brown eyes normal, his sandy beard trimmed into a dull shape. Every time she blinks she forgets what he looks like. She can't keep his face in her mind.

She tells the whole story unabridged, about Joe reporting Richard to the police, about Emma's baby shower, how Richard arrived and broke a window. Was she at the baby shower?

No, she was not there.

Who was there?

She keeps trying to give them phone numbers but can't find her phone. How strange. She looks at her empty hands. She can't find it. Then she remembers Richard breaking her phone at the hotel. She tells them about that.

They're giving nothing away but they're writing every-thing down.

'Richard is dead, isn't he? I panicked, I didn't get that wrong? Did I do something wrong?'

Rugby takes on the job of telling her that he is dead, he's afraid. He looks quite sad.

'Who killed him?'

'Well, we don't know that for certain yet.'

'Joe's my partner.'

'Ah,' he says but she thinks he already knows that. 'The man with all the dogs?'

'Lilah MacIntosh had a substantial amount of cash in her handbag. Do you know anything about that?'

Margo doesn't.

They've finished with her but drag it out. One goes out to ask about something, the other one waits in the room. Then they swap for a while and finally they say she can go.

Rugby escorts her downstairs, through the quiet office building to the lobby and the glass doorway out.

Joe and Thomas are dozing on seats by the door, slumped uncomfortably on fixed chairs. Muttley and Pitstop are sleeping underneath, caked in blood. Margo has to wake them up. Joe has dried blood on his neck and black rims to his fingernails.

He tells her what happened in the flat before she got there: Robertson and Lilah were in bed when Richard broke in. Richard grabbed the letter opener from the dresser and ran into the bedroom but Jack wrestled it off him and then lunged. He only stabbed Richard once.

He bled out really quickly.

'He was a sweet bloke, underneath,' says Joe quietly, 'I don't know if you ever saw that in him but he was …'

Thomas is listening sadly and nodding. When Joe breaks off he steps forward and rests his hand on Joe's forearm, letting his hand sit there. 'Mate.'

Joe nods, acknowledging the rare touch of an undemonstrative friend. 'Yeah.'

Margo kisses Thomas on the cheek because she's bursting with love for him and she takes Joe's bloody hand in hers. She doesn't care that it's covered in gore because it's Joe underneath.

'Let's go home,' he says.

Rugby presses the green button on the wall and the doors open but all three of them stall at the fresh air. They're afraid to leave.

'Go on,' says Rugby. 'Go home.' He's seen this reaction before, she feels. Seen this type of shock. 'Just go about your business. We'll find you.'

They step outside and the doors slide shut behind them.

It's four in the morning. The night is still. The rain has washed the world clean again. She's wearing pink trainers.

Everything is wrong but she has Joe and Thomas, she has a random stranger's dogs and Lilah is OK, but, most of all, she's Susan Brodie's daughter, Susan Brodie of the Whiteinch Brodies, and they can face anything.

41

IT'S TWO DAYS LATER and the road in the Saltmarket still glints with glittery shards of glass. They've been ground into the tarmac by passing cars.

Margo buzzes Flat 2/1. She doesn't know if Lizzie will be in at this time. It's early evening and the traffic behind her is so busy and loud and she has to lean in to the intercom to hear.

'Who's it?'

'Is that Lizzie?'

'Aye. Who's it?'

'Margo.'

Lizzie doesn't say anything.

'Nikki's niece from the other night.'

'Oh. Oh, OK.' The door clicks open.

Margo pushes and pauses, remembering the security measures she took last time. Should she text someone? Normally she would text Lilah but she can't. She doesn't want to text Joe and worry him. She can't text Thomas because he'd tell her to come home. Fuck it, she thinks and goes in without texting anyone.

Lizzie has left the door ajar again but when Margo pushes it open she finds her standing in the hall, waiting.

'Hello?' says Lizzie, breathless and confused. She doesn't know why Margo's here.

'Yeah, hi,' says Margo and shuts the door behind her.

Lizzie waits, nodding encouragement, waiting for her to speak. But Margo doesn't know what to say.

'So ... what is it?'

A dog barks three times upstairs. It sounds like the start of a round.

'I need to ask you about my Aunt Nikki,' says Margo.

Lizzie thinks about it. 'Want a biscuit?'

Margo lies and says she does. Lizzie takes her into the kitchen and opens a packet of Jaffas. They're a fancy variant: dark chocolate with lime-and-mango-flavoured jelly in the middle. They sit down and Lizzie says she hasn't tried these ones before. She's seen them in the shop but not tasted them. She eats one and pays it attention, looking at it as she chews. She declares it 'quite nice'.

'You eat a lot of biscuits,' says Margo, looking around the kitchen.

Lizzie laughs and says, 'I suppose I do.'

She's smiling. She's very good-looking, Margo realises, good skin and grey eyes and chiselled cheekbones, but she's disguised it carefully. Her clothes are loose, her haircut functional as if she's afraid of being pretty, afraid of what that brings.

'Can I ask about Nikki?'

Lizzie tightens her face defensively. 'Only fair to warn ye that if you say anything bad about her I'll punch your lights in.'

'I'm not going to. I just want to ask –'

'Good.'

'I think I hurt her feelings.'

'You did.' Lizzie points at her with her half-Jaffa. 'You gave her the wrong number. She tried to call you and the number was rubbish.'

Margo says she was afraid. She met ex-DCI Gallagher and she told her the Brodies were kind of famously rough. She doesn't believe in the serial killer theory either. She said it was started by Jack Robertson and Barney Keith.

'Oh aye.' Lizzie looks distant. 'Poor Barney went mad. Susan was the love of his life, right enough. He was a changed man after she died. Never got past it.'

Margo opens Facebook on her phone and shows Lizzie Barney's page.

'My God, he's alive …' Lizzie scrolls through the photos. 'That *is* Barney. God, he's that old-looking. He must be a million by now.'

Margo asks if Lizzie thinks he's her dad.

Lizzie looks at Margo's face. 'Probably,' she says.

'Did you like him?' she asks.

Lizzie shrugs. 'He was old. I didn't think about him.'

'Did Susan like him?'

Lizzie grins as if she's going to say something nice about Barney. 'Well, he had a house. She was homeless. It was quite a nice house. I mean, it had doors and none of them were kicked in or anything. He kept it clean and had food and stuff. He had made beds, I remember that was a big deal. Sheets and stuff. Once he had a jar of instant coffee.' She reels.

'Wow! I mean. We were from *nothing*, really nothing. It didn't take much to impress us, you know?'

Margo nods to be nice but she doesn't know what it's like and they both know that.

'But he was steady for a junkie. He did love Susan. She'd have moved on when she grew up. He was one of the stepping-stone blokes. People you grow past. He probably is your dad. We all used condoms on the street, I mean, it was the late eighties, HIV was no mystery.'

'Nikki said he got Susan pregnant when she was thirteen.'

Lizzie nods and cringes and gives a little grunt.

'It's very young.'

She grunts non-committally again, shrugs and takes another biscuit. 'I can't explain that you.'

'Isn't he a paedophile then?'

'Yeah, technically. But then he was still with her until she was nineteen, so then what? He wasn't any more? What does that mean?'

Margo doesn't know. She half hoped Lizzie would say Susan was very grown up at thirteen, but she saw her dead body at nineteen and it didn't look as if she'd ever been old.

'Barney came from some stuff as well. I don't know. I don't know how to make it all right for you.' She looks suddenly very sad. 'It was a different time. We did what we had to. You should be nice to Nikki, you know. She's pretty amazing.'

'I know she's survived a lot.'

'No, you don't.' She puts a half-eaten biscuit down and brushes her hands clean as she speaks. 'See, we know who we are. Me and Nikki, believe it or not, we've survived all that shit: care, deaths, fucking … raped left, right and centre, spat on. We were rounded up by cops and shouted at by drunks, and we were still on the go, like the SAS, we made being outsiders the thing we were. They couldn't break us or make us lie. We knew who we were. If we hadn't become friends I don't know, but us knowing each other, that was important. We never had to pretend to be anyone else or explain, you know?'

'I don't really, to be honest.'

Lizzie smiles at that. 'You're honest. I like that. What I'm saying is that when you're shamed, like us, like whoors, the religious people and all them, they want an explanation: how you got there, what's the worst thing that ever happened, how sorry you are. They want you to hate the punters. I met some lovely men, some I'd have stayed pals with if I had a choice. I still think about them, wonder how they are. Some nasty bastards too, no getting away from it, but those ones weren't regulars, just fly-bys. There was unlikely moments of tenderness there, in vans and lanes and smelly bedsits.' She shakes her head. 'No one wants to hear the full story of it though. I knew an old guy who was in the war and he never talked about it because he said people just thought, "That's sad, he was in a war," but it was a whole lot of things. It was exciting and cheery and funny and he'd pals and that. But to people who weren't in the war it was just sad. That's what it's like for me and Nikki. Fifteen years of our lives, important years but people just want the sad bits or the dirty bits or the Christ-saved-me bits but not the whole of it, the whole messy truth of it. Just the bits that fit their agenda.'

'Doctors get warned about asking closed questions, you know those ones where the answer is predetermined?'

'Aye, "How unhappy are you?", that sort of thing. They're using you as much as the punters because it's usually about how helpful them having a good job and a pension is. But me and Nikki, we know the whole of it. We don't need to lie to each other. She's my sister.'

Margo feels honoured to be in Lizzie's kitchen. 'Then you're my auntie too, in a way.'

'I barely fucking know ye, hen,' says Lizzie and laughs to mitigate the rejection, but she kind of means it.

Margo knows it was a presumptuous thing to say but she'd like it to be true. 'Can I show you something?' She takes out the letters from her handbag and hands them to Lizzie.

Lizzie's face falls as she reads them.

'Oh no,' she says and looks up at Margo. 'Oh no. Where did you get these?'

'They were hand-delivered through my door. I got the first one the day after I met Nikki. I didn't tell her, I thought it would scare her.'

'Oh, honey, no.' Lizzie stands up. 'We need to show these to her. We need to go right now.'

42

THEY'RE PARKED OUTSIDE A white bungalow in the posh part of the East End, on a street lined with villas and well-tended gardens. It's early evening in old-lady suburbia and nothing moves. Front windows flicker with the lights of the evening TV news. In the far distance a tired grey man smokes a pipe and walks a tired grey dog along the street.

Number 52 sits high over the street, built squarely in the middle of an artificial hillock. A lawned garden runs around three sides of the building, separated from the street by a low wall. The bungalow is solid and whitewashed, with new plastic double-glazing and vertical blinds in both front windows.

Lizzie says it would be a bit of a shock to Nikki if they just knock on the door. She might start crying and embarrass herself. She makes Margo call on the landline number to warn Nikki that they're here and they're coming in.

It's answered after one ring by a breathless old woman. Margo asks for Nikki. The woman asks whom may she say is calling, please? Margo gives her name.

'Oh, for fucksake,' mutters the woman and yells, 'Hey! Nikki! Phone! Quick!'

Margo can hear talking and then Nikki grabs the phone. Oh! Is it Margo? She's surprised to hear from her, to be honest. She tries to hide her annoyance about the wrong phone number but it tumbles from her mouth. *Unob-tainable*, she spits. Margo tells her the truth: she was frightened and didn't know if she could trust her. She says that she felt a bit swamped and overwhelmed, when Nikki shouts at someone in the background to SHUT THE FUCK UP YOU OLD BITCH. Not you. There's someone else here. Margo doesn't feel she needs to excuse her reticence now. Nikki has made her case for her.

'I'm outside your house in the car. Lizzie's with me.'

'Whit!' The vertical blinds on one of the windows gape. She can see a long slice of Nikki's face. 'Is that you? In the Mini?'

Margo waves. Nikki waves back manically and beckons them to come in.

They get out and lock the car. The street is completely empty.

'Fucking creepy place to live if you ask me,' says Lizzie as they walk up to three brick steps leading into the garden.

'D'you see your family, Lizzie?'

'Well, most of them are dead. One in prison down in England.'

'You in touch?'

'Nah. Never really got on. Wasn't like Hairy and Nikki. There was always a bit missing in my family, you know? We didn't really like each other.'

'Were Nikki and Susan close?'

'Aye.' She stops at the front door. 'Nikki's the nicer of the two by far. Susan was a mental bitch. She was brave though. Took zero shits from anyone.'

Nikki opens the door to a white hallway. The carpet is white, the walls are white, a small white table sits off to the side. A very old woman is behind her, leaning over a standing frame. Age-related degenerative disc disease. She's so stooped that she has to strain her neck to look up and she has been like that for a long time. Gravity has marked her face, so that her jowls and cheeks sag forward instead of down. She's smiling at the floor.

'Oh, aye, yeah: this is Betty,' says Nikki. 'Our auntie. Isn't that right, Betty?'

'Aye,' Betty tells the carpet.

'So she's your … great-aunt?'

'That's right, aye, that's right enough.'

Nikki takes Margo's coat in the narrow hall, opens an immaculately tidy hall cupboard to hang it up on a wire hanger, while Betty shuffles about on her frame trying to follow the action but getting in the way.

Nikki asks Lizzie how come she's here with Margo and Lizzie covers up kindly by saying that Margo wasn't too sure where it was and wanted to see her. She needs to ask her about something.

'What about?' she says as Betty jostles her trying to turn around and face the company.

'Maybe we should sit down?' suggests Lizzie.

'Oh.' Nikki thinks it's something ominous. 'Aye, OK. Come away in.'

She opens the door to a pristine white kitchen with a big white table and six high-backed chairs. Everything in the house looks brand new.

'This is a lovely house,' says Margo as they file through.

Lizzie smiles. 'Nikki keeps it lovely.'

There's a faint citrus tang of Flash coming from black granite worktops that sparkle under white cupboards and another smell too, a comforting smell of melted cheese.

Nikki is helping Betty manoeuvre her walking frame through the doorway and Lizzie says that Nikki cleans all day and spends every night making lists of things she can clean tomorrow. She's one of those obsessive compulsives. 'She's a bit OCD.' Margo says she's not sure that's what it's called but Nikki takes the odd diagnosis as a compliment. 'I do my best.'

Betty stumbles twice on the way through and Nikki scolds her. She shouldn't be out of her chair after the bad night's sleep she's had, she's just showing off in front of Margo.

'No one's impressed,' she says.

'She's a bit impressed,' says Betty, grinning at the floor.

'I am, actually,' says Margo.

'My next trick's a handstand so get your pennies ready to throw.' Betty delivers these jokey asides like a tired parent who is jollying themselves along rather than trying to appeal to an audience. When they get to the table Nikki pulls out a chair and Betty backs in carefully, making a beeping noise like a lorry in reverse. No one laughs or even acknowledges that she's doing it which makes Margo think she's probably made this joke many times. Nikki hovers until the back of Betty's legs make contact with the seat and then holds it steady as Betty counts backwards, 3–2–1, and drops onto it. Effortlessly, as if it was on wheels, Nikki pushes the chair with Betty in it to the table.

'OK. Tea.' Nikki seems very different in this context, solid and distracted. As she makes everyone tea in matching mugs Margo asks how they came to be living together.

Nikki says that when she got clean she had to move out of the flat she shared with a load of other addicts. She was homeless and Betty needed a carer. 'It's nice.' She smiles. 'Nice way for things to end up. We get on OK, don't we, Betty?'

Betty turns her shoulders to Margo. 'She has me prisoner here. Call the filth.' And they all laugh, though it might be true for all Margo knows.

The tea is served and finally the parliament is assembled at the table. Nikki asks her what it was she wanted to talk to her about.

Lizzie steels herself. When Margo brings the letters out of her bag and puts them on the table Nikki's hands retreat across the table.

They stare at them. The letters are folded but unfurl as they watch. They can see some words: *Ram, PS, smell, youre cunt.*

'Is this a dagger I see before me?' It's Betty, singing in a wavering, theatrical voice.

'Fuck off, Betty,' snaps Nikki. 'This isn't funny. Where did you get these?'

Margo goes through the times and the two different addresses.

'So they're following you?'

'I think so. I saw a green car a few times. I think it chased me once.'

Nikki nods at the table. She's tearful. 'I got one when I first moved in here, didn't I, Betty?'

'Hm.' For once Betty doesn't make a joke. 'It was to scare her.'

'So,' says Lizzie, 'who is writing these letters?'

'Who has been writing them for all these years?' says Margo. 'Are there consequences? Did anything happen after you got the letters?'

No, Nikki says, there wasn't anything really. Just upsetting her, letting her know they knew she'd moved, keeping the wounds open.

Margo tries to minimise it. 'What if they don't do anything?'

'I know,' says Nikki. 'It was the thought that someone who knew you would stoop so low. It was so *mean*.' She looks at the letters again, fearful, blinking back tears.

Feeling as brave as Susan, Margo picks them up from the table and crumples them into a ball. She shoves them back into her handbag. 'This is crap. I'm going to put them in a bin on the way home. No more significant than a supermarket receipt, are they? I thought they might be from Barney Keith.'

'Barney?'

'Barney's still alive,' says Lizzie. 'She's found him on the Facebook. Show them!'

Margo pulls up his profile on her phone.

'God!' says Betty, her face uplit by the phone. 'He looks as if he's melted. He's a lot fatter than he was though. Must have got clean. I just assumed he'd be dead, being so old and that.'

'He's younger than you,' says Lizzie, 'you're still alive.'

'Yes, see: I'm immortal.'

'Really?' Lizzie sounds interested.

'Yes,' says Betty casually.

'Lucky you.'

'Ironically, I crave death's sweet embrace.'

'Do ye, Betty?'

She tuts. 'Auch, jus' in the mornings. Afternoon I'm usually right as rain again.'

'But Barney loved Susan,' Nikki nods to Margo. 'He was good to her in his way. God alone knows what he'd have done when she got it together and left him.'

Margo isn't willing to accept him as a tragic hero. 'He got her pregnant when she was thirteen. He sent her out to make money on the streets.'

Nikki sighs and sucks her teeth loudly. 'Hm. Susan wasn't really one to be pushed around. She had the upper hand there, really, I think. See, Barney was the one doing the cleaning and all of that. He kept the house and she did what she wanted. He was on the sick. He was never very well. He wasn't in charge of Susan, not by any stretch of the imagination. She was a wee besom at times, your mum, you know.'

Margo sits back. 'Has anyone got anything good to say about Susan?'

The three women struggle to think of anything.

'Well, she had you,' smiles Nikki.

Lizzie and Betty grin but it's Nikki they're smiling appreciatively at.

'I do,' says Betty and sits forward, hands clenched in front of her like a newsreader. 'She got off the drugs and that was hard and she did it because she thought she'd see you again.' She stops and clears her throat, looking at the table. Then she clears it again.

This, Margo thinks, is Betty in a state of high emotion.

'She thought she'd maybe get to see you again one day. When you were grown up.' She struggles again with her throat and blinks hard, her eyes reddening. 'And she wanted you to find her in a nice house, a nice clean lady. It's what she wanted. She tried so hard for you.'

Margo feels the spirit of Susan at the table with them and reaches out and squeezes Betty's hand. Betty can't look at her but squeezes back.

'She wanted you to be proud of her,' whispers Betty. 'She was never proud of where she came from. She was changing her life for you, getting off the streets, away from Barney, for if you came to look for her. But that never happened.'

Margo squeezes again. 'It's happened now.' She gestures around the kitchen. 'And look what I found.'

Betty smiles gratefully up at her, shy, because she's being sincere.

'Did Barney know she was leaving him?'

'Yes, I'd think so,' says Betty, 'Susan wasn't famously diplomatic. Barney was part of the shit she was shedding.'

'Wasn't he angry about it? Why is everyone sure he didn't kill her?'

Betty tuts. 'She was physically restrained. Barney Keith couldn't hold a tissue down in a high wind. Susan was very strong.'

'Anyway,' says Nikki, 'he was in Amsterdam that week. He'd been there since the Monday or something. His passport was marked and everything. He showed us.'

'What was he doing there?'

Betty looks uncomfortable. 'What do men do in Amsterdam? He wasn't trying on clogs, was he?'

Margo remembers the newspaper interview. 'He was interviewed just after and said he'd seen Susan off in a taxi that night.'

'No, he was in Amsterdam when she died. It came out later.'

'Diane Gallagher didn't think Barney knew Susan was about to leave him.'

Betty shrugs a shoulder. 'Well, cops get played all the time.'

They get back to the letters. Whoever sent them knew Margo's name was Patsy, they knew that she had seen the other letters. Who knew all of those things? Only Nikki and Lizzie. Did they tell anyone else? Nikki told everyone she met, apparently. Some people were told several times.

'She was pretty excited,' explains Betty.

Nikki is worried about Margo staying in Janette's house on her own but Margo says don't worry, she's staying –

'DON'T TELL ME!' Nikki shouts melodramatically and then explains. 'You're making yourself vulnerable. What if it *was* me? Or *Lizzie*?'

There's a dramatic pause.

'Was it you?' asks Betty casually, ruining the moment.

'FOR FUCKSAKE, BETTY!'

But Betty is chortling away to herself, laughing to them all, looking for an ally in mischief. Finding no takers, she whispers to Margo, 'Drama: it's a family illness.'

Margo smiles at her. 'Why don't you have it then?'

Betty raises her eyebrows. 'I got it out of my system.'

'When you were a stage psychic?'

'Yup. I was good.' She rolls her eyes around the nice kitchen. 'Big in the eighties. Sold out Motherwell Civic Centre. I was kept busy. That's why I was such a shite auntie to the girls.' She reaches out to Nikki.

'You did your best,' says Nikki.

Betty hums. 'No. I abandoned them because I was scared of Patsy, their mum. However troubled Susan was, she couldn't hold a light to Patsy.'

Lizzie says she'll call an Uber because she wants to get home. There's some football match on and she can't watch it here because Nikki doesn't have the right channels. She orders a car and it's four minutes away. Nikki goes out to the door to see her off and leaves Betty and Margo alone at the table.

Betty grins at Margo, open-mouthed, eyebrows bobbing as if she's encouraging Margo to do a trick.

'So, Betty, are you psychic?'

Betty frowns, drops her voice and glances at the door. 'She said you were a doctor. You don't believe in all that sort of thing, do you?'

Margo was trying to be respectful of other people's beliefs but Betty seems disappointed in her. 'I don't, not really. Nikki's convinced though.'

'Yeah.' Betty lifts a shoulder. 'It was a living. I started holding séances for fun and then for money and then I moved the act into halls and it took off. Lucky guesses, mostly. Like that Robertson man and his book, you can't know because you weren't there, but sometimes you can work it out. Variety hall entertainment. I made a good living at it, all legit. Bought this nice house.'

Betty stays her with a hand when Lizzie calls goodbye from out in the hall. 'Don't quote me on that to Nikki,' she hisses. 'She's a true believer. BYE, LIZZIE!'

'BYE,' echoes Margo.

The front door shuts and Nikki comes back in. 'Just nip to the loo,' she says and crosses the kitchen to a large bathroom built onto the back of the house.

Betty waits until she's out of the room. 'I was very lucky. I like to think it brought some comfort. You meet a lot of people in pain, you know? But after Susan died my heart wasn't in it any more. I had to keep going for the money. A lot of people thought I got better at it then, afterwards ... I don't know.'

'Were you close to Susan?'

'No. I didn't really know the girls that well. Their mum was a piece of work, I'll tell you. I didn't want to be around Patsy. Our family –' She glances guiltily at the bathroom door. 'They're nutters. Real hard cases. Getting away from them was my only ambition when I was young. I squatted in an old factory down at the docks because I knew they'd be scared to visit. They'd fight a gorilla but they couldn't take spooky. There was a deserted factory below us and no lights in the street or anything. Banging noises all night from the old pipes and holes in the roof. Spookiest place I've ever been. I was away from them and that was good but I didn't get to know the girls. I was scared of their mum. She used to batter me and steal my money. She died coming up to rob me. Fell off a stair. I felt like I'd won a watch. She was a scary bitch. I remember sitting on that broken floor looking down at her, wondering if it could be true.' She smiles softly to herself. 'Best night of my life. Never felt religious but I said a prayer of thanks that night. I didn't do right by the girls, though. I visited them in care sometimes but I was young myself and before I knew it they were off doing their own thing.'

'How did Susan's death put you off it then?'

'I saw another side. Psychics, people I knew, they were on telly getting involved in Susan's case. I know what they were doing, I was in the game. So I see them, people I know, people who know me, call in tips, ringing the papers. These are people I've talked to about what we're doing: guessing, talking shit, working the crowd, you know? People I've been honest with. On telly doing that. That soured me.'

'Maybe they were genuinely trying to help?'

Betty sighs and shakes her head. 'No. We talked about that con between ourselves, how you'd get great publicity if you were right, but I thought it was harmless. Just say something vague like "a place of water". See the grammar in that? Spooky. Not "a pond" but "a place of water". It's an act but if you get lucky and the body is found in water, it could make your career. I mean, to some that's worth a punt. OK, fine, it's part of the game, they're trying to get publicity for a tour of Fife, but it feels different if you're in it and the police're looking for "a place of water" instead of the person who stabbed your niece to death. Everyone has a limit in a game and that was mine. It's about power, having power over other people. I never really wanted that. You have to not care about the people you're working. Turns out: I was the people.'

She sips her tea and puts her cup down.

'Betty, who do you think killed Susan?'

She gives a sad shrug. 'Could have been anyone.' She nods at the toilet door. They can hear the faint hiss of Nikki spraying air-freshener. 'I remember one of the punters was on the radio at the time, anonymously, he was from Birmingham and they asked him why he came up here to see prostitutes and he said "because up here *we can do anything* to them. The cops don't care". I heard him. That's what he actually said. Are you a gay?'

'No.'

'No, me neither.' Betty frowns at the table. 'I wish I was. D'you ever wonder about men? About men and sex? The dark side of it? What's going on there? Animals and children, grabbing at people, violence and all that mad pornography stuff ... I mean, what's *wrong* with them?'

Betty is genuinely asking but Margo doesn't know the answer. 'Baffles me, to be honest.'

'I don't know either. Nikki wants it to be a monster that killed her. Loads of folk do. Know that bit when everyone is surprised he was quiet and kept himself to himself? It's cos they want it to be special but it's not. It's part of normal. It's careless. I think it was someone's dear old grandad. I think an ordinary man killed her and then went off and got on with his life and they'll never find him.'

'Maybe you're right. It's so long ago.'

'I'll tell you one thing: if you sat him down and showed him a film of him doing it he wouldn't remember. He'd see it differently. They always talk about how victims can't remember properly, don't they? I bet the men who do those things push it right to the back of their minds. All the un-solved murders, the men who did them, they're all out there, wandering about, having Christmas Days and living with themselves.' She nods to the window, as if the men are gathered on the lawn outside.

The door opens and Nikki comes out of the bathroom. A synthetic stench of flowers trails after her and assaults them at the kitchen table.

Betty wrinkles her nose and waves her hand in front of her face. 'For fucksake, Nikki, you're the only person I've ever met who shits roses.'

43

HEAVY RAIN IS FALLING when she opens the door to leave. They bid each other a fond farewell and arrange for them to come over to Janette's for Sunday lunch this coming week. Margo offers to come and get them so they won't be too nervous walking in and meeting Joe and Thomas. They're all living together while they clear Janette's house and have decided to stay on there for a while. Tracey's going to buy the house but she's more than happy to wait until they're all ready. Margo wants Nikki and Betty in Janette's house when she tells them about the baby. If it's a girl she wants to ask them if she can name her Susan.

Having arranged a time on Sunday, Margo insists that Nikki and Betty stay inside as she runs to the car. She knows a door-step goodbye could take an hour and the rain is fierce and cold, sweeping across the beam of street lights in blustery waves.

She runs to her car, gets in, turns the engine on and pulls the seat belt on. She's about to switch the headlights on when she glances at the rear-view mirror and sees the Honda.

She freezes.

The bonnet is long, the beam of the front lights probe around the edge of the garden wall. Margo slides down in her seat.

The Honda pulls out into the street behind her, drawing slowly down the road, coming past her. The rain is too heavy and she's too low in her seat for the driver to spot her. But she can see the back of a head as they cruise slowly past, head inclined towards the bungalow, looking at the window. Hardly breathing, Margo watches the car turn right and drive slowly away around a side street. Is the car parking? Does the driver live here? She considers getting out to go and look for it but her hand rises to the car door and locks her in.

She's sitting low, trying to decide what to do, watching sheet rain on the windscreen, when she feels the rumble of an engine at her back. The Honda has come full circle around the house. It's passing her again. The driver checks Betty's window more boldly this time, turning their head to look up and Margo can see the face. She recognises them. The Honda passes, gets a hundred yards ahead, missing the right turn they took last time, speeding up as they head for the busy Baillieston Road.

Margo sits up, takes the handbrake off and follows.

She has learned from their mistakes and she stays well back and leaves her lights off until they hit the main road. The rain helps, visibility is diminished, but she keeps her small car tucked neatly behind 4x4s and vans. They're a careful driver, cautious, but they clearly know this route well. They indicate long before they approach a turn, slide into turn-off lanes before the road signs are readable. They have done this drive often.

They're on the M8, slipping past unpretty housing schemes hidden from view by thin trees, bypassing windowless shopping malls, sliding through Glasgow city centre to join the four lanes heading for the Kingston Bridge.

They cross high over the Clyde and Margo stays in the wrong lane, knowing that they'll be checking their mirror on the long straight bridge. She stays in the airport lane as they peel off into the left-hand lane that feeds into the M77. Half a mile along she changes lane, staying far behind, tucked in tight to the back of a supermarket lorry. She follows the Honda for two miles until she sees it slow down for the slip road. They leave the motorway together.

She knows, long before they get to the address, who she is following. They take a roundabout, turning towards Nitshill, driving slowly and carefully along broad, potholed roads, turning corners, crossing more roundabouts, following the path to Barney Keith's house.

He parks in a' disabled space outside what looks like a terrace of modest houses. Margo has done home visits to houses like this.

She can see down the open arch that runs through the middle of the building. There are four front doors inside the alley, a white plastic handrail runs along the close and a concrete ramp leads up to it for wheelchair access.

This is two-up two-down social housing, good quality, single level housing for people with access and additional needs. It's run-down though. Litter is stuck in the scrawny hedges and communal wheelie bins stand sentry outside, lids open, one lying drunkenly on its back in the scrub grass.

Barney Keith opens his car door and gets out. He's carrying a steel walking stick with four feet, an aid for the unsteady, holding it in the middle like a spade. He locks his car, and, hunched against the heavy rain, hurries across the pavement, through the gate, and up the path, glancing at the toppled bin as he gets into the shelter of the close. She doesn't see which door he goes into but after a moment a bright light snaps on in a ground-floor window. The blind is down but she knows he's ground floor, left.

Margo waits, watching the street warp through the rain on the car windows, listening to the hiss of the heavy downpour as it bounces high off the pavement. She sits, clutching the steering wheel, getting angrier and hotter, until she throws the car door open, gets out in the cold veil of rain and trails Barney Keith up to his front door, skirting the fallen wheelie bin, hearing the open one filling up with rain.

Nitshill is on high ground, ten kilometres from Glasgow. Barney's close is open at both ends and the bright lights of the distant city glint warmly through the open arch at the back, blurred and inviting through the curtain of rain.

She does not want to be here. She doesn't want to meet him but she knows there's no avoiding this moment. She'll be afraid until she tells Barney Keith to fuck off and stop following her. This is why she rings the door bell.

At this point she doesn't mean for anyone to get hurt.

44

SHE HEARS THE SHARP electric buzz of the doorbell zapping in the hallway. Feet shuffle around inside. The spyhole on the door darkens but Margo steps to the side so that she can't be seen from inside.

'Who is that?' The voice is high-pitched and anxious.

She doesn't answer but reaches over and presses the buzzer again.

After a moment the front door opens a crack. It's fastened inside with a chain. Warmth floats out to the cold concrete close carrying the sweet smell of curry.

Barney Keith peers out at her, recognition flaring in his small eyes. 'Who're you?'

'You know who I am,' she says.

He looks her up and down and shuts the door, slips the chain off and opens it wide. He's using the walking stick now, leaning heavily on it.

Barney is thin and hunched and bald. His eyes are deep-set like Margo's and she sees faint traces of herself in the narrow set of his jaw. He's seventy but still wiry, with a watery paunch. He has dry, yellowed skin, his liver hasn't been functioning well for a long time, and his gestures seem uncertain.

Feeling himself seen, he smoothes a tense hand over his head, as if shielding himself, and his fingers tremble a little.

He has changed out of his rained-on clothes into a T-shirt and grey jogging trousers, greasy around the pockets. His feet are bare and she notices that the toenails are clipped. That's telling in a man of his age. Most geriatric patients aren't agile enough to care for their feet but Barney is able to bend down. He's keeping up the impaired act though, leaning heavily on his stick, shuffling from foot to foot as if his legs hurt.

She's instantly glad she followed him here. She's four inches taller than him. She's younger than him. She's a doctor and has never raped a thirteen-year-old. This man is nothing.

'What'd you want?' he says.

'You're following me. I've told the police but I'm giving you a warning: stop.'

He titters, incredulous, 'I don't even know –'

'I've got photos of your car outside my house,' she lies. 'The police've got your name, your car registration and this address. Stop following me.'

'Oh ... They know you're here, speaking to me, do they? Because you're not supposed –'

'No, they don't know. I'm just warning you to leave me alone.'

'OK,' he smiles faintly.

This is the moment when she should turn and leave but she doesn't. She's waiting for something, an admission that he's her father, for him to show he's not an arsehole, she's not sure what, but she hesitates.

He slumps, looks hurt and says, 'Are you Susan's baby? Are you Patsy?'

But she's sure that he knows perfectly well who she is.

'Stop following me. The police know who you are.'

He opens his mouth to speak but stops. He looks her up and down. The rain at either end of the close is suddenly heavier, a loud shushing in the street.

Barney whispers at her feet, 'You look like her.' He covers his eyes with his free hand and sobs, exhaling so hard that his knee buckles. He staggers sideways, almost losing his footing and Margo has to resist the reflex to reach into the hall and steady him. Barney doesn't need support. He's a fake. She stands looking in, wringing her hands as he corrects himself. He drops his hand from his face and she sees that his eyes and face are dry. Barney Keith is full of shit.

'It's ... I've – osteoarthritis.'

'Huh?' It's a crippling condition, a painful inflammation of the joints, mostly diagnosed by self-reporting, perfect for the mendacious malingerer.

'Aye. You'll maybe have to watch out for that ... I think I might be your dad?'

Margo shrugs. 'Someone said that, yeah.'

'... *Someone* said that?'

'Someone, yeah.'

'Wow! Me, a daddy. Imagine that.' He mutters, almost to himself, 'I'm actually in a lot of pain.'

'Right?'

'Aye. Painful,' he says, looking past her, his eyes hooded, his mouth drawn tight. It's an odd, expressionless kind of look. She doesn't know what it means.

His eyes trace her face and it's not wrong, exactly, but it's odd and uncomfortable. She considers the possibility that he's on heavy medication and maybe she's reading too much into everything.

She looks behind him into the hall. It's clean. The walls have been painted recently, not very well and in a dull battle-ship grey, not very nice but he has made an effort. A blue poly bag hangs off the hall cupboard handle, filled with empty foil food containers. He has eaten a take-out curry and left the bag there as a reminder to bin it and stop the smell lingering. Margo has done house calls to people who were not coping and the signs are clear: Barney is able. He's painting his house, enjoying food, having a life. She finds him looking straight at her, a faint smile flits across his eyes.

'You're my Susan's double. I have been following you, I'm sorry but I seen you at court that day. I just wanted to look at you again.'

She thinks about the bean growing inside her. If she had to give up her baby and then saw them as an adult, she might follow them around. She might scare them with the ferocity of her interest. She might seem this pathetic.

He opens the front door wider and looks hopefully into the living room. 'Come in for a minute?'

She shakes her head.

He holds up a staying hand. 'Fine, no, it's fine. Don't want to make you. Just you do what feels right …'

They stand there, looking at each other.

'What I want you to know,' says Barney, 'is this: I didn't want to give you up. Susan did. I want you to know that.'

He thinks Margo is angry about being given up, he's wrong, she's not, and he's blaming Susan when she isn't here to defend herself and it seems like a cheap move.

'Well,' says Margo, 'she did me a favour. It must have been difficult but it was the right thing. It worked out well for me.'

'Yeah, I didn't – wasn't my idea. She didn't think she'd be a good mum. Didn't like herself very much. I told her you'd love her anyway but – well, she was hot-headed, Susan, strong-willed.'

Margo smiles. 'I've heard that.'

Barney smiles back, looking shy. 'Yeah, she was something else. Something else again.'

And they both nod softly, Margo at the scared and proud girl with nothing to lose, Barney at whatever he thought Susan was.

'I wish you could have met her instead of me.' He drops his chin to his chest and whispers, 'I didn't think you'd want to meet a person like me. I'm sorry for following you ... Nothing went right for me since McPhail killed her.'

'Barney, who told you it was McPhail?'

'I worked it out.' Barney tips his chin defiantly. 'Cops barely investigated Susan's death. The girls would only talk to one of their own and they all knew me, knew Susan, knew how much I loved her. They talked to me.'

'Someone told you, didn't they? Was it Jack Robertson?'

'No!' he laughs. 'No! *I* told *him*. It was me that told him and he put it in his book. I mean, I don't mind, I just want justice for Susan. Jack's a great guy. Have you met him?'

'Yeah.' She doesn't want to tell him that Jack has been charged with culpable homicide. 'Jack's unbelievable.'

'The girls trusted me, most of the journalists wouldn't listen to a low-life like me, scum like me.'

He leaves a pause for Margo to contradict him. Maybe he is scum, she doesn't know. 'But who told you it was McPhail? Was it one of the women?'

'I don't like ... it'd break a promise to someone.' He looks down the close. 'But it was *a* woman, yes.'

The weight of the rain is causing a cold draft at either side of the close and the warmth from the overheated flat seeps out and seems to stroke her cheek. Barney shivers. 'It's awful cold out there. Sure you don't want to come in?'

She half wants to but she knows too much about him. She blurts, 'You got her pregnant when she was thirteen. You were thirty-two.'

'She was fifteen.'

'No, she wasn't. She was thirteen.'

'*She had nowhere else to go.*'

'She was in a childrens' home.'

He leans heavily on the door frame and looks desolate: 'Susan was planning to kill herself when I met her. She wasn't safe. They were at her every night in there. She came to me. Where should she have gone? No one cares. It's happening right now and no one cares. People only care after, when they're growed up and there's nothing to do, then they're all sad about it but it's happening right now and no one cares. But I *did* because it happened to me. I cared. I was the only one. She wanted to be wi' me. Someone that loved her. We were happy. We loved each other until that bastard McPhail killed her.'

'Who told you it was McPhail?'

He hesitates, almost answers but then says, 'You can come in if you like ... I won't bite.'

Margo looks behind him into the hall and he takes that as a yes. He shuffles back, making space for her. Wary, she steps into her father's house.

He shuts the door behind her. "Scuse the mess,' he smiles and points her into the living room.

It's a strange room, wide and broad with a large picture window onto the street and a paper blind drawn down over it. He has painted this room the same dull grey colour as the hall. There's a brown sofa, worn flat and shiny where he has been sitting, with a small concrete breeze block next to it for a table. An empty beer can sits on it. But the whole situation feels odd and wrong: the bulb in the central fitting is too bright, the light is blue and forensic and a row of three old laptops are open and lined up on the floor. They all have external DVD burners and power leads snaking around them. At the side wall sits a full cardboard box of unmarked DVDs. Some of them are in yellowed sleeves, some dusty, some clean. These are the DVDs he is copying, not the ones he's making.

She doesn't know what's going on and it makes her uneasy. She has her back to him but is aware that he is standing quite close behind her. She shuffles forward to get some space between them and sees something hidden behind the window blind. A white and blue pastel porcelain figurine, a lamb sitting at a shepherdess's feet and around its neck is a yellowed-glue garrotte. It's exactly like the one Janette fixed, the one in her collection.

'So nice to have you.' Barney's voice is thick with emotion.

Coming here was a mistake. He's too close. Margo spins around and shuffles back, pointing at the laptops. 'What's that about?'

'Auch,' he says, 'pirate DVDs. Just some daft old movies and that. Sell them cheap. OK, it's not legal but – wee bit of pocket money …' His cover story is wrong. He doesn't seem to know that people don't buy pirate DVDs any more, they just download films for free. She doesn't want to know what's on the DVDs but she can guess.

'Why are you burning them three at a time?'

'Everybody wants the same ones, don't they?'

Barney is different in here, he's standing steady on his feet now, too close, his expression is off. It's not anything specific, she just knows that this isn't safe. Barney, this Barney, is why Susan gave Margo up. She wanted to get her away from him.

'D'you like films?' He's looking at her mouth.

'Some.'

He is standing between her and the door.

'I've got some films you can watch …' His hand darts out and touches her neck and she jumps back.

'Fuck are you doing? Don't touch me.'

Barney smiles as if the last two seconds didn't happen. 'And were you a happy wee girl?'

'What?'

'Growing up: were you a happy girl?' He's smiling and tilting his head. 'Because, me and Susan, that's all that mattered to us. That *you* were happy.'

'What's on those DVDs?'

'You can take one, if you like.' He smiles, 'Or we could watch one together.'

She needs to keep him talking. 'Who said it was McPhail?'

'Hey, listen: have you *seen* your Auntie Nikki?'

'Nikki?' She's shuffling around, edging towards the door.

'Aye,' he's grinning. 'Your wee Auntie Nikki. You seen her?'

'Was it Nikki who told you it was McPhail?'

'Nikki's doing good these days, eh? She's did well, eh? Living wi' Betty and that.'

'Have you been following her too?'

'As if! Dirty whore –' He's smiling and nods at the DVDs. 'You can take one of they wee films, see if you like it ...'

Margo doesn't want to leave her fingerprints on them. She doesn't want to touch anything in here. 'Who said it was McPhail?'

'Diane Gallagher. She telt me. She said he'd killed Susan. Gallagher telt me that herself.'

Margo looks at him and remembers Diane saying he was the most pathetic man she'd ever met. Gallagher would never have seen this version, no one with any power would. Just Susan and the other small people.

'That's a lie. Gallagher knows it wasn't him. She's always known.'

'A lie, is it?'

'Diane Gallagher would never say that.'

'You were there were you?' He's suddenly angry and, somehow, profoundly different. The skin on her neck prickles.

And then he stands with his mouth hanging open, stands still for too long. His eyes are hooded, his expression blank. There's something really wrong here. She doesn't know what it is.

Margo's eyes flick back to the base of the porcelain figurine on the windowsill. She picks it up, holding it in her hand, looking at it. The garrotted lamb gazes up at her, trusting, loving. This is Janette's figurine.

'Have you been in my house?'

'Wha'?'

'Have you been in my house?'

'What the fuck are you saying?'

'Did you break in and piss in my kitchen? What's on those DVDs?'

Barney Keith looks her in the eye and straightens up. Suddenly, she's not taller than him. He holds her eye and reaches down, picking up the walking stick by the stem, pointing the four rubber-tipped feet at her.

'*Smart bitch.*' Barney lifts the stick over his head and smashes it down on her face.

Margo hears a crack as the bridge of her nose snaps. White lights burst in her eyes. She lashes out blindly at Barney and her fist hits something. A snap, she thinks it's her finger but it isn't: she's still holding Janette's ornament. She panics, drags it along something and then reels back as the pain roars through her eyes. It takes the breath from her. Her knees sag. The pain doesn't register in her nose but her whole body and she's suddenly afraid she's going to faint or vomit.

She does neither.

She stands still, panting and blinking until she can see blurred shapes in the bright room.

Barney is gone. The room is clear. The doorway is empty. Shocked, she steps forward, hands out, and her foot lodges on something heavy.

She looks down, blinks hard and sees Barney on the floor. He isn't moving. She staggers away to the door and looks back but she can't see.

She wants to leave but she's a doctor. She can't just leave. She has to help.

She stands, panting, shaking – here come the shock shakes she's seen in other people – and shuts her eyes to clear them.

Barney has fallen, smashed his temple off the concrete block and rolled onto his side. She keeps blinking hard and each time, in the second before her vision clouds over again, she sees him clearly, in snapshots. His skull is fractured, deeply compressed above his left eye. He's dying. Time is limited. She needs to call an ambulance. The shepherdess lies shattered on the floor, and a deep scratch from it gouged into Barney's cheek. His eyes are flickering, the lamb's body is stuck in his eye. But she's shocked and shaking. She should call an ambulance on her phone. But the police will come and she's already in trouble because of Jack and Lilah and Richard.

She staggers out to the hallway. She should fix it. Fix this situation. Tidy this situation. Sort things out. Sort Janette's house, tidy up. She's so sorry.

Out in the hall she falls against the cupboard door, frightened and repentant, knowing she should do something, she lifts the blue poly bag from the cupboard handle and takes it outside.

She shuts the front door behind her, pulling it tight. Her eyes are swelling up, she can feel them starting to narrow.

She's a doctor. Time is of the essence. She should phone.

The cold rain is a salve on her hot face. Her face is swelling, she can feel it, and she looks up at the flickering lights of Glasgow glittering through the rain, red and yellow and white. Taking her phone out of her pocket, she taps in the security code and dials 999.

She can hear it ring out on the other end and sees her situation through a stranger's eyes. This does not look good. Just act normal. Tell the truth. But it looks bad. She finds the blue bag of Barney's rubbish in her hand: why did she take that? She drops it into the open wheelie bin, hears it splash in the gathered water. That seems suspicious as well, binning bags of his rubbish, what's she doing? Flustered and confused, she slaps the bin lid shut.

'Emergency services,' says a small voice from her phone, 'which service do you require?'

Margo stares at the bin lid.

'Hello, caller? Are you there?'

Cold rain patters on her head, worming through her hair to her scalp, running down her neck.

'Caller, I can hear you breathing ... Are you unable to speak?'

A sign is taped to the lid, a message to the neighbours. She stands still, knowing that Barney is dying through the wall next to her.

'Hello, caller? Do you need police, fire or ambul –'

Margo hangs up. She doesn't need an ambulance. She slaps her hand flat on the bin lid and scratches at the tape, peeling the sign off. She's taking it with her. She walks away. She'll never tell anyone she was here. She gets into her car and drives back towards the city.

Three miles away she stops at a red light and looks at the wet sign sitting on the passenger seat.

It's handwritten:

PLEASE folks keep this lid shut.

The hand is distinctive. The letters slant forwards, as if they're in a hurry to get to the edge of the paper. The 't's and the 'f' are all small and straight.

Acknowledgements

A great many thanks, as ever, to my editor Jade Chandler, for pretending to be surprised that this whole thing ended up being a bit more complicated than it was when I initially suggested it and ably pretending I don't say that about every fucking book. Also to Jon Wood and Henry Dunow for all of their support.

Thanks, as always, to my family: Steve and Owen and Edith for the dinners and shoulder punches during the long days.

Special thanks to the many people who took the time to talk to me about their experiences and for their grace in allowing me to use bits of those interviews in a fictional-ised story. I tried to understand and be kind but where I failed please know it was never deliberate.

And a huge thank you to Nanette Pollock and Routes Out Of Prostitution for all their time, patience and help in researching this book.

Denise Mina is the author of the Garnethill trilogy, the Paddy Meehan series and the Alex Morrow series. She has won the Theakston Old Peculier Crime Novel of the Year Award twice and was inducted into the Crime Writers' Association Hall of Fame in 2014. *The Long Drop* won the McIlvanney Prize for Scottish Crime Book of the Year 2017 and the Gordon Burn Prize. *Conviction* was the co-winner of the McIlvanney Prize for 2019 and was selected for Reese Witherspoon's Hello Sunshine Book Club. Denise has also written plays and graphic novels, and presented television and radio programmes. She lives and works in Glasgow.